V

Chapter 1

Lacie could tell her day would be dull without leaving her dorm room, and she lied in bed and stared at the dust on the windowsill, illuminated by obnoxiously bright rays of light that pierced through the half-open window blinds. Her brown shoulder-length hair was as messy as her bed; and her shady but sociable roommate was as distant as desirable food in the mini-fridge. And for a groggy second it seemed like there was color in the dust, until her alarm jolted her and remedied her comatose state. So the pale white girl let out a zombie-like moan and forced herself to sit up.

The eighteen-year-old girl rubbed her eyes wishing she could take her chances with dreams instead of going to class. The room was cheaply decorated around her, one of the few things she had done with her roommate; but now, even in a blur, its initial charm was wearing. Lacie reached for the familiar glossy sensation of her frames, towards the table next to her bed where she usually kept her glasses. She knocked over a notepad and prescription bottle with a drug for depression and anxiety, stacked on the top of other notepads and books, before restoring vision to her earthy brown eyes.

Lacie immediately noticed that almost all of her party-animal roommate's things were gone from the room. She got out of bed and went sifting through the closet once shared with her distant roommate, and found more vacancy there. She stared into the shadowy, half-empty closet, and a familiar and strengthened sense of loneliness washed over her like a tidal wave.

The brunette snapped herself out of it enough to move again. She grabbed what she needed including broken-in blue jeans and an old shirt that had the white-lettered name of a restaurant on it from further south in the state. Then, she retreated to the restroom to get ready and try out the strawberry shampoo she had bought the night before.

After Lacie got her class materials and outfitted herself in comfortable clothes and the familiarity of her trusty brown boots, she headed off into the residential halls. There were fewer people drifting around the campus than usual this Tuesday-- probably staying in, sleeping in, or already in class. Various information was posted along the white brick of the walls. Lacie would peer at the posters on occasion, but she was still overwhelmed by her environment.

A blond-haired girl around Lacie's age approached; the girl was the resident assistant who was in charge of watching over the hall, though she wasn't any taller than Lacie. The RA was wearing well-ironed professional clothing and always had her long hair in a braid.

"Lacie! Just who I wanted to see. I like your shirt." The RA smiled as a group of other students walked past.

"Thanks.. it's green." Lacie replied awkwardly.

Amanda laughed but it came across as somewhat faked or rehearsed, "Okay, just a heads up. But your roommate is leaving college. Apparently something happened and she's going to rehab."

"Oh." Lacie let out a sigh as though she wasn't surprised.

"But there's a girl that should be coming to move in with you tonight or tomorrow."

"Alright," Lacie couldn't help but smirk at Amanda's mask of optimism. "Thanks.. for the heads up."

"No problem." Amanda beamed. Lacie picked up on some kind of glimmer of blue and green, like the thinnest lines of color in Amanda's eyes.. and then a flash of red and maybe yellow, and then orange. It all happened quickly and then disappeared, and it startled Lacie so much that she couldn't say anything back to her.

"Well you have a good day." Amanda said.

After parting ways with the resident assistant, Lacie ventured through the nearest exit into the bright outdoors.

It was a beautiful summer day pardoning that it had rained the night before and showed in the parking lot. Puddles, some blindingly reflecting the sun, were scattered around, only to be hidden by stationary vehicles. There was a fresh and inviting breeze in the air. Students hung out underneath the shade of trees with books, phones, and sometimes tablets and laptops. But regardless of the embracing weather, Lacie felt a deep and lingering sense of isolation. She couldn't help looking at the puddles and thinking of the rain the night before.

The English major made her way in a hurried walk, past the other students going about their day, past the wide parking lot, and various buildings to where her class was. She entered the corridors, similar to the resident halls, but with tiled floor hiding years of wear behind the last time it had been buffed and waxed. And seeing that the door to the classroom was ajar Lacie simply let herself in.

The classroom was an average English college classroom but had nobody in it. Lacie looked at the clock on the wall. The young woman realized that she was early, but it was strange that nobody was around. In the habit of being a private person, the girl made sure that the door behind her was almost closed.

Upon taking a seat and opening her book to the page the class would probably start from, she found in the vacancy of her surroundings-- a perfect opportunity to sleep in.

Lacie knelt the side of her head against her now crossed arms and shut her eyes. She remembered the colored dust; maybe it was the medicine she was taking, or maybe it was just a dream, or a fluke of the mind. Then the whole world, or the last of it, seemed to slowly disappear into sleep-- like walking through an unknown door into a pitch black room, always with the hope that a light could be found.

~

Lacie awoke, lifting her head slightly. Upon seeing her surroundings she jolted upright, which caused her glasses to almost fall off her nose. She found herself in a clean-cut restaurant, but how did she get here? Surrounding her were windows filled with darkness rather than daytime, and the artificial lights that accompanied it. She remained unaware of her shirt, which now read, "Out of

Business."

Lacie noticed a large desk in front of racks full of donuts. Some of these pastries were floating in the air. Behind the desk there was a young woman who was of a complexion pale enough to compliment Lacie's lack of a tan.

Upon seeing Lacie bolt upright, the slightly taller employee had a look of surprise, biting her lower lip and widening her eyes. The strange girl behind the desk had ocean-blue eyes accented with black eyeliner, long black hair with red tips, and a solid black dress hidden by a crimson-colored apron that was covered with a wash of donut residue.

Lacie looked down at her charred English book and then fixed her glasses, "Where am I?"

"Mr. Bagel's Donut Shop." The employee spoke with a meek British accent, but seemed indifferent to the scattered donuts hovering in the air around her.

There was a pause where Lacie's mouth opened but nothing came out. While the young lady behind the counter stared off to the side, twirling the bottom of her long hair with her lower lip still in her mouth, as if she hadn't had a customer in months.

"Mr. Bagel's Donut Shop?" Lacie asked, in a condescending tone of disbelief.

The employee stared at a chair on the other side of the room.

Lacie looked back and forth before returning her gaze to the strange girl, "How.. what's-- what's your name?"

"Elizabeth." The employee stated directly.

"Where is this place?"

"Mr. Bagel-"

"No! I mean the town, where is this?" Lacie almost demanded in confusion.

Elizabeth stopped biting her lip and began cracking her knuckles from under the desk, "N'Qevna."

"Mr. Bagel's Donut Shop? N'Qevna?" Lacie sighed and shook her head. "No, no.. I must be dreaming."

Elizabeth had finished cracking her knuckles and stood in silent, attentive listening to the four-eyed girl across the room ramble on about her predicament.

"I was in college and I fell asleep in class. I couldn't have woke up here. Why does this feel so real?" Lacie looked down at the remains of her open English book lying on the table with the sudden urge to throw it across the restaurant.

"Usually.. usually people come in here to buy food." Elizabeth stated nervously.

Lacie stood up with her chair loudly

sliding backwards across the tile which caused Elizabeth to squint her face with a tinge of fear. The college girl ventured to the front of the counter, "Look, my name is Lacie. Was there someone who brought me in here?"

"No.. One minute there was nobody here, then you appeared with your book, sleeping there." Elizabeth mused.

"Well.." Lacie glared at a floating, cherry jelly-filled donut. She put her hands down on the hard counter as though it wasn't real. "How do I get back to where I was?"

Elizabeth looked to the upper right, holding the underside of her pointy chin in thought as if scrapping her mind for information, "You could speak to my dear Uncle Herbert. He's very knowledgeable of such things."

"Can you take me to him?" Lacie pleaded, her hands forming into loose fists.

"I suppose, as long as you don't leave me out there alone. Okay?"

Lacie pulled her hands from their negotiating stance letting them drop comfortably to her sides. She smiled as if hoping to wake from a dream, "Okay."

Elizabeth slid her apron over her head and tried to pull it off in a comical struggle while Lacie waited by the door. Then the black-clad girl turned off the machines in back and jumped repetitively trying to grab some object beyond her stature. When Elizabeth was finally ready to go, she opened the front door slowly and cautiously, looking around outside and closing the door before opening it again; this happened twice and bothered Lacie, but she decided not to say anything. Finally, when Elizabeth was really ready, the two girls headed off into the uncertainty of a most vibrant night.

Chapter 2

Lacie gazed in wonder and terror at her environment with Elizabeth trailing close behind. The sky had streaks of indigo, violet, pink, and red cloud in contrast to underlying, mysteriously equal streaks of pitch black and midnight blue that were filled with the white glow of stationary and shooting stars. In a center streak of jet black sky, there was a full moon with smoke rising around it, from its bottom half over its top.

Worn-down franchises and businesses mostly one-story-high littered the sides of the road with light. On Lacie's second glimpse of a burger joint, the entire structure flew up out of the ground, and up into the air with the force of a giant rocket. The burger restaurant had no fire and no smoke underneath it, just the blunt sound of its separation from the ground and the intensely loud whistling of the wind as a result of its speed.

"What!?" Lacie yelled as Elizabeth screamed, both alarmed by the building's flight. Lacie hunched down with her hands out, as if she was frozen in fear on a surf board made of sidewalk; while Elizabeth grabbed Lacie's shoulders and hid most of her face behind Lacie's back. They watched as the building charged mile by mile upwards until it was a speck, the night returning to its deathly quietude.

"Is.. is it coming back down?" Lacie asked.

Elizabeth didn't reply.

After the young women realized everything was safe from the sidewalk square that they occupied, they started to cautiously walk again.. continuing to look around as they did. A few other buildings seemed to randomly change their appearance completely as though they were unaware of their existential state. There was a far-off cluster of people venturing around in the distance with one muffled man's voice booming out from them. Pairs of men on the exterior of the distant crowd carried stained-glass windows. Skeletons, mostly human and maybe plastic, were scattered around various places.

Lacie found herself in shock of these wondrous and terrifying surroundings and attempted to retain her sense of sanity with one of many questions, "Why is the sky so weird?"

"The sky has always been this way." Elizabeth said quietly.

"Okay.." Lacie followed Elizabeth's quietude and lowered her own voice, "Why is the moon smoking?"

Though it was warm outside, a breeze

appeared and freely gave up its comfort. However, the moving air of the night did not have its direction decided upon, and would rock back and forth in various intervals of minutes from different directions. Elizabeth's hair shifted with the different directions of the confused wind, "The moon has a smoking problem."

Elizabeth spotted a skeleton grinning at her, its arm outstretched towards the manic hues parading against the smoky pallor of the moon. She attempted to hide inconspicuously behind Lacie.

"What are you doing?" Lacie sporadically turned, hair in her face.

"Don't stop walking." Elizabeth pleaded.

A black and red cat darted from the parking lot of a nearby business where lights flickered and cars were parked upside-down. The fully-grown feline lingered between the girls and followed them inconspicuously, its greenish-yellow eyes in a dim stare forward, a small cactus atop its head.

“Why are you hiding behind me?” Lacie asked with tension forming in her voice. “You're scaring me.”

"I'm afraid of the dark." The black-clad girl stated timidly.

"You're dressed in all black and you're afraid of the dark?"

Elizabeth furrowed her eyebrows, "I try not to ever leave the donut shop."

The girls both passed the low, mumbling voice of a male for some inaudible speech in the distance, "I know, I've seen her. She doesn't."

Lacie noticed a shadowy stranger in a black trenchcoat, sitting on a bench from a few businesses down. She guessed that it was a guy, though the face was too dark to be visible. The figure and his surroundings were outlined with blue light from the restaurant behind him. He had a lighted, metal sign next to him that pointed to him and explained, "This person is eating chicken at a sea-food restaurant."

"So I just keep going down this road to that four-way up there?" Lacie adjusted her glasses trying to ignore the creepy, dark figure, and the sign about creepy, dark, sea-food restaurant chicken.

"Yeah." Elizabeth had noticed the stranger by now. "I'll be right behind you."

As the girls made some distance from the stranger, Lacie began prying Elizabeth's knowledge. "So where are you from? You're not originally from here are you?"

Elizabeth looked down, "I don't know, I don't remember. But we need to get out of the endless dark."

"Endless? Is.. is it always night here?"

"Yes, and it is quite unpredictable in certain places." Elizabeth twirled the red and black tips of her hair around her finger and bit her lower lip.

Lacie adjusted her glasses nervously, "Like where we're going?"

"Yes," Elizabeth replied softly as though the world was eavesdropping. "And right now out here."

Lacie got a bad feeling in the pit of her stomach, and kept walking at a brisk pace along the sidewalk.

Upon arrival at the intersection a new car barreled forward from the abyss into a traffic pole which caused both of the girls to jump.

The sound of the collision was made to be so eccentrically loud that an orchestra appeared from the shadows of a nearby driveway, increasing the volume of the event with a single orchestral hit of sound-- which triggered a small, overhead explosion in the sky; afterwards the orchestra faded, returning to the dark. And this alerted the nearby religious crowd.

The driver who emerged from the wreckage was a husky black man in formal dress with glasses over large brown eyes. The man boomed with his hands on his head, "This can't be happening. I had everything worked out for her, she was paid off!"

There was a huge puff of white smoke that materialized from out of the car's exhaust pipe with a loud poof. As the smoke started to clear, fence appeared all around the wreckage of the car. Lacie did not know how to respond and stood in shock which led Elizabeth to shyly chime into the driver's predicament. "Are you okay?"

"I'm fine." He scratched his head in a pause, then formally held out his hand towards Elizabeth. "I'm Mr. Dreary-Gravy, but most call me Mr. Greary."

The girls introduced themselves and shook Mr. Greary's hand.

Lacie was amused fairly, "You uh.. You smell like beef gravy."

Mr. Greary chuckled drearily, "Hence the name, young lady."

"But why dreary, Mr. Greary?" Elizabeth tried not to seem shady.

Mr. Greary sighed wearily, "Such is the dreariness of beef gravy."

The nearby religious group was in the vicinity of the four-way now. Outer pairs lugged around heavy stained-glass windows full of multi-colored pictures of rocks. A grey-suited preacher in his fifties made way through the crowd holding onto a large book with a collection of rocks on the cover; the preacher had an exuberant demeanor and grey hair pointing out diagonally at the sides in the back of his head.

The preacher introduced himself, "Hello, my name is Thomas Limestone. By the rocks, I believe we were destined to meet!"

Lacie and Elizabeth just looked at each other as though they didn't want to converse with the man. There was something odd about him and he was covered in gravel dust.

"I really must be going, I have to go buy eggs." Mr. Greary hastily impressed.

The preacher cried out almost squeaking at Mr. Greary, "You sir, who smells precociously of Thanksgiving, who admits to idolatry of eggs-- have you yet discovered the profound beauty of the rocks all around you!?"

"What are you talking about sir?" Mr. Greary seemed intrigued.

There were people from the group of all ages looking over the rocks in the road and their patterns. They were completely enchanted with the rocks around them. A little girl in a pink dress fell into the rocks and began crying; she had skinned her knees and they were bleeding. The sky began sprinkling with rain.

The daughter's father came to her aid, picked her up and with a calm voice, "Shhh. That's just part of the rocks' plan hunny."

The preacher held out his open hand out at the little girl in a pointing manner, "Why can you not see?"

"I'm sorry, but I don't think I want anything to do with that." Mr. Greary stated calmly.

"Life is a rocky path, you might skin your knees on the rocks, but someone might come to your aid and be your rock as well." Thomas Limestone replied with his loud and squeaky voice. But Mr. Greary seemed politely unresponsive and more intent on pursuing his minimalistic grocery shopping than a religious discussion in the road.

Lacie turned to Elizabeth while holding back laughter, "We should probably go too."

"I'm all for it." Elizabeth half-whispered in fear.

Mr. Greary overheard the two young women, "Are you headed off to All-Mart?"

The girls noticed much commotion in the environment. Far-off trees came to a sort of consciousness, uprooted themselves, and flew around like out-of-control airplanes. Some trees however, felt more like individuals in refusing to leave their places, even to the point of moving their branches like crossed arms in certitude. Two of the buildings to the left broke apart into pieces, forming themselves together into a kind of arch across the road ahead: from here, hanging light bulbs were in constant swing on their electrical cords. Shadowy creatures with colorful markings, around the size and shape of squirrels and turtles, scurried about, visually obscured by their distance.. barely in the streetlights as they ran across grey and green grass, grey and black cement.

"Excuse me to have bothered you all." The preacher steamed, his joy dissipating. In a fit of disgust the preacher led his congregation backwards, literally speaking. Pairs of men huffed as they heaved, back-tracing with the stained-glass windows.

"Ye- Yes. We are heading to All-Mart." Elizabeth half-turned her head at Mr. Greary, both her and Lacie were breaking from the spell of the craziness and curiosities going on around them-- as much as one could.

There was a nearby pounding on the ground. Soon after, a menacing, six-foot-tall statue with wings and horns came barreling through the intersection, stepping on Mr. Greary's car, further damaging the vehicle and knocking over some of the surrounding fence. The middle-aged man put his hands on his head again in shock.

As the gargoyle ventured further away the faint rainfall subdued.

On Lacie's face, behind her spectacles,

there was an expression of both fear and general confusion, "We should get inside a building as soon as we can."

And so without further hesitation, the unlikely trio made their way down the road "You Is Twenty-Three", towards the enigmatic fortress called All-Mart.

Chapter 3

Lacie and her newfound accomplices found themselves in a massive parking lot expanding over a vast area of land (with All-Mart due North of their general direction). The store itself was one-story but expansive, with red and blue brick, and the name "All-Mart" in huge, white lettering with a black outline. Fake, robotic birds with copper wire nests were perched atop and within the store sign, with parts of the birds' machinery showing as they twitched or rotated their heads and wings.

There were thick, black clouds, at a much lower altitude than the enormous colorful streaks of cloud high above them; the black gas looming with width over the All-Mart area, blocking out the colorful sky from anywhere nearby. Further away, seldom giant fissures could be seen in a conjoined parking lot, next to an even more distant and run-down mini-mall where all the businesses appeared closed for the eternal night. Near the center of the parking lot was an empty trailer with rust on one end and a fresh coat of black paint on the other.

There was also a group of six, fancy-dressed senior citizens with veiled and masked faces. They were sat down at a black metal-frame table, chatting in front of the store in various foreign languages. There was an identical table next to the old people three times larger that was vacant and seemed to be more enshadowed.

Elizabeth spoke quietly, with anxiety, "Well it seems we're in company."

Mr. Greary turned to Elizabeth and smiled, pointing his finger in the air which made him seem like some sort of cheesy superhero. "There is always company at All-Mart young lady. Now to the Dairy aisle!"

Elizabeth's ocean-blue gaze widened for a second as though Mr. Greary had lost it.

Lacie suddenly noticed rips and scratches at random intervals in her vision of the world around her and she became fearfully preoccupied with them. She reached out gently at one of these rips, out of both fear and curiosity, and teared it by accident. Her vision went starry black and she was filled with a feeling that she held an unstable piece of some cosmic structure. As her hand slightly pulled away at something like a paper-thin wall of liquid, there was a sensation as if she was dreaming and the dreams were switching so fast she could barely process them. She quickly released her grip in more terror than wonder, as though having just touched a hot stove-top.

The table that was three times its size fell over and crumbled into pieces of debris, and the black clouds above had ceased, allowing return of the colorful sky above the store. The six old people sitting at the adjacent table were now six new, maskless people in their twenties, but continued their normal, inaudible conversation. The bricks making up the store were completely white with the All-Mart logo's lettering gone black and inverted. Now in the center of the parking lot, there was a shouting man in suspenders and a pink hat who stood next to a pile of pink hats that towered at least a hundred feet into the sky from the once empty trailer. Mr. Greary had simply disappeared.

Lacie felt her knees weakening, "I feel dizzy. I think I just need to-- where is Mr. Greary?"

"He's.. waiting for us inside the store." Elizabeth replied unknowing of what had just happened.

"Oh.. okay." Lacie wanted to ask Elizabeth if she had noticed any of the changes, but didn't want to scare the gothic girl anymore than she already was.

The girls attempted to pass by the unstable tower of pink hats without being bothered, but the man in shoulder straps and a hot-pink fedora boomed at them, "The end is near! Get a pink hat to protect against The Fifty! Giant bunny rabbits descend upon us! Fifty giant bunny rabbits will wreak havoc upon our world!"

Lacie was sucked in by the idea of defending herself against any aspect of this town, "How much is a hat?"

"I have a bad feeling Lacie, we should probably go." Elizabeth whispered, peering in fear at the unstable tower of hats as though they could fall at any moment, as a new and growing black cloud appeared some distance away. Upon seeing this dark cloud, the young people conversing at the table from in front of the store all vanished simultaneously in puffs of grey smoke; Lacie didn't notice.

"Well they are free of course, as a measure of survival for a universe void of towels; and some of my hats are as high as the moon." The hat man made his statement with certainty, though Lacie didn't understand exactly what he meant by the last bit.

Lacie took a pink sombrero, put it on, and then stared blankly at Elizabeth from behind her spectacles. "Aren't you going to take one just in case?"

"I--" Elizabeth seemed frustrated for some reason. "I guess."

The gothic girl went for a pink trilby, similar to a fedora with a shorter brim.

The man with a pink fedora grabbed her wrist, "No! One from the outside, this whole tower could fall!”

Lacie's face changed to concern and she froze for a second from the man's sudden outburst.

Elizabeth stood meekly as the man continued, holding herself to keep warm against the undecided breeze that began to hit in gusts of noticeably different temperatures, at least to her.. she whispered again to Lacie, "Please can we go. I have a bad feeling."

Unbeknownst to the donut shop employee who now kept her eyes shut, a treadmill had materialized in the ground underneath of her; this caused her to move backwards at a slow crawl.

The man had quite an attentive attitude to his tower of hats, "I'll help you find just the right one. Let me see, hmm.. The cloche seems too much like you've got a bag on your head."

From the black cloud a man appeared in solid black: a longcoat with a sash, gloved hands, boots just over the ankle, and a wide-brimmed fedora with one middle crease higher than the other; underneath of the hat was a head made of similarly dark marble, with a mostly hidden face and hair-- like that of Augustus Caesar's statue. And he began treading clomp by clomp towards Elizabeth, a trail of thick, ebony cloud behind him.

The man in suspenders paced around looking through his extensive hat collection. "This cowboy hat is too tom-girl, that baseball cap is too common and the top hat over there would clash with your personality.."

Lacie crossed her arms and spoke with anxiety-laced optimism, "Whatever works, so we can be prepared."

"Machinagess! THE NEWSBOY!" The man seemed extraordinarily excited about hats. "Or newsgirl as you would probably have it. The question is what news do you have to bring?"

The marble-headed man was behind Elizabeth now and cupped his hand over her mouth covering her scream. Thick, black clouds surrounded them both (and the treadmill).

"Elizabeth!" Lacie ran to the jet black cloud frantically, but was too afraid to touch it, and watched helplessly as it dissipated. She looked around the area, but it was too late. Elizabeth and her captor were gone (and the treadmill).

The man in the pink fedora sighed, "It's my fault, I spent too time trying to find the perfect hat for her."

Lacie deduced the captor was probably the blue-silhouetted stranger that the two girls had seen earlier.

"No it's mine." Lacie's voice broke in unison with a crackle of thunder in the sky. "I left her without seeing it."

“Was she your friend?”

“No, she was my guide to get out of this weird place.” Lacie replied.

"It's only a parking lot.” The man offered up the newsgirl hat, “Take her hat, maybe you'll find her."

Lacie walked over to him and took the hat, "Thanks."

The student descended past the man and his tower, past the solid table and table rubble, to All-Mart's crooked entrance.. with two welcome mats in front of it that had been torn to pieces, and some holes from bullets or golf balls at the top of the glass doors.

Chapter 4

All-Mart's automatic doors opened with a haunting laugh booming from the walls surrounding Lacie, "Testing, testing, is this on.. Okay. Hahahahaa!"

Lacie looked around, clutching the pink newsgirl hat and holding down the pink sombrero in fear of losing them, and out of nervousness beyond them.

The top and middle of the entrance's glass doors behind her had suddenly and mostly been painted in shades of blue, save the bottom of the entrance glass. Small hands from outside continued painting the unpainted bottom glass with shades of blue, the world swirling out of view with the laughter of three children. The suddenness of it creeped Lacie out. And she decided not to walk back near the doors to see who was on the other side.

Lacie shivered and crossed her arms, she could see her breath each time she exhaled. There were huge snowdrifts all around the foyer to the extent that they leaned against benches, pop-deposit machines, and a few random carts. The Ladies Restroom had the doorway rotated ninety degrees as though the entrance was laying down. The Men's Room was blocked off by a flickering soda machine with a puddle underneath it that looked like urine. What was even worse, "Nobody Was Here" was written in large print on the floor tiles, with what appeared to be blood.

The bench nearest to Lacie was covered in snow. There was a plaque above the seating that read, "Bench Reserved For Odis."

The bench next to that bench had a sleeping older black man hidden behind the snowdrift; he looked like an old Blues player with swimming goggles on his forehead, slip-on shoes that showed his brown socks, and a white cotton dress-shirt with tiny polka dots. The wooden sign above this bench was more make-shift and read, "Odis's Vacation Bench."

Lacie decided it would be best, before entering the store, to wake this man and ask where to find Herbert. Anyone wearing polka dots and swimming goggles should be friendly, Lacie thought. But first, Lacie had to go to the restroom very badly.

So Lacie crawled through the ninety-degree doorway whose long way touched the floor, trying not to touch the tiles too much with her hands, since they turned out to be sticky from soda recycling residue. She found the room quite normal if not a bit dimly lit, where the temperature had went back to the warmth of the outside night. There was even a couch.. but with two more uglier couches on top of it.

Lacie went to open one of the two stalls and came across a fishbowl sitting on the top of the toilet, full of water with a comical-looking skeletal fish facing her from behind the curved glass.

The skeletal fish spoke, "I am the last remaining mystical repository of knowledge in the vicinity of your unkept toilet.."

“What the fuck!?” Lacie backed up as the fish spoke.

Then the fish jumped into the toilet which flushed immediately. After this.. event, Lacie decided to use the other stall. When the young woman was finished with her business she found that instead of hot water the sink pumped out hot chocolate, so she washed her hands with it.. and then inconspicuously tried some of it.

Lacie crawled back through the doorway finding that the store temperature immediately dropped again, and she used some of the snow to get the sticky hot chocolate off of her hands.

Lacie was now ready to wake the old man sleeping on his bench. She adjusted her glasses and ventured towards him, "Excuse me sir."

The man just continued snoring.

"Sir!" Lacie screeched.

"You wake me up again I'll steal your

shoes!" The ancient man caused Lacie to jump back, losing both her hats and almost causing her glasses to fall off.

The young woman readjusted her glasses and left the hats on the ground, collecting herself.

"But I'm wearing boots." She mused.

The old man's eyes jutted open, "BOOTS!? Who the hell around here wears boots? Are you on drugs?"

"I.. I don't know. I don't even know how to process all of this." Lacie replied.

"Well what do you want?" The old man corrected his posture.

"I need to find someone named Herbert."

"HERBERT!?" The old man's velocity made it seem like he was straining his throat. Lacie was becoming physically annoyed by the old man's shouting. She could tell he thoroughly enjoyed it as a mode of cheap vengeance for having been woke.

"I don't know anyone named Herbert except that chain-smoking, drunken animal in Aisle Three. You can't see him until you go to the Technology Department to get feed for the technacles.. Oh.. if you find a man named Victor tell him he owes me cheese. Now if you'll ex-cuuuse.. me!"

"But--" Lacie whined.

Odis quickly shut his eyes and tilted his head into an "asleep" position.

Finding that any more conversation with Odis would be futile, Lacie picked up her pink sombrero and newsgirl hat. She left the foyer through the second set of automatic doors which had already been painted over in swirls of blue.

Growling bass poured out as the second set of automatic doors opened to a well-lighted store in utter disarray. Lights flickered occasionally, sometimes in different colors, and exchanged dishes of food with seemingly invisible limbs-- two bulbs in particular were somehow conversing over Japanese customs. A couple jump-ropes hung from the ceiling, one straight while the other was in a noose. Strangely-colored tumble-weeds flew at high speeds over the aisles, some of them venturing with dark brown or blue hats. Most of the aisles were crooked and full of curious collections of things. There were a couple huge, dangerous-looking sink holes in the floor some distance ahead.

A muscular young guy around Lacie's age stood next to the automatic doors, with a cooler full of ice and beer, and a stereo system currently blasting hip-hop music. He was dressed head to toe in pink with star-shaped sunglasses. His shirt had white-letters saying,

"Fo' the chicks."

The shelves to the right of Lacie were mostly full of cobwebs, sand buckets, bouncy balls and miscellaneous products. A rough-looking man rested on one of the bottom shelves with his back turned. He was fearfully mumbling to himself about multi-colored talking cats and unions.

The young man in pink offered Lacie a beer, "Welcome to Null-Mart, you will never find a more wretched closeout of scum and villainy."

"Thanks, I guess." Lacie replied.

"Nice hats, care if I have that sombrero as your ticket in?"

Lacie reluctantly gave the young man in pink that hat and declined the booze. The unofficial greeter promptly put the hat on and beamed a huge smile.

"So.. from your angle, how sexy is the hat? Would it look better with stunna shades?"

"Uh.. it's fine.. What's going on here?" Lacie asked.

"It's a party up in here till the whole place comes crashing down!" The man in pink gestured with both hands.

"Null-mart? Crashing down?"

The greeter cocked his head up looking over the store like security. He cracked open the beer in his hand and took a sip, still grinning, "Inside, we call it Null-Mart. It's all comin' down tonight though, soon as the time comes and the Technology Department empties, the technacles are gonna rip the foundations down.. Might as well get plastered for the show!"

In the distance there was a young man in all black, including a trenchcoat and circular shades, but he did not have a marble head and was human. He sat on a reclined, beach chair atop shelving between aisles and seemed quite drunk. Some sort of large, black, dog-like creature flew some ways behind him from the ceiling and into an aisle-way, and left a trail of black smoke laced with ash. The stranger raised his non-beer hand in devil-horns with a black magic marker grasped in his fist.

"Hey, could you put your hands on your head?" The greeter asked.

"Why?" Lacie inquired.

"I want to smell chocolate-covered strawberries."

Lacie looked away from him for a second in embarrassment, afraid that she might be blushing.

An individual in his fifties or sixties emerged from a nearby aisle in a shimmery blue suit with tiny, flashing blue lights poking out of the clothing's rayon material. He also had blue eyes, white hair littered with glittery blue, and a short white goatee with a similarly surreal color at the hair's bottom half.

The theatrical old man grabbed a brew, and joined Lacie and the man in pink, proving to possess a deep, Scottish accent as he spoke, "That *'Nobody Was Here'* outside-- half of that was done with the blood of Red Squad, the other half with Russian salad dressing. Trouble is, there may not be a difference. Ha ha ha ha!"

"Damn." The Man In Pink shook his head smiling.

Lacie decided to pretend that the Scotsman wasn't being serious.

The Scotsman took a gulp of beer which had turned a similar glimmer of blue as the tip of his pointed beard-- though you couldn't see it through the brown glass. He shook hands with Lacie who appeared speechless, "Hello young lady. You may call me Cuithbeart Cobalt. The youthful renegades of The Midnight Brigade have been painting all the door windows in sways and swirls! But forgive me, what is your name?"

"It's Lacie and why are they painti--"

"Lacie! I don't really care for that, I think I'll call you Four-Eyes McPhee." Cuithbeart had the matter settled upon himself.

"That's kind of offensive." Lacie remarked.

Cuithbeart raised his thick eyebrows, "Well at least it's not defensive. Ha ha ha ha!"

"I need to find someone named Herbert." The girl inquired.

The Man In Pink scratched his dirty-dish blond hair, "Yeah, Aisle 3. Hope you got some DVD's or something."

Cuithbeart pulled out an action movie from his suit pocket.

"Well, I suppose I'll take you to the furry bastard. No true Scotsman would call him anything else!" Cuithbeart laughed.

"Furry?"

Cuithbeart's face went sly, "You'll see. Oh.. so furry."

"Okay.. thank you." Lacie expired.

Cuithbeart picked up another bottle of beer and put it in his pocket. With a deep, grizzly resonance of his Scottish accent, "..one for the road.."

As the Scotsman spoke, the light reflecting from the floor seemed to reflect just slightly brighter, if only for a second or two.

Chapter 5

Lacie and Cuithbeart made their way past countless, unmanned cash registers and nearby aisles with the rap music behind them abnormally dissipating. One further aisle had countless balloons rising from it, going up through one of many crevices in the ceiling. The registers were all open and filled with soda-soaked confetti, junk food, and small bells. The floors were covered with green and violet tiles; the tiles were stained with black and white paint and popping out at different corners; and from the holes in the popping corners, smoke rose, and from behind the smoke came distant, echoing screeches from some unknown form of life.

More jump ropes of neon colors dangled from the ceiling, some of them knotted together and swaying or swinging almost to the floor. Other jump ropes worked together to swing a third jump rope, though there didn't seem to be any form of mechanics powering them. Lacie was aware enough to duck.

"Ah! Damned jump ropes!" Cuithbeart tried to navigate the ropes while keeping his beers from shaking up. “What a bunch of magical bullshit!”

Lacie quietly giggled at Cuithbeart until

her laughter was cut short by the loud rushing sound of water. From afar she could see a group of ceramic frogs playing instruments in melancholic melody atop thin, white shelving. Further back, a huge tidal-wave of green water was approaching. Cuithbeart, Lacie, and Cuithbeart's beers (which spoke through bubbling) all yelled in unison, unable to run or evaporate. The ceiling-high wave of emerald water rushed over them with a lidless plastic pitcher or two.

Lacie was hit by the wave with great force, and forced to swallow some of the water, which tasted like a Lime-flavored drink. The tide rushed her across the store ceiling until it finally subsided, dropping her alone in a new aisle with the newsgirl hat next to her. She lay on her back looking around at her blurry surroundings, quickly realizing that her glasses had fallen off of her face. She slowly got up as something strange handed Lacie her glasses.

Towering in front of Lacie was a large, fluffy rabbit who appeared to be wearing an adequately-sized, black, Victorian-patterned vest. He was holding a human-sized cigarette in one big paw and a whiskey glass of some bronze liquor in the other. She noticed a sign above the distinguished bunny which read, "Aisle 3".

Lacie also noticed small, tar-like writings on the diversely-tiled aisle-floor, but not the one behind her which read: 'Heavens it's eleven of eight on the nineteenth fate of four, then down and around to seventeen, almost zero, seventeen again, till twenty-four for sure. Thirteen is bad luck maybe, fourteen a bit better than thirteen say thee, eighteen a time to run, four should watch out for the sign of thirteen, eighteen might have weight next to more of four.'

"To whom do I owe the pleasure?" The giant rabbit asked, patting the watch in his vest to make sure it was securely ticking. The shelves around the rabbit and Lacie were filled with what seemed like stylized, yet clunky, odd devices from the Victorian era or the Industrial Revolution.

"Uh.." Lacie gasped. "Are you Herbert?"

The rabbit sipped his liquor, "And you, some sort of green fanatic? With your tee-shirt and your lime drink?"

From the rabbit's words Lacie noticed that apart from a few green puddles, it was as if the lime drink had abnormally dissipated, but she otherwise ignored his sarcasm. "I think your niece has been kidnapped."

"I don't believe you." The rabbit was smug.

"Why not?"

"Because most refer to me as 'my dear Uncle Herbert.'"

"But.. why?" The girl's face crumpled with curiosity.

"I'm an aniecetheist."

"Wha-- So you don't even care?" Lacie asked.

The smoke billowed from Herbert's cigarette as he took a puff and followed it with a kind of sip of his drink that would be precocious to the average giant bunny. The bright lights caused Herbert's white fur to glow, but that was the only part of him doing so. His eyes looked of someone who hadn't slept much, his long, puffy ears perched downwards to the side. The rabbit's nose was wet, but his stare had a dry enthusiasm which seemed unable to falter, "Who kidnapped who?"

"A marble-headed man took Elizabeth!" Lacie exasperated in frustration.

"Oh.. the donut girl," The large rabbit laughed. "That was no kidnapping.. First of null there were no kids involved."

"Then why did she look so scared?"

"Because the man who took her is one of them.. And they are the reason that skeletons sporadically litter these empty streets."

Lacie started to get upset, “So why did

he take her!?"

"Because he likes donuts." Herbert laughed.

"Then why did he kidnap her like some creep?"

Herbert held his cigarette in the air like a French philosopher as he spoke in his deep British accent, "Since the donut girl is the only one I know of who can make donuts, and she has disappeared from the donut shop, I would wager it is because of that."

As Lacie took a breath to speak again she felt her entire body weaken intensely. She peered down as her brain and face felt like it was tingling. The floor beneath her was dissolving into gas following with her lower torso. Somehow she did not lose height. As Lacie looked up her vision dissipated into a strange kaleidoscope of her surroundings.

Just as it seemed she might start to have a panic attack from this alien sensation-- her being was restored.

The aisle had expanded with a road appearing over the floor that was glowing intensely with light. Rainbows came off of the road everywhere as though it was some sort of intense and futuristic prism. Lacie could feel slight heat around her feet. She quickly collected herself to whatever degree she could and asked Herbert, "What is going on?"

Herbert (who's fur now shimmered even more intensely) sipped his drink and puffed on a new cigarette, "This is The Ultra-Violet Road, once a prominent grid-work of unspeakable beauty.. all that is left of the road remains in remote, flickering fragments."

Lacie could feel warmth and intrigue stirring within her which misplaced some of her previous fear. She was mystified by the rainbows all around her which reflected in the brassy instruments and inventions closely sprinkled around the shelves. But the road began flickering like a dying light fixture, and each time it turned off the normal tiled floor appeared.

Moments later, the road was gone, and the aisle seemed to shrink back to normal.. shrinking like the vision of someone with great fatigue-- as if the aisle returning to its normal size was a problem with Lacie's vision as much as it was a tangible change in her physical reality.

The girl held her open palms out towards the floor, and took a deep breath before returning her posture to normal, and speaking to Herbert again. "Okay. Who made this road? Can it lead me back home?"

"The answer to both of those questions is no." Herbert replied.

Lacie slumped down to the floor with

her knees out, staring down at the tiles and cradling her head with her hands. She moaned in distress, "Oh.. what's going on?"

One of Herbert's long ears twitched as he let out some sympathy with a large puff of smoke, "It seems you are the one in need of saving, dear. That is all that is going on.. Tell me, do you play croquet?"

"No." Lacie almost whined.

Herbert chuckled heavily to himself before taking another sip of his liquor.

The voice of a man in his forties came from the end of the aisle.. "Well Syll, are you able to find Muenster?"

"Get up. Take another deep breath.. and have a glass of scotch." Herbert remarked looking down at Lacie.

Lacie rose her head up, dropping her grasp to her semi-scrunched legs, and catching a glimpse of the distant man; he was long-faced gentleman somewhere in his forties with an expensive yellow bathrobe and a silver cane under one of his hands. He suddenly stepped forward, while talking to whoever 'Syll' was, and disappeared from sight.

"I think I've been drugged already." Lacie lowered her eyes to the floor again and sulked, returning her attention to herself.

Herbert reached for a scotch bottle from the nearby shelf. His big, fluffy bunny paws hid most of the bottle and all of his glass. He poured himself a refill and chuckled, "Not in this world you haven't."

There was a pause where Lacie thought of what to say.

“Is there any way out of here?” Lacie asked, lifting her gaze from the floor.

“The exit.” Herbert replied with dry snark, finishing what he was doing.

“Will that take me out of this world?” Lacie asked in frustration.

“I suppose the question is, do you really want to leave yet, and leave Elizabeth's fate up to chance, or do you feel a strange, driving mixture of terror, curiousity and guilt?”

Lacie stood up. She thought for a second and tried to find the words for her emotions. Her shoulders tensed up and she clenched her fists against the front of her legs, “..is this girl.. Elizabeth, in danger?”

“She could be.. I don't know for sure.” There was a pause before Herbert spoke again, where he gulped down some alcohol. "I can help you search for Elizabeth if that's what you want."

“Elizabeth said you know how to leave this place.” Lacie said sternly, loosening her hands but not her shoulders.

“From my observations, scant as they are, each person's exit is different.”

The girl took a deep breath through her mouth and nose before speaking again. "How do I find my exit?"

“Curiousity and guilt.”

Lacie paused and pondered for a moment.. “So if I find Elizabeth I can leave?”

"If you tried to find her and it was a waste of time, you would risk getting stuck here-- from there, here.. going mad or dying are the greater possibilities. Or you could look for another exit, another way, and another risk. It's really your choice. But when 'She' completes The Nocturnal Migration, you will be out of time."

"She?" Lacie asked, standing up with fervent curiosity.

"That smelly, leathery-faced hag 'She'.. is the leader of The Nocturnal Migration, and the migration is said by some to power 'here.'" Herbert replied, before going into a short coughing fit.

As much as Lacie wanted to leave this crazy and creepy city, she wanted to make sure Elizabeth was okay. And as much as Lacie wanted to make sure Elizabeth was okay, she wanted to leave this.. well, you get the idea. She decided to go with her gut, and let her guilt and curiosity lead her, since it seemed like the safest option.

Lacie picked up the pink newsgirl hat

and placed it snugly on her head, "Alright then, where do I begin?"

Chapter 6

Null-Mart was particularly bright as most large stores are, and there was a loud mechanical humming which must've been coming from air-conditioners that echoed through the ventilation system-- but the store's normalcy had limitations. The store leaned inwards from some of the outer walls. And parts of the ceiling made loud creaking sounds, while bent and broken metal in the ceiling made a rare showing of black clouds shifting across the bizarrely-colored and starry sky.

Peculiar creatures went flying at random intervals across the open gaps in the ceiling. A few of the creatures stayed in the store and began flying around lower, each looked like a cross between a dog and bat with large wings, four eyes, and two protruding mouths; to make matters more curious the creatures had black smoke trailing from their faces, though one of them littered both black smoke and ash from his.

Herbert belched before speaking, "Somewhere in this store is a young woman who thinks.. she is a bird."

With arms crossed, an awkward expression came over Lacie's face, "What?"

"You need to find this person and bring

her back to me if you want me to help you."

"Why?" Lacie coughed from the smoke pouring out of Herbert's mouth.

"Curiousity and guilt."

"Oh.. okay." Lacie replied, feeling that she was starting to annoy the rabbit too much, but also that he might be insane. As the girl took her leave past Herbert she noticed a caterpillar cocoon hanging off the inside of an empty bottle of gin.

As if coming from the end of the aisle behind Herbert, the young lady heard the low, crackly voice of an old woman, "No more glasses, camera-eyes."

The area around Lacie's eyes tingled. Feeling around her eyes it seemed as though her glasses were melting to the bone of her face, but with a kind of tingling and numbness rather than pain. She cupped her hands over what felt like strange mechanical devices which had formed over eyes. She gasped in fear. Her eyes felt similar to the two small ends of a microscope that a person would look through.

She blinked instinctively.. and when she blinked, she felt her eyelids make tiny clanks.. Lacie's eyelids were now metal shutters at the ends of her scope-eyes.

Behind Lacie, the world appeared all fuzzy, and some distance away Herbert's back seemed two-dimensional like a cardboard cutout.

Lacie was frantic, "Oh my Null! Null!? What's happening?"

A pale-blue wool suit appeared atop the aisle division as though an invisible figure was filling it, with rounded-out holes in the neckline and sleeves. A deep voice bellowed out from the wardrobe, "I am the lead romanticist for the modern age, I have bought the dance and I have bought the grave."

The robed, long-faced gentlemen looked from across the aisle, "Young lady, are you alright?"

Lacie glanced at the gentlemen who held a silver cane with a silver lion's head at the top-- though presently, the bottom of the cane did not touch the floor. He had dim blue eyes, and slicked-back, greying brown hair, and a thin mustache-- of similar normal color. And underneath his bright yellow bathrobe was a black suit and tie with a white dress shirt. Then Lacie looked at the vacant space, where the empty suit had just been.. then Herbert's back (who was now normal looking with an enormous puff of smoke emanating above him) with the sharpness of her vision returning to the bunny's side of the aisle-- and finally she peered back at the yellow-robed man.

"No!"

The man kindly protested, "Well maybe there's something wrong with your sight, how did you come to have microscope eyes?"

"They formed from my glasses." Lacie explained with frustration in her voice.

A light above the man flickered as he was taken aback, realizing he had further upset the girl. Tears welled up from the ends of Lacie's mechanical eyes while a drizzle of raindrops echoed across the top of the Null-Mart ceiling. Some rain fell through the ceiling's crevices, one of which was right above the robed and suited man.

There was a distant pounding which only seemed to worry Lacie. She recognized the sound, but was unsure from where.

From the right of Aisle 3's end came a Japanese woman around mid-thirties in white garments. From her clothes, strips of cloth hung down fading into warm colors like some sort of mummy fashion model-- though her bandages stopped at her neck. She had gold jewelry, brown eyes like Lacie's normal eyes, and well-styled hair. What was most noticeable though, was the warm smile on the lady's face and the cart she pushed full of different cheeses. Upon seeing the scene the woman spoke, "Victor, who is this lovely girl you are upsetting?"

Victor's forehead was wet with rain. He

went to Lacie and wiped off some of her tears as if he was a close relative, "I apologize if I upset you."

"No it's fine." Lacie said.

"Well by now you should know my name. What is yours?" Victor replied.

The pounding got louder and the college girl replied awkwardly, "It's Lacie."

The beaming Asian woman left the cart behind and was now next to Victor. She shook Lacie's hand making Lacie feel even more nervous, "Hi Lacie, I'm Syll."

There was some indie rock music Lacie could hear playing throughout Null-Mart, nothing sounding like the old rock songs they played constantly on the radio back home; the music was audible underneath of the loud, nearby pounding. Syll had noticed the heavy hits against the floor, but Victor had not just yet. The robed, old man looked up at the dark creatures flying above in the ceiling gaps, his precious hoard of cheese, and then Lacie, "Syll is a lovely creature from the Something Prefecture. And I'm from-- what's that loud pounding?"

The same suit which appeared to be worn by an invisible figure had reappeared, it had shifted next to the cart of cheese as though it was about to steal the cart, its invisible hands on the handle.

A huge, ugly statue came barreling through a Null-Mart wall into the aisle division, cracking and denting the floor, crushing the pale blue suit and almost knocking over the cart. Lacie, Syll, and Victor quickly got out of the monstrous statue's beastly pounding feet-- and Herbert's face was thrown into surprise as he lost his cigarette to the floor-- hopping out of the way as the statue bolted past him. The empty suit spoke as its fabric changed into sparkling black sludge that oozed out onto the floor, with the words coming from it now inaudible.

The ends of Lacie's mechanical-eyes fell off hitting the floor with a clink. She gasped, reaching around her glasses and face to find them immediately back to normal.

Victor and Syll peered down the aisle-way. Syll pushed back excess strips of cloth dangling from her torso and looked for her pockets as Victor spoke, "There goes that gargoyle again."

Lacie looked down at the microscope lenses wondering what the heck just happened, and if she should pick them up, in case they would come in handy later on. They were antique brass, and they appeared old and Victorian, with an etched and repeating pattern of a heart, an eyeball, and the side view of a hand with its palm up, running along the middle border between the two segments of each eyepiece.

Lacie's eyes went back to Victor and Syll, "Why does he keep doing that? Wait.. He runs when people are crying, and rain comes down?"

"Gargoyles were originally designed to direct that." Syll informed.

"Oh.." Lacie jolted. "I have to get going, I'm running out of time!"

"Where do you need to go?" Victor asked, peeling off the wrapping on some cheese.

"I have to find the woman who.. thinks she's a bird." Lacie replied timidly.

Victor arched an eyebrow in curiosity, "Interesting. I've not yet had the privilege of meeting her!"

"Oh!" Lacie remembered. "Uh.. I have to tell you that someone named Odis wants your cheese..?"

"Ah.. I'll deal with him later on then.. Let's get going." Victor put the half-eaten cheese in the cart with a serious, almost grim look on his face.

A familiar smokey voice bellowed out from behind Lacie. "That you should."

It was Herbert, "All your noise is annoying my distorted senses."

"Sorry.." Lacie's apology was barely

audible as she looked down and scratched the back of her head.

Annoyed by Herbert, Victor left Aisle 3 and started down the Dairy Section on the side of the store and at the ends of many aisles. Herbert hopped back over to his familiar spot; the large rabbit's hops were quite a hilarious sight to Syll and Lacie who tried to contain themselves from laughing.

Lacie looked down once again at the scope-eyes on the tiled floor. It seemed like they vibrated or shook for a second, and then she heard the old woman's voice whispering to her, “No more glasses.. alchemy..”

Syll motioned, "Are you coming?"

Lacie knelt down and picked up the lenses and put them in her pocket with some kind of instinctual reflex. Maybe they could come in handy. Especially in a place as strange and potentially dangerous as N'Qevna.

White, black, and purple confetti poured from Null-Mart's dead light fixtures, with mad strangers underneath the lights and confetti who seemed from different worlds or perceptions. In Aisle 4, a woman in dirty rags cried out for her husband in gripping distress, but all that was left in front of her was what seemed to be a rotting apple. Aisle 4 itself looked like an old library of ancient books and rotting fruit filling the shelves.. with an occasional couple of involuntarily-moving squirrel skulls and a pumpkin.

There was a white-masked individual in a bear suit with the head and mouth of the imitation animal as the hood. He or she used a lengthy, crotchety branch as a walking stick, their back and spine bent with a stupor. The person in the bear suit was atop an aisle divider full of rolled carpets. He or she was laying out the carpets one by one-- save the place where a lone clothes dresser covered in aged stickers laid on its side with a missing drawer. At the top end of this aisle divider and shelving being carpeted was a little girl; she was covered head to toe in a shade of light blue with a dripping watering hose, trying to get the end to unplug.

Lacie quickly ventured to Syll with Victor not far away from them. Ahead was the back of some husky man, some feet away, who seemed to be inspecting eggs to the left. And the same black-clad youth who Lacie had spotted when she entered Null-Mart was still on the top of a further aisle division, drinking at a corner. Further away, men in medieval and military outfits of great differences were now locked in battle with the giant, flying bat-dogs.

Chapter 7

Elizabeth peered curiously at white, metal beams connected underneath metal, blue square platforms that came together like a three-dimensional maze in the black fog and wild sky. On the blue platforms there were random cement or metal blocks with their edges sanded down, from which thirteen-feet-long crooked streetlights rose and pierced the darkness. The marble-headed man, still wrapped in expensive leather, stared in fixed expression at Elizabeth from a nearby, opposing platform.

He spoke with a deep fluid tone as his hard jawline crackled open, "I've rescued you."

Most of the pieces of marble from the man's jawline made their descent downwards through the platform's blue chain-link holes as black cloud formed around the man's face recreating it.

Some of the platforms tilted back and forth just slightly as towering, illegible neon lights flickered on and off in the gaps of the structural maze. Wingless red birds somehow flew from light to light, some ghastly, some ghostly. Each bird had one fin on their back, a narrow beak, and long, waving skeletal tails. And the great lights were held up by numberless, smaller metal beams which sank down into a dark gray smog.

"Rescued me? You grabbed me! And you wasted a perfectly good cookie!" Elizabeth stood up and replied angrily as one of the huge signs literally ripped off of its hinges with the ringing of the English girl's voice. Hundreds of feet in multi-colored light detached in a frightening fall downwards.

The marble-headed man reached out to Elizabeth with his leather-gloved hand as if to stop the event, "Please don't be angry with me."

Moments later both heard the enormous crash of the sign and the marble-headed man sunk his arm down. Elizabeth held her anger back with a calm question, "Who are you? Are.. are you the individual who was eating chicken at a sea-food restaurant?"

The man shook his marble cranium negatively, "A marble-headed man would have no business eating chicken from a sea-food restaurant.

"No.." The man bowed deeply with his right arm just above the waist. "I am Monsieur Malluso of The Presiding Manner. And you are Elizabeth of Mr. Bagel's Donut Shop."

From the darkness, snakes with bacterial-like bodies the size of dragons began appearing. Their bright-golden skin was dotted with other colors and semi-transparent. The surrounding, animated neon lights lit up against the sweeping exoskeletons of these organisms, splashing them with color. They fascinated and scared Elizabeth enough for her to with withdraw from speech and keep anxiously centered on her residing platform.

"Monsieur, why do you think you rescued me?" Elizabeth asked politely.

"That young lady you were with. She was endangering you, I could not let her."

"Lacie?.." Elizabeth wondered out loud. "How do you know my name?"

"Because I was assigned to keep you at Mr. Bagel's." Malluso kindly stated.

"By whom?" Elizabeth inquired.

"Forgive me, I can't say for your safety.."

“Is it Mr. Bagel?!” The rising of neurosis in Elizabeth's voice caused creaking and breaking sounds from the pipe-like foundations of the enormous towers of light.

“It's classified for your safety.”

"Well then I want to leave. I don't like this place."

"Okay, okay. Just stay calm, or you could crush us to death." Monsieur replied.

One of the dragon-snakes emerged from the dark. This one in particular had crimson skin; the carriage on its back was a wealthy mix of engraved gold, brass, and silver, and hiding bits of strange technology in the seating. The creature halted for Elizabeth while still squirming around from the tail and making low-pitched, multi-vocal 'Ong' sounds.

"I'm not sure where he'll take you at first," Malluso eyed the dragon-snake. "But I know you'll eventually get back to the bakery."

The sound effect of a disc scratch echoed out from one of the lights like a disc jockey was stationed inside one of the towers; indeed she was, some girl named Eris waiting for key phrases such as 'back to the bakery' to accompany with sound effects on a commissioned basis. She also made the cookies for Monsieur, but had thus been unsuccessful in charging him an arm and a leg. It was rumored that she was a closet nudist when no one was around; she might've been, but nobody in the black cloud could see anything half the time.

"You are awfully concerned with my safety." Elizabeth furrowed her eyebrows at Malluso in a look of confusion that matched her voice.

Monsieur did not reply. But instead, pulled a double chocolate-chip cookie from his pocket and took a bite out of it. As a breeze came in shaking the tails of Malluso's coat he murmured very quietly to himself, "Mmmm..

Crumbly, but good."

Elizabeth gave Malluso a brief annoyed stare before venturing up the steps of the carriage hovering to the left of her. After opening the carriage door she found countless seatbelts around her, as though installed at every opportune space. She promptly buckled herself in with a few or five, and after closing the door, held onto the bar in front of her.

Arrays of crystallized wings grew from the dragon-snake's back. Then the creature moved swiftly through the air flapping its wings almost quicker then the eye. She jolted through layers of mist and ebony cloud as fierce winds rushed around her.

* * *

In an instant the black-clad lass found herself transported back at the donut shop in such a manner as to cause chairs and tables shuffling away from her with life. A severely tinged, smoking circle was impressed upon the floor around her, followed by some hearts, smiley faces, stick men, and other inked doodles. This mess and losing her chair for the floor generally caused her some distress. A paper came floating down in front of the girl, a bit singed itself, explaining the process of teleportation.

With underdeveloped diagrams the paper outlined such a process as 'Transporteriffic Splenditransport'.

After reading the teleportation notation, Elizabeth got up off the ground and checked the double doors of Mr. Bagel's Donut Shop to make sure that they were locked. The door certainly would not open under any pretenses but smashing the glass, which she found a small comfort. A multi-colored feline with a cactus hat or head went rubbing against the doors, but missed the young lass's attention. Elizabeth looked around for the lock unable to find it on the doorknob where it had been, until she heard a slightly muffled, sarcastic voice stating, "It's locked, give it a break already."

The employee decided the voice was right, and decided to give the door a break.. by not breaking it.

* * *

Malluso stared at the space between two street lights letting off their guidance in the enormous black cloud. A dark voice created a wind current behind him, "No more next'uses, Monsieur."

From the black particles of cloud came the whispers of many tongues, "The future is Five! The future is Five!"

There was a huge breeze behind Malluso, "Caravans are coming, Monsieur."

The great creature that was behind Malluso went flying in an enormous gust of wind knocking a couple towering signs down accidentally as it made its swift exit.

Some of the glowing dragon-worms were being chased by sinister and hungry bat-dogs; black smoke poured from these dogs' double mouths and nostrils, and here, in this place, there were endless trails of ash pouring out from each creature's four eyes. Malluso drew a rapier with a black and gold contorted handle and prepared to fight the large bat-dogs, or as he put it under his breath, '..those foul caravans.'

A fierce crowd of caravans ripped into the exoskeletal bodies of the dragon-worms causing them to screech in elongated "Ong" sounds. Three of the bat-dogs bolted towards Malluso from different directions. Malluso ducked and stabbed upward, ripping the stomach open of one of the foul creatures and dodging the other two. The struck caravan yelped, collapsing on the ground where it let out its dark rasp and dual voice, "Indigestible Monsieur, why will you not let us feast on delicious tropical carreras?"

Monsieur sheathed his sword back by the left side his coat. He pulled out an entire platter of strapped-down double chocolate chip cookies from the right side. Malluso's jaw (which had healed from its previous speeches) crackled open with little pieces of marble flailing everywhere, "These tropical carreras are vital to powering the lights which hold the contrast to the black cloud that sustains us. If those lights go out, this cloud will begin collapsing in on itself. I've explained this before.."

The caravan on the ground had already began to heal with black gas forming around its body. The other caravans swirling around the sky had stopped their wrath and listened in angry attention at the sight of baked goods. The dragon-worms, or tropical pharisees, were subject to random intervals of intelligence--but they had all made a fair account of such intelligence in the distance they made from their terrifying hunters. The winged-dog on the ground in front of Malluso growled from both of its mouths, "How many cookies do we get?"

Chapter 8

The refrigerated aisle, from Dairy to Horror, was quite long-- spanning across the left side of the store, for anyone looking towards the back of the store (let it be noted, that this understanding and distinction between left and right has become an imperative fact for those who find interest in the basics of geography, and is heavily agreed upon by individuals standing side-by-side one another, while contested to this day by some who do not [citation needed]).

All sorts of assortments littered the shelves, including a wooden shelf.. and piles of cheese. There was a bearded, gruff man who looked a little 'provolonely'; a real 'Monterey Jack' standing in a vat of a cold colby cheese sauce and making new shelves with a hole-ridden saw resembling a slice of swiss. There were various people smoking, drinking, or sleeping on the cheese, absorbing its iconographic powers.

But the travesty of the far-off Meat and Horror sections were much more nerve racking. And this wasn't just because bologna was on sale. It was not Russian dressing dripping from those distant shelves holding what seemed like animal carcasses recent and ancient. Here was a section full of opened packages of bloody meat and half-visible discs offering dial-up internet-trials running on into a section of people who were sleeping or maybe worse. Red liquid that was mixed with water and liquor was spread across the floor and sinking into one of three large sink holes.

Mr. Greary was stroking his chin impressed and dazed upon the selection of eggs in front of him unsure of what to buy. He already had one twelve-egg carton under his arm.

Lacie waved at him frantically, "Mr. Greary! Hey. It's me! Lacie."

Mr. Greary turned his head, "Lacie?.. Lacie!"

Before anything more could be said, a large and green pointed limb rose from the nearest sinkhole, stretching high and upright in front of Mr. Greary. The green skin of the tentacle was covered in sections with material similar to computer motherboards and all sorts of fans, hinges, devices, and valves for the massive intake of caffeinated beverages: a technacle. The technacle had a plethora of artificial eyes, and other more primitive protruding lasers which seemed designated to scan areas, detecting heat sources and really good movies. Where a normal tentacle would have suction cup like holes, the technacle had cupholders.

Victor rose his arms in front of Lacie and Syll, purposefully brushing Syll's breasts. He spoke with an ounce of deviance, "Wait, don't get any closer."

Mr. Greary and his lack of technological giftery was detected immediately by the present technacle-- just like the man in pink had hinted at earlier. The technacle wrapped itself around Greary, and he was nabbed down into the sinkhole screaming.

Lacie felt a paralyzing surge of fear as she saw Mr. Greary pulled down into the hole by the monster limb.

Syll pulled Victor's arm away, "Victor.."

Victor dropped his arms and chuckled, "Quite.."

"What the hell are those things?" Lacie asked.

Victor twiddled his adorned silver cane, contemplating the gap before them, "Technological tentacles, media lovers. Technacles. They'll pull you into those terrible sinkholes if you don't bribe them. Then who knows what danger might befall you."

There was a look of sad concern on Syll's face, "I'm sorry about your friend Lacie. Hopefully he should be okay. Or.. err.. I guess that's two friends?"

"Okay.." Lacie retorted. She didn't

know if she considered anyone here a 'friend'. She hadn't had someone she would call a 'friend' since before she left for college.

Above Lacie, Syll, and Victor there was a group of three people in mostly Victorian garb standing on top of the aisle divider and shelving. The trio all had scope-eyes that were darker compared to the ones in Lacie's pockets. A pattern of a tiny skull, a bird, and an eyeball were laced around the middle of these strangers' mechanical and ocular protrusions, though Lacie and her newfound accomplices couldn't see it.

Two of the three strangers were unfriendly-looking women wearing both dresses and corsets. One woman was young, in her mid-twenties with pink and dark brass scope-eyes. The other woman was in her fifties with dark red and dark brass eyepieces.

The male looked to be in his thirties and worried. He was in back, behind the two women, sporting similar 1800's garb. He had on a male surgeon's corset (which was straighter than its female counterparts) and a modern doctor overcoat. He also had protruding lenses from his face that were dark brass with thin streaks of indigo and violet. He had two ghostly instances of him on his left and right, totaling in five, and every instance of him looked like an unstable hologram that would randomly blur, tremor, or shift, making it impossible to tell which of his appearances was the real one-- or if one appearance was more real than another.

The youngest female, some years ahead of Lacie, had garments of underlying black, with thick stains of paint that was strangely similar to an area of the ceiling above her. Shadows crept across her body as if invisible lights or lack thereof rotated around her. The girl's coiled strands of hair shifted from a pink at the roots and into indigo, while orange pipe-cleaners that matched her hidden irises zigzagged outwards from her hair.

The young women was hunched over slightly, holding her open hands in the air like a cat with its claws out; her fingers were covered in sharpened finger-rings, like metal claws that were painted in all sorts of colors. Her porcelain face looked down on Lacie in disgust, and the bottom of her face was stained with dark gray, orange, and purple, in such a way as to make her look like she had been drinking paint.

"Give me that hat or I'll kill you!" The strange girl yelled.

Lacie retreated backwards holding onto the top of newsgirl cap, "This is my hat!"

The blurring and unstable man spoke up in a relaxed tone that did not match his face, taking speaking turns with his faded clones, "Ratty, don't hurt.. Ratty, don't hurt the poor girl, it's her.. poor girl, it's her hat.. it's hers. Let's, take the cheese.. let's, the cheese."

Victor's eyes narrowed, standing in front of his cart with his arm on the handle in a kind of parental protection, "Now listen here you ghoul--"

The scope-eyes of the older woman rotated in and out under strands of her shoulder-length, scraggly white hair. Her flowing dress was splattered with dark colors; the dress had a long collar made up of partially-dyed rib bones. The scent of cinnamon, blood, and rose emanated strongly from her. She stood quietly with a striking and unpleasant presence.

"Look.. wait." Lacie pulled her hat off with strands of brown hair going off in all directions. She decided to give the hat away since it hadn't protected her in any way and Victor's cheese was at risk. Lacie held the hat towards Ratty with her voice shaking and her eyes on the razor sharp claws, "I'll give you the hat I just need to ask you a question, please?"

"Go find your own cheese." Victor spoke angrily with his cane gripped defensively.

Atop the shelving, the older woman laughed snidely and the man in back moaned to himself in the pain of his multiplicity.

Ignoring Victor's words completely, Ratty jumped down, snatched the hat from Lacie and spit in her face, "No, bitch!"

Lacie sneered, bolting at the hat in Ratty's hands to grab it back. In reaction to this, Victor held Lacie back from her ribs with his cane and Syll followed by holding her back from the shoulder. Ratty had a malevolent grin on her face and was ready to slash Lacie with her free hand.

The Japanese lady tensely inquired upon the two older people on the top of the shelves, "This girl needs to find someone, a woman who thinks she's a bird. That's all we need to know, we'll be gone after that."

Ratty's grin changed to smug satisfaction as she placed the pink hat on her head. After that she seemed to freeze in place, her orange eyes widened-- albeit hidden behind her scope-eyes, and her hands stayed stuck on the top of her hatted head, while Syll ripped off a strip of her mummy-like cloth to let Lacie wipe the saliva from her face.

Ratty began making gestures with her arms. She started dancing, as if in a sports-like behavioral taunt, but still wide-eyed, and one of the pipe cleaners fell out of her hair. Lacie threw the strip of cloth on a nearby shelf, and her, Syll, and Victor took some steps back from the dancing girl.

The man and his ghostly copies moaned in echoes, "Ecila.. my Ecila."

Lacie was nervous with everything going on and forced the question through her voice breaking, "Is.. that who she is?"

"Tell them nothing." The older woman's voice crackled angrily. She took a few steps forward, and then rose up her hand and snapped her fingers

Syll, Lacie, and Victor looked around to see if something had happened. Victor became dumbfounded with horror. His pile of cheese was melting rapidly through the cart, giving off steam as it left a puddle across the multi-colored tiles of the floor. The old man fell to his knees, the light fixture above him flickering in and out, his cane dropping to the side as sad violin music suddenly began playing through the PA system. He scooped at the assortment of cheeses and plastic all melting together, quickly realizing the heat.

Victor drew back from the pain in his hands, landing on his butt, which stopped the violin music-- he wiped the hot material on his pants to get it off his hands. The witchy old woman cackled and snapped her fingers again causing Syll, Lacie, and Victor to feel a deeper panic as they looked around with terror at what this leathery-skinned villain was capable of.

This time had backfired though, and the woman found her hand had turned into an enlarged cardboard hand, while Ratty generally stayed in place in some kind of popstar-like “dance trance”.

The black-clad young man who had been some aisles away drinking had retreated from his beach chair. He had pale skin, short black hair, and a possible Vitamin D deficiency, with small circular sunglasses that had red chaos stars centered on the black of the lenses. And he wore a black trenchcoat with red markings on it, and military boots, a shirt, and khakis colored like the coat; and he sported a black cane with a bowling-ball sized, silver chaos star atop it-- the tips of the chaos star dipped in red paint, with the metal center where he normally rested his hand. And that's enough of that.

This twenty-something stranger hung from a bar supporting the ceiling using the top of his cane, somewhat unsure of his idea of being there in the first place.. and trying to remember how he got there.

"Hanging out here.." His booted legs dangled and fear filled his stomach. As he spoke he was noticed immediately, "I pay tribute to my counterparts, the lost boards and pieces from which they host the differences of compassion. It is not me however farce, who outputs separation from which loss is found wholly without parties who would be so dispassioned."

The young man's cane finally slipped from the bar. He dropped like a rock, a black-clad rock, vanishing in midair-- in a puff of white smoke. Lacie tried to make sense of the young man's words in her head, while Syll went to help Victor up, who was suddenly in a heavy laughing fit.

Syll pulled on Victor's shoulders from his clothed armpits, trying to get him to stand up, but then she stopped. "Why are you laughing so hard? What's so funny?"

"That was Thee Chaotician, I know him.. the Chaotician.." Victor laughed hard to himself with a red face and wiped away a tear, "..solves problems that don't exist."

Lacie and the trio on the above aisle stood in wonderment, save Ratty who continued dancing in a varied fashion to tune of the store music, which had changed to synthpop. The lighting around Ratty's form remained unnatural.

"So what does that mean!?" Syll practically yelled in confusion.

The face of the old woman on the top of the aisle division grew more vindictive..

Victor was on his knees, shaking his head as he continued laughing, "We're by the

Dairy section!"

Chapter 9

Having been bested by Thee Chaotician, the old woman at the top of the aisle shouted out a command in rebellion, "Ratty, go and show that girl with the glasses your claws."

Ratty only continued dancing to the store music in a goofy manner.

"Stupid girl." The woman atop the aisle sneered. Then she turned her back revealing the brunt of her high collar made up of variously-colored ribs, "Come Manchester, let's leave.. Now!"

Manchester made a motion for her to stop, "Wait Mona!"

As Mona walked down the aisle division, pieces of her began disintegrating into the air. She turned into dust until nobody could see a trace of her but a white strand of her hair which mimicked a bird shape for a second before floating to the floor.

A sudden flash of light hit Lacie and she found herself in a vacant black and white aisle. The grayscale floor was all covered with wet, multi-colored paint stretching down the aisle-way. The paint read in large letters, "Oh that wall has nothing bad behind it, but we keep jumping to see if there's something more, trying to break the fear don."

'Don?' Lacie thought. 'Did someone forget to put in the letter W?'

Pieces of burning paper with alien writing flew around Lacie as she looked up to see the gray monochrome sign in front of her read 'Aisle 9.'

The floor crackled and Lacie gasped. The tiles rose up and broke into pieces, forming into disfigured humanoid figures on both exits of the aisle. The colorful paint from the letters on the floor dripped down the monochrome floor tiles that made up the evil figures' bodies. Lacie was frozen in fear, but noticed tiny golden ovals on some of the monsters.

"Where is all the color to everything? What is going on?" Lacie asked frantically, as though expecting someone invisible, like the former old woman's voice she had heard, to answer her.

The creatures somehow rattled as they stumbled towards her, while the blazing writings and their smoke swirled everywhere. Lacie coughed, and shielded her face from the papers, catching a glimpse of some trailing violet blur from above the aisle with what looked like red and white running shoes underneath of it.

Behind Lacie, there was a chocolate-frosted, marble cake contained in glass which fell upside-down from a hole in the ceiling. The glass container the cake was in shattered in front of the figures behind her, and she turned to look at the dessert. Completely surrounded by monsters made from the floor, Lacie pulled her long lenses from her pocket and put them over her glasses in some instinctive attempt to get back to where she was, and save herself from the madness of Aisle 9.

Lacie then found herself back in the refrigerated aisle with the strange lenses feeling like they were grafted to her face again. She was relieved to see Syll and Victor who looked as if they didn't know she had left. Ratty still danced away to the music coming from the store with the pink newsgirl hat atop her head. The strange shadows that had surrounded Ratty were now gone and she seem completely possessed by the newsgirl hat.

As though Lacie had never disappeared, the man with ghostly copies on each side of him made his plea, "She wandered to the East following a flock in her head.. no chirping. I couldn't follow, she went through an aisle of mirrors, so I couldn't follow."

Victor took a bite of fanciful, apple-shaped cheese, "An aisle of mirrors you say, ghoul?"

The copies merged and Manchester

became one defined shape, "Ah, the television was fixed."

"Television?" Syll and Lacie asked near the same time.

"As I've said before, no time to explain. You'll have to find a nearby sinkhole. This particular sinkhole has a stairway, you just have to land on it. I think there's still a way from there.. to get to the aisle of mirrors."

"Okay." Lacie and Victor replied simultaneously.

A medium-built, dark-skinned young man in Shakespearean clothing appeared at the end of the nearest aisle opening. He yelled at the trio, "Which one of you killed off the first black character!?"

"What the?" Lacie turned around, mumbling to herself.

Victor pulled his cart of cheese close, Syll had her arm wrapped around his other arm with his hand firmly leaning on his cane.

"We have no idea what you are talking about." Syll replied.

"Bullshit. Where is Mr. Greary?" The stranger didn't let up.

A hefty, light-skinned guy appeared in a similar classic play get-up, sipping on a large soda from across the other end of the aisle. "C'mon Jeffrey, anyone with common sense knows these actors are in an elongated dream sequence."

Jeffrey pointed at the plump young man, "I'm not up to put up with your shit Geoffery. Go back to soldering electronics and watching science-fiction."

"Wonder what'll happen to you." Geoffery almost sneered at his friend like an angry bull that liked chicken wings.

Jeffrey was muted for a second, gawking at the colorful girl who continued to dance as if possessed. "Who's that fine girl dancing?"

Amidst what was now a pulsing house song on the loudspeakers, there echoed a muffled voice, "The sun is coming up in another world. Shut your eyes to see the time."

Lacie heard the loudspeaker and tried shutting her eyes.. or her lenses. She saw some kind of fanciful clock ticking under the darkness of the metal shutters. The twelve on the clock was larger than any of the other numbers and appeared to glow more than the image of the golden timepiece. And the hands of the clock contorted off of its base in a three-dimensional stretch before returning towards the actual time.

“I.. I think I can see the time we have left.. I think.. We should go.” Lacie said quietly after she opened her lenses to Syll and

Victor appearing some feet away waiting.

Ratty jumped down and followed the three.

Jeffrey scolded, "Hey wait a minute! Where do you think you're all going? Backstage!?"

Manchester waved to Jeffrey from above as he began dissipating into the air like Mona had, "Tweedledurr."

Jeffrey gave Manchester an unenthused stare.

"So I guess it's just you and I." Geoffery took in the final contents of his drink leaving an annoying bubbling sound. "Well, I'm leaving. I have work to do for the technacles."

"What are you doing messing around with them?" Jeffrey groaned.

Geoffery threw his empty soda on the top of the aisle divider and began walking away.

"Hey! ..wait!" Jeffrey tailed, running down the aisle.

* * *

Victor scratched the back of his head with the silver handle of his cane, "Well here's the nearest sinkhole, the one that Mr. Greary was sucked up into.."

"Yeah.." Lacie looked around. A bunch

of kids with blue war-paint on and blue-dripping paintbrushes went running past the end of the aisle to her right, 'Aisle 10', where a bonfire had been abandoned. A mess of cooking ingredients surrounded the fire; the ingredients had been pulled off the shelves, and in their place was tired livestock wearing appropriately-sized clothing. The mostly-clothed animals, who were mostly on the shelves, were watching a small, black and white television from across them connected to what looked like a white solar panel.

Victor pressed forward.

Syll reached her arm out, "Victor wait. We won't even be able to get to the stairway if there is one. That technacle will grab us."

Just then Ratty dashed out from behind the three and went straight up to the sinkhole.

A technacle came up and grabbed the girl, pulling her down past the floor so quickly that her hat flew off her head. But the headgear met with gravity and fell through the sinkhole after her.

Lacie closed and opened her lenses with a quick glance at the clock which pointed to 9:02. "I don't know if I should waste any time with N'Quevna being crazy at it is. But I don't want to die. Do you guys have anything to offer it?"

Syll smiled warmly at Lacie, trying to

reassure her, “It'll be okay, there hasn't been any screaming when people are kidnapped.”

“Oh shoot." Victor palmed his face in embarrassment as a gunshot rang off casually in the distance. “I’ll stay behind and take care of this cheese. You girls go without me.”

“Oh.." Syll was reluctant but then smiled for some reason, "Alright.”

Syll bravely inched towards the sinkhole, and Lacie followed her with a knotted stomach produced by an extreme anxiety, as though she had eaten too much cheese.

Chapter 10

Surrounding Lacie and Syll was an enormous, cavernous, courtyard-like space, underneath All-Mart's floor, which was so large that it was highly unexpected to both women. The space was filled with blue, green, and violet lights. But there were also bulbs of flickering white hovering around or bouncing off of giant cement walls and towering descending stairways. Most of the cement was covered in graffiti, occasionally exploring mathematical algorithms in abnormal and nearly indecipherable writing styles, but curiously it stopped towards the bottom where the painting would be easiest to do.

The women were dropped off at the top of a massive stairway by a technacle which had grabbed them and then used its jets to fly downward and vanish after hearing some beeping below like from a microwave. Equally skyscraper-like stairways around the two women were underneath other sinkholes, with often risky falls to get to them, and with small, but deadly gaps in all of the stairs as they lead downwards; on some of these other stairways, technacle bullies waited to grab people's technological sacrifices.. or the people who did not pay up.

"It.. let us live." Syll remarked.

Lacie raised her eyebrows, "Wait.. you didn't know that was going to happen?"

The two females felt fortunate to be alive and further took in their surroundings.

The cavernous floor was also covered with writing, and though it made Lacie flinch at first, she found that if she focused the right way, her scope-eyes would rotate, and her vision would zoom-in on things like a camera; her zooming vision pinpointed the writing on the floor to be programming code along with all sorts of devices, electronic parts, and occasional junk food wrappers scattered around. Then there were technacles here and there below, with blue or green skin covered in gadgetry. The bases of all the technological tentacles were hovering metal boxes with small, jet-like exhausts attached to the bottom of their metal boxes or bases, which gave off low, pure white flames.

Further off was a giant fortress made up of a collective of giant metal panels that were connected by long plastic connectors, the connectors were engraved with symbols resembling technacles and intricate designs somewhere between modern and Victorian. Strange markings from all sorts of languages were engraved across the metal walls similar to the bordering cement walls that had such markings in paint. There were large multi-colored beetles around two feet long that randomly screeched, walking across the metal, and engraving it with spikes on the bottom of their front feet.

Lacie and Syll noticed the squeaking sound of pulleys some ways away above them.

"Let's see what that is." Syll said, and the two women ventured cautiously to the edge of the stairway to follow the ropes' trail downward with their eyes. Far below there was an old man in all blue, with a giant, wooden wash-bucket that was connected to a rope and rising to a sinkhole like a makeshift delivery system.

"Hey," Lacie pointed at the far-off old man, "I think that's someone I know."

As the two women stepped down the first step, some of the white lights which had been bouncing around stopped flickering, floated over to the front of the them, and started moving with the duo like electronic faeries or the lamps of invisible goblins.

Some twenty steps down Syll stopped, "I better tighten these bandages. I'm afraid of what would happen if I tripped down these stairs."

Just then, the stairway started to tremor slightly and move, and the pieces between the gaps in the towering stairway rotated to form a downward square-shaped spiral. Lacie huddled towards the ground, frozen in fear, with her hands trying to grasp the stairs and her mouth agape as Syll nonchalantly tightened some of her bandages. As this was happening, an adult owl flew by and spent some time falling in order to flick the two women off with its wing.

There were hundred-foot gaps in each corner of this new stairway, where something that looked like metal liquid formed from out of thin air into cylinder-shaped slides which connected the stairs from their gaps. More mock hieroglyphics covered the outside of these slides, reaching all the way down the lengthy tubes to the flat-floored beginning of each segment of the stairway. The gaps in the stairs were now as non-existent as ladders, and the chutes gave Lacie and Syll a way to get to the ground.

"Woah." Lacie was taken back from the structural change and her microscopey face stayed concerned. "Are those slides even safe?"

Syll finished wrapping one of the loose bandages around her leg and tucked it in, "I hope so."

Lacie pushed her glasses back, "Why do you wear those anyways?"

"To protect me against security of

course.” Syll stated clearly.

“To protect you against security?”

“One should never seek too much security if they want to be secure.”

“And how do bandages protect you against that?”

Syll scratched her head while looking up, “Hmm, I guess I don’t recall if they ever have.. I don't remember.”

“Here, I guess I shouldn’t be surprised.” Lacie mumbled before looking down to suddenly see Ratty attempting to dance down the stairs and slides. The familiar pink cap of the forgotten newspaper saleschild had somehow made it back on the vindictive girl's head.

Lacie's attention was broken when what appeared to be a naked female mannequin, crawled its way out of the nearest slide.

“What the?” Lacie flinched.

The mannequin made its way over to Lacie and tilted its chipped head to the right with a cheery voice, “Hi, my name’s Same. Why, what’s your name?”

“Uh.. It's Lacie.”

The mannequin straightened her spine and clenched her fists, “No, I don’t want that to be who you are. I will give you another name as someone else with a different past.”

Lacie‘s voice broke, unsure if this

mannequin was going to be another Mona, "I don't know if you're serious, but please don't."

The mannequin tilted her head again, "Haven't you ever wondered what it would be like to lose your past and name?"

"Then what would I have?"

"Why, another one I suppose. A new identity."

Powerful and dingy-smelling drafts started to blow through the area and the mysterious strands of large cobwebs floated throughout the industrious, cavernous air. Syll rested her hand over her chin in thought, with the ends of orange and yellow bandages drooping off her arms and flailing with the breeze.

"But then I wouldn't be me.. and I'm sorry, but I have limited time and I have to go." Lacie retorted, thinking of what Mr. Greary would say, and taking a quick glimpse at one of the stalking white lights that circled her and Syll in the two adventurers' stationary state.

Same walked off the steps, maybe on accident, falling a long ways down until she crashed. Lacie looked down and zoomed-in. Same was as stationary as the floor and near her body Lacie read the letters in what looked like ranch dressing, "Nobody Was Here".

"I suppose that mannequin got lost down

here and was trying to climb up these slides to get back up. Maybe she was even stuck in one." Syll theorized.

Lacie sighed as her lenses, some two inches or more in current length, focused below, "Well.. this just keeps getting stranger. Let's go then, maybe she's alright."

Syll nodded and they made their way down the stairway and its enclosed slides. Lacie's fear of the chutes breaking apart had heavily subsided by the third slide, and she began having fun with the venture; she stayed behind Syll in a single-file fashion due to the absence of rails around the stairs. In technacle fashion, both of them enjoyed each slide's imposition of structural integrity against the risk of some frightening fall.

When the two women arrived at the cement ground they caught their breath, relieved to have made it down without falling. The white lights which had been following them vanished like bulky, old televisions shutting off. The square spiral stairway reformed loudly by sinking into the ground, and the far-away sinkhole that they had come from appeared as a small black circle above them, as though covered up by someone in the store.

They made their way to the mannequin whose arm lied outstretched, detached from her body.

The mannequin looked up at them, "Who are you?"

Syll spoke, "I'm Syll. This is Lacie."

"Who am I?"

"You are Same." Syll replied.

"Same as what?" The mannequin asked.

"The same as Four-Eyes McGee!" A familiar voice interrupted. Cuithbeart laughed to himself and took a sip of water, his right hand holding an open beer. From closer up, Cuithbeart's washbucket apparatus appeared like an elevator for the daring.

"It bothers me that you keep calling me Four-Eyes whatever." Lacie stated.

"You don't seem to feel any remorse for calling me an alcoholic." Cuithbeart retorted.

Lacie stomped her light-brown boot and clenched her fists, "What!? I never called you an alcoholic, Cuithbeart!"

"Well I guess you're right! I must have you confused with the beer. Ha ha ha ha!"

Cuithbeart's blue beer bubbled.

"And who is that girl dancing?" Same asked.

Lacie noticed Ratty who seemed to be sweating profusely as she was still engaged in dancing. Four-Eyes went over to Ratty and took the pink newsgirl hat off of her head. The hat disintegrated in Lacie's hands.

“I’ll kill you!” Ratty yelled as she wrapped her hands around Lacie and started choking her.

Lacie instinctively grasped the clawed hands around her neck, trying to pry them off, “Wh.. why..?”

“You almost killed me!”

Cuithbeart laughed heartily and took a swig of beer. “C’mon now, that’s no reason to choke Four-Eyes McLouie!”

With struggle, Syll pulled Ratty off of Lacie’s neck. The Asian lady made her plea, “We didn’t know that hat did such a thing. We’re sorry.”

Ratty backed away, scrunching her face at Syll, Lacie and Cuithbeart. She booked it, running off towards an entrance leading into the strange fortress.

“Well, I think she's heading into the direction we need to go.” Syll said.

Lacie shut her eyes for a second to see the gold clock had inched a good fifteen minutes from the time she had last looked at it somewhere on the stairs. Similarly, Cuithbeart discarded his last beer at a fifteen minute mark.

Chapter 11

Victor had passed the cheese, deli, and miniature appliances (a small exhibit for the small consumer), as well as the expired deli, and a room full of vending machines-- and he was now amidst refrigerated human beings as still as death: the Horror section. The aisle directly to his right had its end covered with what looked like the vault door of a bank. Above him, breakfasts and multi-colored cinderblocks rained down from the sky thudding against Null-Mart's roof.

"Geeze!" Victor flinched, as a red cinderblock came crashing down to the floor through a hole in the ceiling some thirty feet from him.

His cart was almost twice as full as before with all sorts of cheeses due to his grandiose plans, similar but different from the modest breakfast food tastes of Mr. Greary. The wrinkled, classy gent strolled through the Horror Section on the store fringe, content with his future purchases.

He looked down affectionately at his stockpile, "..cheese.."

In front of Victor some feet away was none other than Malluso, who was holding up the arm of a body for a second before dropping it. A leaping caravan far behind Malluso went making some noise as it busted a crevice in the ceiling open further, chasing after a miniature hot-air balloon that was drifting up towards the sky. The marble-headed man turned his head over to the cheese enthusiast and stared, his face unable to do much more.

The army of people in medieval and military outfits, of various degrees of authenticity remained scattered across the store in battle with the caravans. Only one would-be warrior remained near, in kevlar, laying sideways on the floor, and running in a circle like his left arm was the bottom end of a top.

Victor pushed his cart next to Monsieur with a faint smile that subsided at the sight of the bodies stacked across the refrigerated shelves, "Sleeping in cold places can never be good for dreaming."

Malluso nodded before his jaw crackled open, "But science proves it is good for sleep. It is also good to put bread on cookies to keep them soft, and bread's sponge-like properties help toothaches. I occasionally come here and dump bread on these people with hopes it may help in some positive attribution."

Victor eyed the various bread products which were sprinkled about the dreamers.

"Your savior complex proceeds you Monsieur Malluso." Victor chuckled, opening up a bag of cheese, pulling out a slice and dangling it in front of him. "But are you a fan of cheese?"

"I would buy all the cheese here if it would stop the protests outside. Why do you have so much of it?"

Victor ate the cheese and straightened out his spine to an uncomfortable verticality in conflict with his utilization of a cane, "I have thoroughly planned out a Haunted Cheese Party."

Malluso took out a red handkerchief with thin black patterns proceeding to wipe his mouth, though it seemed he hadn't ate anything. "It sounds like quite the idea. What prompted it?"

"I am not sure," Victor shrugged, pulling some warm string cheese out from his pocket. "I have always enjoyed the exquisite nature, texture, and taste of cheese."

"Something to contemplate." Malluso replied, his hand on his chin.

"It leads me into contemplation.." Victor held up a cheese string, it dangled in front of his eyesight, hanging between his thumb and index finger, "That there must be some underlying intelligence in our existence which governs my taste and tastebuds. But I wonder if the terms of consciousness are something else entirely, or secretly the same. What do you think of these things I speak of, Monsieur Malluso?"

Malluso searched his mind under a particularly pointy, softball-sized light-bulb; the dangling light gave holographic-like visibility to surrounding bacteria, luminescent heat in the vein of the star.

"I am only sure of practices altruistic and sweet, which bring about a grand contentment.. and well.. high blood sugar." Pieces of Malluso's jaw hit the floor like rocks and pebbles.

Victor tilted his head slightly, bending his back to its normal place, his string cheese eaten. He placed both hands on his cane and took on a full smile, "Somewhere in all that marble is a little boy clawing and gasping for air."

"Ha ha ha ha!" Malluso laughed heartily slapping the edge of the shelf with his leather-bound marble hand. "Not quite."

* * *

Syll and Lacie made their way through the inside of the underground fortress's narrow halls. Electronic torches pointing in all directions lit the corridors, with some torches inside indents in the metal walls, as if forcefully placed there. The walls were in sections, slanted inwards, and connected by large triangular bolts. Empty picture frames dangled off of the ceiling from kite strings and tiny fragments of mirror glass trailed across most of the floor from the center. Lacie saw the floor and thought that Ecila and the aisle of mirrors might be close by.

Meanwhile, Cuithbeart stayed behind to take Same up in his wash-bucket apparatus, and have her repaired with the help of The Midnight Brigade.

“So.. are you and Victor an item?" Lacie asked.

“Oh no, we just came here to buy those." Syll replied.

Lacie‘s left eyebrow went up. “...”

To the girls’ right there was an enormous-sized, plastic bear-shaped container a little less then half-filled with honey. Seeing as the technacles didn’t have mouths, Lacie wondered who would’ve used it.. and on what dish. There were scratch marks on the face that read, “DO NOT TOUCH. Abdon's honey.”

The two eventually came to a shut door on their left.

“Well.. should we go on in?” Lacie asked Syll.

“After you microscope spectacles.” Syll said warmly.

“I forgot all about these.." Lacie replied feeling her protruding eyes. "I guess it doesn’t matter if I leave them attached.. I hope.”

Lacie wasn't sure if she could even detach her eyes on her own. And the thought of what could go wrong scared her. Slowly, the girl turned the doorknob in front of her and pushed open the light-blue door.

Lacie and Syll ventured into a medium-sized room with crab grass that was growing out of soft soil floor. There were walls made of rock, excluding where the doorway was, with a silver and white checkerboard ceiling, and a glimmering pond with rainbow fish. There was a large dry-erase board up behind a hefty, pale, middle-aged man with his badly-dyed brown hair combed to the side. He sat on a lowered, padded stool with a white dress shirt and light beige pants with black dress shoes. He had a disturbed face, and was facing the empty space and doorway, and stared without blinking.

“Uh.. hello?” Lacie raised her hand in the air as if to wave but not actually moving it beyond that.

The stranger had a raspy voice, “Hello Lacie and Syll. I knew you were coming because I am a book. Come, have a seat.”

After looking around for chairs and not finding any-- and being afraid to ask their host about it, the two visitors reluctantly sat down on the organic ground.

"So you are a book?" Syll asked.

"Historians are prone to the end of their history. I am a history book. One of N'Quevna's five. I was drawn into creation rather than written. Drawn as a book. Posing as a man. Neither, nor." The man adjusted his small glasses, his big nose pointing out downwards from underneath.

Syll posed a hand on her chin, strips of cloth dangling from her arm, while her blank face showed eyes of irisless interest, "How strange."

The history book looked at Lacie with a gleam of urgency, "You live in this madness until it has lived in you."

"How do I leave this place?" Lacie plead, unsure in asking.

Syll dropped her arm back down to her lap alongside the other one and sighed as if being insulted.

"One way might work, it also might not. Based on history, you simply must find a child and say firmly and out loud.." The man or book got up from his seat with a lean, and the rest was whispered into Lacie's ear discriminately before he sat back down.

"But why.. why that way?" Lacie's voice broke and her eyes would've welled up with tears again, but it was too hard with them being microscope-like lenses.

"I make no guarantees. After all, I'm balding."

"Well then.. where-- where is Elizabeth?!"

"Elizabeth is where you first found her. But do not be fooled, there are important matters at hand. You will be in great danger if you do not stop the fearful events of fear which have been put in place by The Black Cloud. Though there are different results for different choices, calories and all."

"What do you mean?"

"Your best bet will probably be continuing to do whatever it is that you intend. I cannot predict the future and have no more information or suggestions for you. Please leave."

"But--" Lacie returned.

The man went back into a stare at the doorway and his form shifted into a drawing on the board behind him.

Lacie stood up dumbfounded.

Syll slowly got up having been silently thinking to herself while the two talked. She placed her hands on Lacie's shoulders and looked her in the lenses, "Stop worrying, we'll find a way. With little to no security."

Chapter 12

A mass of a shadow rested in the empty baseball field of a park where the wind rushed downwards like a suffocating blanket. The shape of the shadow took up a great space on the field with the surrounding fence bent in all different directions. Of all bases, only the home base which had been ripped in half by something, was left in sight. The trees were all bending and bowing under the smoking moon, and underneath waterfalls of color that poured in the distance up high, from the colorless clouds that almost enveloped the colorful night sky.

Near-translucent forms of people with opaque lower torsos floated under the park lights. Their upper bodies were the shades of a leafless, tree-ridden, cloudy blue sky before its descent into the evening. Their heads were weighted down, giving off dim, yellow stares towards the ground like miniature street lights. As if they were reflections of some parallel world.

The tall park lights were lit with an eerie fluorescent glow cast over its paved trails and the grey and green grass around them. On the side of one of these black paths there was the occasional park bench painted over wildly and sporting dangerously calligraphic, metal ends. Onward the path went into two connected, wide-roofed, wooden bridges full of picnic tables which had been tossed around; more than occasionally, a table would make a dangerous jump into the air like a popcorn kernel, and one had made the tricky descent between the railing and the roof-- and into the creek below. Across the bridge, the pavement ventured straight between two rows of forest into a most potent darkness.

The mass in the baseball field opened its greenish-yellow eyeballs to its surroundings. Its large, black scales shimmered with enough blue shades of light that it was as though the blue reflections were in constant failed attempt to penetrate the monster's flesh. The creature stretched its two great, webbed wings, raising its head to a flock of different kinds of birds emerging in the distant night sky.

The great monster had a giant human skull in proportion to his reptile body with the bone covered in similar scales; the skull split into fours which met at its jaw, while the center of the skull was full of black shades of toxic smoke, mostly staying trapped lest he speak. Some of the toxic black and green smoke poured from the winged reptile's nasal cavities as it breathed heavily in wait. A h'ragon.

In a sky losing its color, flyers of different sizes and colors flapped their flying limbs against the raging wind. Among them, twelve mostly noisy black crows, five vicious white, brown, and black sparrows, and a bald eagle with an eyepatch descended. There were also two white, black spotted downy woodpeckers (with a red die taped to the red backs of their heads), three red and grey, homeless house finches, eight black and red northern cardinals from the South; and two light-brown ruffed grouses in tacky, miniature roller-blades.

Also among the crowd of flyers were four white-breasted nuthatches in tiny t-shirts, a wild turkey with a fitted top hat, and a white, black, and grey tufted titmouse (whom is actually a bird). Lastly, there was six red, white, and black ruby-throated hummingbirds (some mutes).. nine grey and white rock doves born from various boulders, and a winged brown shoe piloted by a black mouse who held onto the tongue in sheer terror.

The flock formed together into a humanoid shape: Mona. Her hand had healed from its cardboard status, but some of her pride had flew away. She appeared to be middle-aged now, though her style of dress was near the same-- mysterious, colorful bones still jutting from the collar of her dark

Victorian wardrobe; and her hair remained a messy white. Mona kept many feet back in order to breathe fresh air, rather than the poisonous fumes spewing towards her.

A deep choir of growls poured from the h'ragon's throat and redirected the wind with a great ferocity, "The tasks?"

Mona lifted her arm and the ground rose underneath her hand into a stationary shield that swirled in color between brown and grey. Fidgeting bird wings birthed at random like fast growing seedlings, from all sides of the upturned dirt barrier. Abbadon's toxic vapors hit the upturned ground and spread away, keeping Mona from harm. The scope-eyed woman replied with a tone that said her presence there was a waste of time, "The defrag's are at 4 A.M."

The breeze followed fiercely again towards the middle-aged woman with the h'ragon's voice, "No, Mona. The other tasks."

Mona grinned wickedly, "I've locked away the trouble, she will give no more gifts to strangers. As you might know from the Above floor, someone made sure that Fear will soon take five forms. Five or six, anyways."

"I leave you to your rotten will." As the h'ragon spoke, Mona's earthen shield began to visibly crack from the wind pressure.

"The lesser of many evils, Abbadon."

Mona chuckled under her breath until it turned into a full-blown laugh, interrupted at its pinnacle as her human form retracted into its flock. The group of flyers retreated from Abbadon's green-streaked black breath with an intense speed.

From a nearby bench facing the field a Mexican man appeared in a timely puff of white smoke. He had long hair split on each side between blue on the left and red on the right; a small tuft of blue sticking upwards at the back top. The man also wore faded jeans, red and white shoes, a brown aviator jacket, and orange-tinted, aviator sunglasses. His head was tilted downwards under the light in sympathy to the specters scattered everywhere around the park. He rose up his hand which was covered in silver and golden rings. And in pointing at the sky he drew out the loud sound of an engine.

Diego's glasses reflected some of the colorful streams from black clouds in the distance, "Future of chemical tragedies, the milk has gone spoiled."

Abbadon turned his massive skull and sneered forth a green-streaked black cloud from his mouth and nostrils, "Diego Caprice."

Diego pointed his finger down as a two-man plane emerged from the sky, "Desert made of tenants, screams the concrete motels."

The plane glided downwards towards the center of Abbadon. Seconds later the aircraft crashed between the monster's wings with feasible force. Pieces of plane went everywhere and Abbadon gritted his teeth. But the h'ragon shook it off; and its eyes met the running blur of red and blue with a fury.

Diego had dodged the h'ragon's first toxic cloud. His speed was so great that to normal humans he left a dark violet streak in his path. His heart-rate had increased, but was not yet a hindrance, and he raised his hand again.

Abbadon inhaled a building's worth of the sweet, nocturnal air before entering a pause as his cold glare followed Diego, his skull cocking back like an organic cannon. Diego made a split decision to redirect the new object at his disposal and sent it hurtling into the ground at the appropriate distance, running backwards from where it was going to fall..

An enormous mass of ice engraved with the Mona Lisa came down like a defensive wall, pounding into the ground as the h'ragon let out a life-encroaching, green and black cloud of staggering proportions. The black gas appeared to be acidic and began to melt the ice, surrounding his Mona Lisa shield as he expected.

Diego paced back in a quick jog, some

fifteen-feet out of reach of his death-- he noticed dead moths scattered here and there on the ground, near a streetlight that had been surrounded by the toxic smoke. The long-haired man held his outstretched palm towards the sky, four fingers and a thumb all covered in precious metal bands.

"Calm hunting in Restless Park. Children sell their madness." Diego whispered as the outline of a white, two-story house came rocketing downwards from the sky.

Diego pulled two crimson twenty-dollar bills and two similar fifties out of his pocket. He knelt down, flashing the money on the field like a hand of cards. The bottom of each bill read, "Illegal tender is to be used towards the resources to live."

The long-haired hunter disappeared in a puff of white smoke as the house he sent from the sky came crashing down upon Abbadon's head. The metal plumbing of the house hit Abbadon first, causing him to let out a loud, screeching roar as his wings twitched and froze; the creature's head was smacked into the ground as pieces of the house and its insides flew everywhere. The red cash on the field rushed upwards against the wind, drifting into the monochrome sky until it vanished into a section filled with fluctuating lines that did not leave stars.

The baseball field was left in a poisonous smokescreen from Abbadon, and the melancholic specters rose their glowing eyes in anger at the unconscious beast..

Chapter 13

Lacie and Syll cautiously treaded up a steep, new staircase towards an arched doorway with elegant, out-of-place moulding. There were giant quote marks on the double door ahead, one mark etched into each door, and a third doorknob placed on the wall at the bottom right-- either pointlessly or to make a point. Bright light pierced through the crack of the doors into the dark of the stairway. Syll opened one of the doors as quietly as she could muster, and the women peaked out at the well-lit room before them..

A big beetle, like the multi-lingual writers outside, lay upside-down and maybe dead on the abnormally-shaped, dark silver floor. The tiles were like large, blocky puzzle-pieces with small, slanted edges across a big room full of wires and technical equipment. There were also many small rows of filing cabinets, but it was anyone's guess save the proprietor, as to what was in them.

Some pieces of floor rose up and were shaped as blocky chairs; they faced desks full of various-sized monitors that were stacked on books to support good posture and simultaneously, a good mood-- though technacles didn't seem to need them. One computer screen on the far left was black with grey text on the top of it, another beside it blue with grey text on most of it.. to the far right a screen with a role-playing game, and the fourth in the middle with some Sci-Fi strategy game. ALL WERE FLAT-SCREENS, DAMN!

The metal ceiling was smooth and slanted, but rumbled randomly as though something was trying to get in. Around the space of the room, bent metal plates rotated in collections in the shape of spheres, hovering between twelve and thirteen feet over the ground; they cast down vivid holograms blurred at the boundaries of settings and their subjects.

One illusion cast down from a sphere was a group of cardboard houses in an abandoned library. The top windows of the library were being broken into by a group of teenagers. One of the boxes had a familiar, hand-shaped hole. Another box had the cut-out of what almost looked like four narrow root systems, two of which were smaller. Lastly, there was a barely visible hole towards the end of the elaborate cardboard fort that looked like a head-sized oval.

Lacie looked at something in the cardboard with curiosity, but didn't voice her thoughts out loud.

Under no sphere a technacle hovered in the furthest reaches of the room with a shimmering golden base and light-green jet exhaust. The technacle had extravagant lasers and spherical eyes that both scanned a fancy desk full of monitors. The screens portrayed strange codes and shapes running every which way almost in flux. After a few moments, the technacle started hovering in a circle around the desk with masses of papers in its mechanical grasp, while the vision of it and that of the desk was distorted like desert air.

Soon, the golden technacle warped and vanished without a trace.

Another sphere to the far right pictured an eerily empty 1960's living room: television trays hoisted X'd out calendars from 2012 and other 'apocalyptic' dates. The thermostat was set all the way to 90. An elephant stood to the right of the room while the bones of another lay with used syringes to the left. There was a regal speech blaring from the glow of the television, "For a short time I will hold exclusivity to this world.."

Another sphere cast an image mimicking the room it and everyone was in, with a cactus-eyed, green-striped, brown, black, and tan cat who sat frozen on the floor mumbling, "I'm real.. I'm real.."

Geoffery was standing next to a long

computer desk watching Jeffrey who just paused a game and minimized out of it. Geoffery stacked a programming book on a pile of other literature, technical and fiction; his left hand held a cola slushie, "Run on sentences don't make things more descriptive, because they're too hard to read."

"Yeah, but making an unnecessary new paragraph for easy reading just promotes stupidity.." Jeffrey said. "I mean, what ever happened to classic literature?"

Geoffery froze for a second trying to piece together something. Then he took a sip of his slushie and post-gulp, "Pray tell a lying truth as the roots of thine caprice, brah."

"No you didn't." Jeffrey shook his head. "You did not just say something that stupid.."

There was a green technacle behind the argumentative duo manipulating lasers on ball-joints from its normal-hued metal base. The green lasers, acting like computer mouses, used a strong wall as a mousepad that was attached to the desk across from the technacle.

In one corner of the room, near the door, there was a brown, indigo-spotted llama smiling and nodding his head to the side as he sang in a muffled voice, "See without borders, son. See without borders, son. Scapuuula."

The animal only garnered attention from Lacie and Syll who saw it as the last thing they noticed before making their entrance into the room.

Geoffery, Jeffrey, and the hovering technacle immediately eyed the intruders.

"What are you doing here?" The technacle spoke with a voice like an American butler coming through a radio.

"We.." Lacie looked up at the unstable ceiling with fear before lowering her head back to the technacle. "We came down here because of one of you."

"And..?"

Lacie's gaze pointed up and to the right as she recalled everything that had previously happened, "To look for a girl who thinks she is a bird, a husky man named Mr. Greary who was taken down here, and--"

"And if she can help us find the other things, an angry young woman named Ratty." Syll said.

"Hold up, can you give me her number?" Jeffrey interrupted, picking up his cell from off the desk.

Lacie glimpsed at Jeffrey and ignored his request, returning her gaze back towards the technacle, "..and someone named Ecila who might be the girl who thinks she's a bird, and was last seen in an aisle of mirrors."

"I see. I'm afraid I can't be of much help. But I can tell you your body-fat percentage."

"Ah. No thank you." Lacie replied, disappointed.

"Though it's nice to meet you both. I was once XO823, but now everyone calls me Dave. I have graphs on the subject.." The technacle bowed down and gave Lacie a handshake. Syll's eyes widened when Dave's gesture was extended to her, and she simply stepped back and waved awkwardly at the floating, mechanized, biological entity.

"I'm Lacie and this is Syll." Lacie retorted, her lenses zooming in and out slightly at the orb-like eyes of the technical creature doing the same.

"Unfortunately as for the bird girl, there is more than one of this or that who thinks they are that or this. I have graphs on the subject.." Dave elegantly ignored the tremors from the ceiling.

Syll attempted to redeem her lack of a handshake, "Not with the intent to be rude, but we are surprised that you can speak, and that you seem so civilized."

"We are firm in keeping order, but not really violent. The rumors you've heard are an insurance policy for our low numbers. Of course, we intend to bring Null-Mart down at The Second Midnight, I even have graphs on the subject.. So I would ask you two to leave this store before then for your own safety."

"The Second Midnight?" Lacie inquired.

"Yes, it comes after the first midnight."

A mass of the ceiling had been forcefully unbolted and peeled open to reveal the shape of something monstrous, outlined by the darkness and accompanied by floating debris.

Lacie, Syll, Jeffrey, and Geoffery stepped back.

Dave pulled out ten sheets of graph paper with retractable metal hands and pincers, bending his point backwards and focusing his visual processing sensors and lasers above.

"Dave, dude, you got to be crazy. Get back!" Geoffery perspired.

The technacle assured Geoffery of his stance, "Both entropy and elegance fuel my autodidactism."

Dave began graphing various traits of the creature.

The multi-legged creature above roared in a tone as though it was both male and female with a voicebox turning on itself.

A slightly rusting, metal sign came rocketing through the huge, new hole in the ceiling and clanked onto the floor, reading, "SATIRE FOR SATURDAYS".

Jeffrey knocked over Geoffery's drink as he stood up and made a run for it. Though the cola slushie had turned to small, orange cheese crackers.

"Hey!" Geoffery sneered before coming to his senses. "Five second rule.."

"We need to find a way out of here." Syll said frantically.

Dave pointed his head towards the back of the room, "There's a glass exit behind one of those illusions. But only one form can go through the glass every twenty-five hours. I have graphs--"

"What!?" Lacie asked, hearing Dave perfectly fine, but afraid to leave Syll and the others behind.

"The glass is half-impossible." Dave said, inking out graphtacular information about the monster above.

"Go." Syll said to Lacie as she grabbed an unplugged waffle iron off a nearby desk. "I'll catch up with you if I can."

"But that's a bagel--"

"It's a waffle maker. Go!" Syll pointed towards the back of the room.

The creature came down crashing into the light of the room to reveal that it was shaped like a spider with a body and head made of tombstones. The spider's legs were culminations of moveable red bricks with differently-sized handprints on them.

Two blank, open tomes with their

bindings attached to the spider's polished cement face, sufficed somehow for eyes. As the arachnid took in its surroundings, illegible writing formed over the pages of the books, their pages swaying back and forth with some unknown force.

Lacie weaved around the downcast illusions. Around the mirror image with the paranoid feline affirming its existentialism. Past the elephants live and dead who graced the paint-chipped and overheating 1960's living room. Past the darkened library where lights lit up from underneath cardboard sculptures. Around a stunning, sometimes real and sometimes cartoon rendition of a medieval planet which panned in and out, sliding around different areas with visual ease and great detail. Past a simplistic geometrical display, and other futuristic machinery.

Jeffery and Geoffery had both high-tailed it out of the room down a hard-to-see ascending stairway to the side, hidden by holograms and a poster of a descending stairway; the computer Jeffery had been on went black with the text: "The reasonable limitations wherein 'anything is possible' have been expanded. Please stand-by(..)."

The spider had Dave wrapped up in web and the tentacle's graphs were now strewn about all over the floor. Syll confidently and cautiously approached the clay and cement arachnid as it let out guffaws of horrible noise at her, dropping the stationary technacle to wrap her up in the death-grip of its webbing next.

"Oooh wooo hooo hoo hooo." The indigo-spotted llama continued singing and head-bobbing unfazed by the events around it.

Lacie came upon the back of the room, its long metal wall had a row of normal windows, leading nowhere, with ugly underlying brick and the tattered remains of distinguished certificates nailed into the mortar.. but there was a thick window in the floor, like a cube of glass, leading through the ceiling of a shadowy hallway. A graph full of empty circles from a hole puncher laid on the center of the thick glass of the one window leading somewhere. And above this window, in the floor there was Old English style text popping out, which read, "BLACK STOCK".

Lacie didn't quite know what she should do, but remembered that the glass was half-impossible and she did not have time. So she jumped onto the glass and frightfully started to sink into the window like it was clear gelatin or fast-acting quicksand. Her heart pounded out of her chest in fear for her life, and she took as deep a breath as she could, before her whole body submerged into the liquid glass.

Chapter 14

Odis awoke on his vacation bench. He was shivering with goosebumps while the payphone next to him rang incessantly. Someone had put nine more goggles on his head in creative ways while he was sleeping. The snowdrift in front of him and subsequent crystallized snow piles around him had grown a few feet, his lower legs surrounded with free-form miniature igloos.

A man with metal hands or gloves was pounding on the wall outside screaming, "Let me out! Let me out of here!"

The voice of a woman was underneath the volume of his, "If you buy one receipt Phil, you'd get two free. Phil--"

A chrome mechanical bird, with no front section of its beak, twitched around the floor with ice formed around it. The bird's free wing waved a toothpick flag with a bubble-gum wrapper comic. Odis shook off the snow from his warmed feet, pulling his legs out of the drift and burying the robotic avian by accident..

Odis picked up the phone which had been painted over in sparkling blues and then with thin, dim yellow lines, "Yellow?"

"Red!" Said the voice on the other line,

as if the caller could see dying glow of the pop-machine obtruding the Men's Restroom.

The store speaker above rang out as well, "Moowahahahahahahaa!"

Odis eyed the public address noise-maker with the phone still up to his mouth, "Oh shut up, you."

"How rude." The voice on the phone replied.

"Or two receipts.." The woman outside murmured to her husband. The man continued hitting the cement with his gauntlets and shouting as if he was trapped inside the outdoors.

Odis stared curiously at the door and changed his tone, "No, not you."

"Then who?"

"Who are YOU!?" Odis asked.

The caller hung up.

"Pumpernickle.." Odis put the phone back on the hook and stood up. He looked down at the surface of the floor that was snowy, icy, dusty, dirty, and in some places lacerated.

It was less than a minute before the phone began ringing again.

Odis picked up, "Hello."

It was Victor, his voice stressed.. "Odis, it's Vigiorno, meet me at 2-20, 2-20 Riley Street, between Aisle 67 and The Department of Unnatural Affairs. Bring sweet-rolls."

"Where am I supposed to get those?" Odis asked, wiping his hand down the stubble on his face in apprehension.

"Just meet me there old friend."

* * *

The clothing aisles were tidy and well-kept, but it was rare to see hangers used. Instead, the clothes were folded over the metal racks in big ol' piles. Cuithbeart stood outside of tan dressing rooms peering around in uncertainty. The dressing room in the middle had giant fans in place of normal walls. Same, the mannequin, occupied this center-row dressing room while the fans turned at full blast. The artificial girl had her arm newly patched up with a couple hinges-- and with The Midnight Brigade's paint supply, she transformed herself in various tints and shades of sparkling blue.

A conglomerate of malicious kids were scattered around the store creating general revelry and disruption. The lighter shades were the youngest between five and six, two girls who painted with azure and deep sky blues, and a boy who used dodger blue. Twin girls around eight mostly did curlicues in alice and maya blue. There were eight through ten year-old boys who were maliciously fond of the medium shades of glaucous, royal, and iceberg.

Multiple shadows of a single phrase shifted high-above across the ceiling as a letter from the phrase occasionally burnt into the metal: "No originality."

Also in the group of kids: presiding somewhere were two boys between eleven and thirteen with the darker shades of yale and ultramarine, along with a thirteen-year-old girl who dabbled with persian blue. Lastly, nearing the darkest spectrum was a fourteen-year-old girl and fifteen-year-old boy-- the girl often found using sapphire and the boy using midnight. Each member of The Midnight Brigade was most-dressed in and named after the main color they used to paint, and nobody-- not even "Cobalt" or other older members, were really in charge of the group and its disarray.

Far away to the right Cuithbeart noticed there was a non-member around eight and his lax mother both standing on their heads as if it was commonplace. The mom had grabbed a package of chocolate-covered wafers and was about to throw them in the cart.

"Put it back! You already have a treat." The eight-year-old scorned.

The Scotsman heard and noticed Dodger

talking to a clothes rack, "Just 'cause I painted you, you can't join. Those are the stiputations."

Cuithbeart turned to his left where he was startled to see 'Thee Chaotician'.

"How am I supposed to get out of here? The room is surrounded by fans." Same inquired, having entered the room before the walls had shifted into familiar, cool-breeze outputting devices with no discernible exit.

The Chaotician turned towards Same and Cuithbeart upon hearing the dilemma. "In other places I do believe, blue is a stable hue. But here, such material-- if it does not deceive, might allow one to pass through."

Same and Cuithbeart stared at the newcomer mutely wondering where he had came from. A thin trail of white smoke faded off from the left side of the dark and flashy figure; he leaned against the tan dressing room to the right with his right shoulder, his bulky cane was on his other side and held by his left hand in a disproportionately diagonal manner that mimicked his body.

Cuithbeart looked at Same, "Well.. it's up to you Statue Girl!"

Same raised a foot slowly towards the great fan in front of her. Parts of the metal casing began bending, screws loosened, the center motor and attached blades fell to the ground, and a hole big enough for someone to pass through formed in the ruins of the once binding device.

"How fantastic!" Same examined the fan-door after stepping out of it.

"How did you know that?" Cuithbeart asked.

'Thee Chaotician' responded with a question, "What is a fitting conclusion to be absolved from that which was once confusion?"

"Ah." The cobalt Scotsman replied in jest.

"I think I saw someone like you before, before they disappeared in a puff of smoke." The blue mannequin stated to the black-clad poet.

The Chaotician straightened his cane with his hand atop the highest point of the chaos star, "Some people disappear in puffs of smoke. Maybe because they have personal expiration dates. Personally and not as a joke, I have never been on a date with expiration.. Maybe I'm already expired, to make the quizzical correlation."

When his words ended, a puff of white smoke surrounded 'Thee Chaotician' and he disappeared.

Chapter 15

Lacie sunk through the thick jelly window, while blurry objects came out from the sides of the gelatin-like window and hid over her head as she sank. She floated like a feather some fifty feet down to the wide, slightly-curvy floor of a wide hallway. A succession of top hats landed on her head, and she felt a heaviness that she had never felt before. Her body had accumulated around a hundred and eighty-pounds of weight. With a tone that was half whisper she spoke to herself in dread, "What?.."

The exit behind her shifted its composition back from gelatin to glass; it was a loud, crackling reform which echoed throughout the shadowy hall trailing lengthily in two unknown directions into the night's darkness; the change in window material was to be so eccentrically loud as to trigger a violinist in the distance who played a shrieking jingle before vanishing.

There were parts of walls that were vacuous, with shelves where cleaning equipment once was; and parts of walls spattered with glowing plastic and paint, in doodles and mostly cosmic shapes, and poetry written in differently painted hues, chaotically wet and dry-- dim and flourescent. Cleaning equipment and muddy, soapy water littered the metal ceiling indicating further foul-play with gravity. And the grey cement floor along with the three-dimensional symbols of sanitation above it gave some sense of being in the back of an average department store, rather than some dry deep diving into N'Quevna's underground.

Lacie felt her hair vertically pointing upward underneath a black top hat that was split down the middle in two pieces save the brim and ribbon. Between the split hat was a longer green top hat, darker than her shirt, and sitting snugly over her head. Atop the black and green top hats was a white, half-sized or miniature top hat-- diagonally placed off to the dented or cut side of the green top hat's top, atop the black top hat. And upon the center of the diagonal white top hat, that sat atop the green hat, that was stacked inside the split-apart black top hat, was a smaller, translucent, upside-down top hat (for those who could spot it).

Lacie pulled on the top hats on top of hats to see if she could take them off, but the hats all held together as though with a strong adhesive, towering over her jutting microscope-eyes.

Printed on the cement around and under

Lacie were a burst of differently colored and shaped triangles all pointing the way down the direction which she faced. As she took a step over the shapes and in their direction, she felt the force of her newfound fat, and found that her clothing, while tight, had possibly changed somewhat to take shape around it. Her spine was slumped and her breathing heavy as she took each slow step, and her artificial eyes proved stuck to her face as she tried to yank them off in frustration.

Amidst her predicament, Lacie couldn't help but notice some large, grammatically-incorrect scribbles on the wall:

Super, I am.
capes are cool!
I can fly too.
can't you?

Some twenty feet forward, two sheets of different paper blew towards Lacie. The sheet of lined notebook paper flew in a whirlwind motion landing to Lacie's side while the blank computer sheet she saw and decidedly caught, just barely, as it tried to fly over her head. She stepped onto the notebook sheet next to her foot just as more wind came rushing through from nowhere. The computer paper read, "11/11/11 – New studies show the scary possibility that paper could be hazardous."

Lacie panicked for a second before reading the second paragraph, "12/13/14 - New studies show that paper is actually not hazardous, and in some cases triggers neurological functions which promote longer life."

Lacie sighed in relief and looked to the next line.

"12/14/16 - New studies show that a chemical in trees may be poisonous and that paper could be carcinogenic."

She became more skeptical as she stared at the last writing on the page.

"N/A - New studies show that I've drank up all of the coffee and pissed-off my colleagues."

Lacie laughed in a hiss of her formal voice. She leaned down with effort and picked up the lined sheet of paper; seeing that the lined sheet was full of text, she stacked it over the computer paper and began reading.

"'Thee Chaotician' walked out of a shadow-beam, the very opposite of sun-beams, which presented themselves through crevices in the vast ceiling. The unilluminated beams stretched all the way to the pet section of Null-Mart's floor, where circular tiles which doubled as thick glass containers spun. The containers were full of the mixed up fragments of a liquid phrases like, 'Settingo descripto.'

To the Chaotician's left was a highly-reflective, fish-filled tank with the bottom, brass label 'WHEREUR@NOW'."

Lacie heard a grunt. She stopped reading and looked around but could spot nothing lively between the shadows of the shelves.

One slightly-rotated blue and turquoise poem (of many different handwritings) caught her attention:

I was/saw between the lines
at dirty, cement hills, sunset setting, selling
shaking visions to askers and anyones.
I was/saw my favorite bargain today,
stu- stutter- stuttering for breath,
decades ago, today.

Lacie pondered the abstract words briefly, but wasn't sure if the poem was even written to make sense. Unbeknownst to her, the hall ahead and behind would contort itself in an almost undetectably slow spiral, similar to the slight structural curvature, or bigly wiggliness, of the floor, which still left sight of the furthest distance not devoured by shadow. She forgot about the poem and continued scanning the notebook paper in her hand.

"Surrounded by the caged and glassed-in

anomalies of the pet section, the Chaotician found himself next to a wooden pallet stacked high with boxes of soda pop halfway into a shadow-beam. The magician of sorts had an egg in one hand and a magic marker in the other. His cane stood upright, or maybe 'downleft' since it was in a left-tilted stand off of the ceiling.

'Thee Chaotician' was inclined to draw a stern, cartoonish face onto the egg with the magic marker. Then he ripped one of the boxes open, pulled out two cans of soda, and opened both. He took one can and dumped it on the egg, acting with proclamation, 'Aloud abuse of language far from credential, seems allowed in still-forming images lost in transformational potential, whereupon the crafter is naught and comfort sought complacent, for the artists wrought with cultural replacement.'

After all this, the egg hopped into the air out of the Chaotician's hand, stealing the magic marker with invisible force. With the same thieving force while in midair, the egg grabbed the large red handle which pulled the wheels underneath the wooden plank of sugary substances. The living yolk evidently took on a diamond's hardness before hitting the floor. The white entity scampered away with the soft drinks at human walking pace, and the label names of the drinks changed from what they were to 'Eggola Cola'.

The Chaotician having purposefully not interfered, was taken aback by the eagerness of the Eggola to become what it now was. He gulped down some pop from the other can and put it down in front of the fish tank. Finding that he no longer had a magic marker, his power was severely limited to a cane; one he couldn't reach nor needed as a medical necessity. Though these circumstances did not bother him, as his attention quickly diverted towards questionably domesticated critters, crappers, and 'clawers.'"

Lacie heard another grunt. Though thoroughly surprised at noticing the slow spiraling of the hall, she followed the gruff sound's direction, tracing a figure in the darkness that didn't seem to be wearing anything, with a coffee maker on a shelf that hid his crotch. Lacie dropped the papers, failing to finish the one she had been reading. The figure noticed her and spoke, "I'M AN INVISIBLE MAN!"

"I don't know about that." Lacie murmured unable to speak louder. Albeit paranoid by the presence of the man, she shut her lenses long enough to notice the glowing clock in the dark of her temporary sightlessness had lost its three, contorted hands. All the numbers on the clock had also switched with the number twelve in their respective clock number rotations.

"I heard that. And it's not like clothes are cheap." The man rubbed his knobby nose with a thin hand, his skin like a coal miner's. "Judgin' by your plump appearance Miss Outta Business, you must be friends with that fat gravy smellin' feller who came 'round these parts lookin' for a cape with his fancy clothes."

"Gravy-dreary? I mean, Mr. Greary?"

"Mister Thinks-He-Can-Fly is up ahead the spiral and down the hall, left through the exit on the right.."

"Wha--? Never mind."

Lacie passed by the man who talked to himself about Mr. Greary expecting her to listen. "Says all he needs is a cape and he can fly! Hogwash.."

Lacie recalled the man said "Outta Business" but made no connection to the writing on her oversized bosom in the tiring process of movement; she wondered if Mr. Greary was the one who wrote the strange poem on the wall.

The large, hatted lass eventually found herself out of breath. Lacie had come to a tall rectangular hole in the wall leading into a large, sweeping room whose inhabits caused the ambiance to swirl with uneasiness. She noticed an inner dome overhead where a surreal rendering of N'Quevna's sky spanned in consistent movement. Large, hunky monsters over half the room's height lumbered in a square dancing crawl with long, barren faces.

Painted cement walls of dingy hues and blurs of white towered in the formation of an outer maze, which surrounded the great monsters. In the center of the room was an oversized manhole which the monsters circled around. The leathery creatures took no notice of the girl as their arms dragged like mops across the floor, their crooked legs barely visible, and the thins of their eyes remaining in a calm focus.

The scope-eyed girl took the first entrance she could find into the maze, where telephone numbers, romantic interests, and insults had long been scratched and marked into physical dominion. At one point, as Lacie turned, a gap in a metal wall came up behind her that she would've been able to fit through before. Now instead, she was forced to walk down a ramp, inwards into black liquid that went up to her neck.

Lacie struggled through the mucky liquid, disgusted and saddened, and came out of the other end traveling up another ramp.

Around the second corner from the liquid was Mr. Greary. The man still had a twelve-pack of eggs under one arm next to his gut. He looked lost, "Lacie? Is that you?"

"Yeah." Lacie replied.

"You've put on weight, muck, and hats."

"Not by choice."

"Same here with the former." Mr. Greary laughed somewhat awkwardly. He continued, "Do you know a way out of here?"

Lacie remembered the way out of labyrinths, "We could always keep taking left turns."

"Better to take rights, they are generally more legal." Mr. Greary insisted with sparks of heroism and nerdiness in an otherwise cautious voice.

The duo decided upon the plan to take rights. The maze walls towering over their heads seemed like they might go on forever. They passed by pieces of trash left on the cement, a woman's head peering out at them from the floor (evidently she was standing in a human-sized hole), and a paper-mache man on a rocking chair, with a creepy face and friendly wave.

Lacie was speechlessly on her guard. Mr Greary noticed and sympathized with the young woman's apprehension, "Imagine if we took left turns."

They eventually came to a dead end with a series of machines which looked like sleek, steel, one-person chambers (some high caliber of technology with human-sized holes). Above the contraptions was an 'EXIT' sign with an indicative glow that hit the stomachs of the lost. Two of six machines had their fronts opened revealing chairs; while the rest of the contraptions were closed on people, save one machine on the end, that was unplugged with an 'Out of Order' paper plaque.

Mr. Greary sat in one of the open machines with his egg carton on his lap, "Well it's worth a try."

Chapter 16

Syll opened up the waffle maker, its brand name, 'Experimental.' The appliance's insides were covered in reflective surfaces. Strips of Syll's bandages and strands of her dark hair pulled forward with the force of the waffle-maker and it acted like a giant vacuum. Dave was behind her in the throes of an automated yell, still tied up with webbing. The technacle watched with validated fear as his graphs were to become battered batter. The hardened arachnid guffawed with inhuman laughter, even as the endless ink was pulled from its book-eyes like opaque webbing entering compressed air.

The spider raised a front leg of brick to crush the woman and would have, but she remained standing-- almost under the arachnid's head with the point of the vacuum in her grasp. The creature's leg began cracking along with the head, and the body followed in a fast-evolving crumble of old bricks and unmarked graves. As the fearful form was being decimated it continued laughing, causing Syll's arms and hands to tremble at its loud and frightful voice.

The arachnid fell into a ruin of clay and stone rubble. Syll jumped back instinctively, though the debris of the spider was sucked through the air into the waffle maker. She then promptly closed the contraption which then steamed from the sides. Dave commented on Syll's reaction, "Best to keep that closed, as fear seldom dies so easily."

From a distant corner the brown and blueish-purple llama still sang. He took some steps forward with a bobbing head, "La di da di daa.."

Syll placed the abnormal appliance down on the ground and looked at the technacle lying on the floor. She remained stationary, her eyes changed to a polished black similar to Dave's own lenses. Dave tumbled around, unable to do anything but propel himself into chairs and desks. In his bound struggle, Dave knocked one monitor over, which had already been on the edge of the table from the waffle maker's suction; BUT IT WAS STILL A FLAT SCREEN, DAMN!

Dave's robotic voice turned full volume, "Aren't you going to help me?"

A grandfather clock fell through the hole in the ceiling where the arachnid had pummeled through. A nearby metal sphere from high above cast an illusion of some quaint, far-away place out in the night. The grandfather clock shattered violently in front of the illusion with large splinters of wood and glass going everywhere.

Afterwards, it seemed that the busted timepiece's pendulum continued, mimicking computer mouses hanging from tables. Monitors flickered on and off, their cables unscrewed, loosened, and wobbled just so. Most of the lights around the room followed in flickers. The clasps of the waffle iron released and a couple handfuls of small spiders poured out around the cement in a disorganized crawl.

Syll reacted to all this chaos by moving back nearer to the doorway she came from.

"Dum di da di doo!" The llama sang.

"It's okay. I believe that means we 'got' it." Dave stated.

Syll did not move.

The technacle was not enthused with his lack of freedom, "We Asians have to stick together. So would you please untie me?"

"How do you mean?" Syll asked, thinking Dave a liar.

"I was made in China." The technacle replied, unable to get his mechanical arms through the webbing.

Syll hesitated.. "Uh.. okay.."

She made her way to the technacle past multiple holograms, one giving show to the molecular level of an eyeball, while another moving-picture was the feed of a camera on a fighting caravan inside the outside. With great struggle, Syll began pulling off one fragment at a time of each thick strand of webbing.

"Hmm.. do you lift weights?" Dave asked.

"A little." Syll smiled slightly, but it was short-lived and mostly feigned.

"If you're able to rip off the webbing of a stone spider, maybe you should lift less often. It's considered--"

"Maybe I should leave you here." Syll glared.

Dave was silent for a moment save the mechanical buzzing of his base, "Awkward."

Eventually Syll was able to pull enough webbing off for Dave to do the rest. While the technacle untangled himself with a free mechanical arm, Syll went and fixed the layout of equipment on all of the desks where electronics, books, and other geeky curiosities had shifted towards an edge, or fallen to the blocky, steel floor.

When all was not said, and done, Dave hovered in front of the spherical illusion and sectioned reflection of the vast room they were in; a holographic cat remained in the middle of this complex image, scared stiff and now laying on its back.. still chanting, "I'm real.. I'm real.."

"Over here Syll. There is an elevator.. though it's not exactly safe by human standards."

The grandfather clock rebuilt itself over a period of minutes and went rocketing back up through the torn-up gap of cavern ceiling where it came from. And the downcast illusion in front of Dave had copied the image of the clock inside of it as though it was ticking outside on a winter night with the lights of some country home far off behind it.

"Oh good, that was one mess I didn't want to have to clean up." Dave said, having hovered to the side of the illusion to seek graphing-view of the self-repairing sound.

A dozen new wooden clocks of different sizes came raining down into the room, busting apart all over the floor; though a couple timepieces first broke as they hit the high-floating spheres. All of the clocks only featured the number twelve, with plastic, wood, and glass twelves either spinning, popping out, or portrayed as shaped holes.

Syll jumped, covering her head and moving forward in a weave as the weighted clocks fell around her. A miniaturized clock, though still quite large, hit the woman on the side of the head. She passed out, drops of blood cascading down the black of her head.

Dave bowed his uppermost point in apprehension at the incident; meanwhile, a medieval-looking swordsman's scream rang out from one of the downcast, spherical camera feeds attached to a flying caravan.

The technacle hovered over, his base tilted forward as it did when he was at fairly high speed. He picked up Syll who was unconscious, "Not all tentacles are rapists, silly woman. I have graphs, manga, and statistics from Tentacle Rights Activists on the subject."

The technacle took her into the elevator which was a kind of steel-cage rhombus, a faulty, three-dimensional rectangle that liked to collapse on anyone over three-feet tall. To the left wall of the lift was an empty retractable bookcase with a missing middle shelf. An animal under three-feet tall was in the right corner of the elevator manning lowered controls, the critter had the body of a small monkey, clothed like a fancy, hotel employee, and the head of a badger-- an elevator chauffeur with a socialite name-tag reading, "Hello, my name is 'Bob.'"

The chauffeur had a disgruntled look, "Going up? Because you're certainly not going down."

"Yes. Going up. As you know, I am not--"

"I know, I know.. you are not properly outfitted to fly all the way up there yourself. And you have graphs on the subject."

"Precisely."

"Whose the broad?"

"A fellow Oriental."

"Right.." Bob commented snidely. "With a synthesized Mid-Western accent?"

"I had no idea you'd gone racist."

"I've met coffee makers that made less generalizations than you, Dave." The chauffeur pressed a black button with a golden 'G.' He looked off into the space with a cold narration from under his wet snout, "Going up."

The folding elevator must've rose hundreds of feet high in a cable climb. In the backdrop below, the steel pyramid-like fortress showed its enormous size. The melodic llama rotated his scraggly head in a circle while his shape and muffled melody faded from the moving compartment. Dave rested his metal base upon the tidy floor while keeping the roof raised.

As they neared the ceiling Syll awoke groggily. A double-door hatch, with a middle permanently opened for the cables, swung open automatically to let the rhombus elevator through into the well-lighted disarray of Null-Mart.

The elevator denizens arrived to see an ordinary road that should've been outside with a centered, yellow dashed-line in the middle of the store. Light bulbs above somehow exchanged half-eaten casseroles and munched on main-courses, often with bent tin-foil covers with the black-markered words "FORGETFUL HEAT TRANSFER". Aisles were plotted loosely around the pavement but never over it, except one aisle division of shelves which had been torn in half and moved. Four large sinkholes surrounded the road, five counting the hole centered in the cement.

By an aisle selling pack-mules that could run, was a scraggly-looking fellow holding a shotgun, buff, with some fat addition, hair in a kind of puff, but not conditioned. He cocked the firearm and shot it at the ceiling, "Everybody out!"

Also standing on the road was a thinner man dressed like a coffee-house hipster with IT-style glasses. He was a programmer (of some sort) and community coordinator (of summed sort). A pile of clocks slowly grew from the aisle-way closest to the malevolent individual like a pile of popcorn that was almost done in a microwave. The man held a medium-sized clock above his head and laughed maniacally with strands of hair dangling in front of his glasses.

Odis, Victor, and a cart piled higher than ever with cheese were on the side of the road. Odis and Victor had looks of terror on their faces, while Odis's head was still covered with swimming goggles. Victor spoke softly and urgently to Odis, "He's recycling animations. But that's the extent of his recycling program. We are dealing with a dangerous, clock throwing man."

The man threw the clock he was holding down into the sinkhole in the road, "I'll throw clocks, then they'll respawn. I'll throw clocks into people's heads!"

Bob eyed the small, blood-soaked part of Syll's head. Then the badger-monkey pulled out a slightly oversized toothpick and started picking at his pointy teeth, "Clearly he's tried."

The man with the shotgun fired off another round, "Listen you fools, we gotta get our asses outta here now! This whole place is coming down."

"Well, not for two or three more hours. I have graphs on the subject." Dave retorted from the elevator.

"Oh please." Bob retaliated with rolling eyes, his hand fidgeting in the act of plaque removal. The badger-monkey jumped with fright as a plastic wall clock was thrown at Dave and bounced off of his metal base.

"How rude." Dave said.

Odis cupped his hand over his mouth as to speak in Victor's ear, "I think I could steal his shoes.."

"Vic?" Syll said from the elevator floor,

noticing the cane and cart while holding her head.

"Syllable!" Victor rushed over to her. "What happened to your head?"

Bob threw his toothpick into Null-Mart space, "I don't mean to be impolite, but could you all get the hell out of my elevator?"

"I'll be going back down." Dave said.

Syll and Victor left the elevator. Syll looked at the blood on her hand and then up at Victor, "I was hit by a clock, I think I might need more bandages."

Bob hit a button and entered a straight-postured, formal trance, "Going down."

The elevator's lift hatch opened, and the wannabe-rhombus room descended, and the hatched closed once more.

As Bob's act was happening, the clock-thrower went to go pick up a sundial from the jutting clock pile-- but a light fixture dropped a glass container which splattered cheesy potato wedges all over the malicious man's head. The clock-throwing programmer halted, cringing, and screamed from the heat of the delicious side dish.

There was a slight squeaking accompanied by the sound of wheels from the front side of the store. Emerging from one of the aisles was a chicken egg with a drawn, yet animated face, its mouth cracked open at the middle, and its yolk like a tongue. The egg had a black marker hanging from its side and behind it was a wooden crate of soda, labeled, "Eggola Cola."

The others watched the Eggola in disbelief as it made one-inch jumps and quirky, high-pitch squeaks almost in tone with the wheels of the heavy pallet; a block of soda pop dragging inexplicably from the ovular ovoid's invisible pull on a lowered, paint-chipped handle.

Ignoring the Eggola, the man with the shotgun held the hollowed end of a spare shotgun shell to his ear. He stood deeply attentive. Then, the odd philanthropist dropped the shell and raised his arms in commotion, "OH MY GOD, THEY'RE GOING TO BLOW UP THE OCEAN!"

Chapter 17

Lacie and Mr. Greary found themselves in different, but similar pod-like machines located in what appeared to be the Null-Mart Electronics Department. The contraptions' glass fronts unfolded to better reveal store displays on the brink of emptiness, virtually ignored by those within their contours. What looked like the corner of a house was popping out of the high-up paint-splattered ceiling. In the center of a rectangular counter scrapped of its registers was a human skeleton, sitting deep in thought with shifting gummy eye-balls.

The skeleton talked to himself blissfully, no, miserably unaware of his surroundings, "The man meets his odds of happiness with the manifestation and consequence of his applied belief in reality. Where his peers praise him, sing along with him in a choir, most often when he is beneficial to their emotions rather than the best possible objective logic at present; or criticize him with zestful lenience on their own worldview.. The criticality more likely with the pertinent need for change amidst the pain of change or lack thereof, for one, or the other, or both parties..

"And if I am to maintain both an allegiance to that which is objective logic, to all available evidence and to its probability, I must hold some uncommon modicum of resistance of lenience to my own emotional benefit and present belief, which, still to me, lends itself to greater pain and uncertainty.

"Damnit." The skeletal philosopher formed a bony fist and banged it upon the counter.

Lacie felt much lighter, she leaned forward with her hands on the glass entry-way of the futuristic apparatus. The first thing she noticed was that her skin felt very hard and that she had the hands of a mannequin-- she had no hats, and had glasses again instead of scope-eyes. She was angry and frightened at having yet another new form-- and thought she might want to close the lid and press the button to make her go back to being the other version of herself, being unsure which was better or worse at this particular point in time.

Lacie's thoughts to retreat were cut short as Mr. Greary leaned forward and stepped out to the right. He was now in the form of a shirtless mannequin that looked like a male model in faded blue jeans; his glasses also curiously remained.

"Imagine if I took the left machine." Mr. Greary jested, sound coming from him but his mouth not actually moving, as if he was trapped inside the plastic.

Lacie laughed, her plastic face in the same stationary state.

The skeletal philosopher turned his head towards the newcomers in an awkward stare which only lasted for thirty seconds before he went back to his logician's mumble. Lacie noticed the desk in front of him had a mounted, crooked, white metal sign that read, "Skeletons, in moderation!"

Lacie got out of her machine and the mannequin duo left the lids of both opened. Lacie looked down and saw she was in a brown three-piece bikini, the kind with a skirt. Mr. Greary looked at her and then returned his gaze to his chiseled abs, "I think we came out of a different store."

There was a man around his thirties with devil horns rising from his head. He played fervently with a custom-made guitar hanging at his waistline where black jeans and a macabre, black t-shirt met. Drops of sweat ran down his weathered face along dangling dreads and sunglasses. He stood on an endless stretch of upturned tiles with a backdrop of busted televisions lining the wall to the right. A few electronic boxes weren't broken but displayed common and not-so-common static buzzing with white noise.

One old television with antennas had a show on that would occasionally be interrupted by static, showing an old television increasing in size, with a narrator speaking. "The allusion of the broken television, the TV that is never used, refers to the *static* lifestyle in response to a *static* counterpart. Those *static* hearts continue hoping, a judgment on the media of the past."

When the speech on the old television was completed the electronic box immediately went into loud static and started smoking from its top.

"No, it must be a bias on my part. To loan pain to uncertainty.. Is a loan just as valid as ownership if the future is by its very nature uncertain? Or is it only that way in regards to pain, as pain is something I am trading with myself in my meandering pondering for the hope of certainty? And if I can successfully trade pain for happiness, or success, or wisdom, or virtue, or do the opposite by some tragic mistake, who is to say what I even really possess? What is the ultimate value of possession and the civilization that comes out of it, starting with one's right to possess themselves, when the reality of death and its limitation of possession underlies both? Possession is certainly necessary for the existence of civilization, but is it really necessary for me, with my aim towards the heights of both happiness and intelligence, or a distraction from my facing the reality of my future death?"

The metalhead halted a solo and swiveled his horned head to the skeleton, "Man, Mycroft, I'm telling you, you've gotta do an intro with all that dark intellectual shit on my new album. Just as soon as I get this solo down.."

Lacie and Mr. Greary peered around in their new forms. Lacie felt drawn to one TV screen in particular that seemed to film a large dark theater from its second floor, though mostly all that could be seen were red curtains stained with blues.

Among the upturned tiles of the department was a large measuring device placed in the floor. The center of the device was a chaos star posing as a compass, with a clock around and above it, then around and above that was an actual compass-- then temperature, nuclear, and so on and so forth. The highest arrow pointed far from the device to big letters written in cursive and Greek dressing, "Nobody Was Here".

"I have been here for exactly thirty days since my ribs were picked from me by that old buzzard of a woman. It's been a trial. I'm sorry James, but I won't do anything other than ponder my existence until I get them back." Mycroft replied, revealing his multi-colored gummy tongue.

James continued his metal solo from the beginning, distortion just soft enough that the noise around the room could still be heard.

Just outside the Technology Department was a walking church with massive windows which required at least four men to hold them upright rather than two like with the last church. Here a priest was in the stead of a preacher; his crooked eyes were green, and he had short white hair, while covered in a long black robe with a rock pendant.

The priest tried to lead his congregation into the Technology Department but kept running into an invisible barrier. He stopped and spoke to those within, with a weak voice nearing squeakiness, "There are no rocks here and so much light, what age is it supposed to be?"

A fifteen-year-old boy in makeshift threads of Midnight blue was scratching short hair that was the same color. He wore layers of clothes just slightly too short or too long, but no skin apart from his hands and face ever showed. He was peering down at the salad dressing which was starting to dry.

"Cursive she have to do it in?" Midnight moaned, "I guess would work in theory.. still."

"Lacie." Mr. Greary inquired.

"Yes?"

"There's a golden wall clock lodged in the back of your plastic head."

Seeing his congregation looking at old, secular movies on sale in the aisle-way, and having no way of entering the more advanced section of the store, the priest withdrew with his group. Some children and one father with the congregation had grabbed some DVD's; and a golden retriever that might've been with them had a stray VHS tape in its mouth.

Midnight ventured over to Lacie without warning and yanked the clock out of her head. He inspected it carefully before speaking, "Has my this name all over it."

Midnight folded like two 2D doors closing in on themselves and he disappeared with the clock in hand.

Lacie felt the fissure in the back of her head, otherwise unaffected by it. Mr. Greary peered at the Lacie's cranial gap and checked the back of his head. He was both worried and relieved, "You, are, okay?"

Lacie shut her eyes (though nothing happened to the mannequin). She found her lack of sight back to normalcy, the golden clock no longer appearing in the darkness. She nodded at Mr. Greary, but secretly felt concern.

Lacie walked past the cashier desk where she saw a teenage girl sitting on the mysteriously upturned floor and leaning against the glass display behind Mycroft and the desk. Her arms were wrapped around her legs which were close together and sprawled outward in tight jeans. She had on a vintage shirt with some long red cloth tied around her neck. Her hair covered half of her face with various brightly-colored reds. Her only showing eye was steel with a glowing, greyish-blue iris surrounding a luminescent white pupil.

The eyelashes of her one showing eye were the teeth of an open zipper with an oversized pull tab that hung off the side like a giant metal tear. The teeth of zippers covered her arms, the few 'zip fasteners' which were opened revealed muscle fibers under translucent plastic sheets signed in marker with the Latin names of insects.

As Lacie and Greary spotted her a long store light fell from behind them and shattered on the convulsed floor. They both reacted with a startle.

"Oh." The girl whined. "The lights always fall when people look at me."

"Don't worry about it Lenore." James said in the midst of experimenting with guitar chords.

"I like your eye." Lacie said. "I have weird eyes too."

"You don't have eyes. Are you making fun of me?"

Lacie remembered her scope-eyes were on her actual body in Black Stock, "No. I mean--"

"Everyone new makes fun of me." Lenore said.

Mr. Greary was consoling, "We're not here to make fun of you. Wait.."

"Oh no.. you changed your mind?"

"No." Something took over Mr. Greary, "That red cloth, is that a cape?"

Lenore lifted her head up out of her palms, "Yes. This cape belonged to a boy who thought he could fly, but something happened."

"I'm sorry.." Mr. Greary said.

"It was terrible." Lenore's voice broke.

"Was it from trying to fly?" Lacie asked.

"What do you think?" Lenore sunk her head into her hands, and another three-inch zipper tag popped through her hair, both drooping from the outer corners of her eyes.

James messed with his tuning, "Don't mind her.. she just got that haircut."

“What is the point or purpose of possession to one such as myself, when my own bones have been stolen from me.. and the police do nothing because I am a skeleton?" Mycroft looked down to the five ribs which had been taken from him. “Do I deserve happiness if I seek the highest intellectual truths in life, and doing so leads me into an endless and painful inquisition of the reality and mystery of the end of life? And for that matter, does anyone? And if the heights of happiness are perpetually in conflict with the heights of intelligence, and civilization is to value one or the other, then what is to come of civilization and its survival as a result of its failures in either regard?”

Lacie gawked at the skeleton, "Excuse me mister skeleton."

James started playing a guitar solo while Mycroft turned to the girl with an uncontrollably cold stare.

"Are you okay?" Lacie asked.

Mycroft's multi-colored gummy tongue flapped from inside of his jawbone in recital, "Is anyone truly okay when faced with the limitations of all language to accurately solve the primordial terror of existence and death that manifests from our infancy?"

Lacie didn't quite know how to reply, "Ah.."

James messed up on his solo and stopped with a sternness directed towards the mannequins, "Look, I don't care if you guys chill around here, but you need to stop talking to me while I'm practicing."

James ran his hand through the top of his long hair, counted without 'four' to five, and continued from the beginning.

"Do you know where I can find a cape?" Mr. Greary asked Lenore, brushing off the agitated guitarist.

Lenore raised her head up at the plastic clothes model, big zipper tags dangling from a rounded face. Her iris shifted to warmer colors before she looked back down at the floor and touched the dusty upturned tiles around the good ones she sat on.

Lenore untied the cape, took it off, and handed it to Mr. Greary. As she did this, each upturned tile on the floor on the department flipped over and returned to a brand new state like the origination of its placement; apart from the salad sigil.

Lenore felt the back of her neck, "You can keep it in case you find the owner."

"The owner..?" Lacie said, mostly to herself.

"Thank you! Thank you!" Mr. Greary knelt down and hugged Lenore; the oversized zipper tags fell off her face and clanged against the floor. Mycroft had stopped talking to himself, and had placed his right hand under his chin, and stared at the spectacle with enormous interest.

James opened his mouth under a brow

of agitation but was stopped by a bony hand raised up in a 'stop' motion. Mycroft spoke, "Stop talking and focus on playing. I understand the intensity of your query.. and if you focus, I shall be on your album."

A great caravan with a strapped-down camera came swooping overhead with a trail of black smoke and ash, and pointy, slow flapping wings. There were arrows in the beast's head and something bloody in its mouth.

"Oh dear." Mr. Greary said. "Well we best be going."

"Okay." Lacie replied, looking at the caravan and then down at her plastic limbs.

They ventured towards the mechanical exits and waved to Mycroft, James, and Lenore who returned the favor-- James only waved because he had screwed up again on his solo.

"I hope this cape will materialize on the other side." Mr. Greary gawked at the machine.

Lacie however, was quick to get in the podlike apparatus she had came in without thinking about it.

"Tuck it into your glasses." Lacie suggested with her hands on the lid, "Are you coming?"

Mr. Greary had hesitated while looking

at his mannequin body. He snapped out of it, and tucked the red cape around his glasses which blocked most of his vision. Then, he sat down on the black, cozy chair in the sleek machine and closed the lid in unison with Lacie.

Chapter 18

Trees leaned inwards with their roots showing around the edges of a sprawling dirt crater. Strewn inside the crater were busted towers made of neon-colored light bulbs which had fallen from disturbances; and occasional street lights left to glow no more with their faces in the ground. Somewhere, an empty honey container of abnormally large size laid half-buried. There were also sleeping, docile, or permanently damaged caravans, misfits amidst the edge of the collective canine barbarism, and destined to the group's scraps at the bottom of its collective hunger.

The land once filling the crater was floating in the sky, just above. The floating island had pitch-black, wooden pavilions whose foundations stabbed through their roofs like shabby giants' knives. Pieces of timber from crooked picnic tables that didn't make it were scattered across the floating land mass, the splinters sometimes floating in the air themselves.

Pressed deep into the hovering island was a vertical labyrinth of thick, metal-linked foundations, mostly hidden by a dark grey base of pollution that, unlike the mostly black gas above it, reached from its grey edges with handless and footless limbs that went into a dark greys and turquoise before each gas limb's dissolution.

Leading upwards from the dirt, pavilions, and layer of ugly grey cloud, was a slowly twirling and monstrously-sized black cloud filled with a wallless maze of shimmering, blue metal platforms, as well as towering LED and neon lights shining in bright colors in contrast to their relatives, colorless and smaller sodium-vapor street lights; the lights gave visibility by separating and hollowing the black cloud just so. The vindictive glow of small creatures' eyes hid where groups of lights were busted; the creatures, though not all small, made brief semi-silhouetted appearances in and out of the mysterious, clouded-over outskirts.

A homeless man with an eyepatch who thought he was a tour guide stood below in the crater, he talked to himself or to invisible people, amongst the crumbs of the various baked goods that Monsieur Malluso once carried. "The crater we are standing in is commonly called 'Below.' While the floating island is often dubbed 'Above.' And these two landscapes constituted the rarely used, 'Crater Park..'"

Underneath a couple of the large, blue square platforms there were rows of computers old and new, alien and human, bolted upside-down with hardware hanging; the machines were running without being plugged in, as if somehow taking power from the surrounding toxins.

Two basketball-sized men with dim eyes, heavy facial hair, and fitted peculiar clothes, waddled around in the gravitational difference of the poorly-placed technological laboratory. Oversized suit ties drooped off their shoulders and severely worn ribbons from their wastes as they loitered upside-down.

"Mirk mirk." One ball-sized man said. His black mustache twirling down into orange as it trailed to the ground. He dodged the wingless, finned red bird which he had spotted. The mirk mirk's skeletal tail took off some strands of his facial hair and ribbon in its magnetic-brained movement.

Gald growled and shook his fist at the bird. "Youch!"

Jitters, the miniature man's long-bearded friend, tapped him on his tiny shoulder, "I believe we'll find it. Gold, Gald!"

Gald grinned at Jitters's twinkling eyes under his ridiculous whitish-pink beard. Gald jumped upwards (which was downwards) but did not return to the floor and began screaming.

Jitters grabbed Gald by one thick strand of his 'stache which caused his eyes to widen as he yelled, "Mirk! Mairk! Mackin!"

"I've gotcha fer the gold, Gald." Jitters swung Gald into the platform back into the abnormal gravity's grasp. Then Jitters started gyrating his hips and jittered with excitement, "Gald, we gotta gald down to thart cretor. Pranto!"

Gald punched Jitters in the face, "Butter my knife, it's a dead end from here. Mackin."

"Don't you worry so much, I land valiantly." Jitters explained in recovery from the punch, grabbing Gald's 'stache and throwing him into a frightening, terrific fall towards the ground, ties and ribbons covering his sight.

Jitters grabbed and waved a disgruntled mirk mirk at his descending companion, "Put some wings into it, chicken!"

Abbadon soared into sight with half his scales pried off revealing leathery, green and blue skin. There was anger written all over the beast's face, and "anger" written (or maybe imprinted) all over his face. Two or three of the black and blue specters, whom appeared like they came from the air in front of trees at early night, held on mercilessly. They tugged onto the creature's thick bony plates and used lose scales to stab at the similarly thick, underlying skin.

Gald fell onto Abbadon whom didn't notice as he was being violently attacked and any sense in him was already violated. Though Abbadon was of a massive size, his mass paled in comparison to the island before him. Abbadon hit a couple towering, impossible to read lights of mostly primary colors as the h'ragon's claws clanged against the platform with his landing; a great number of the bulbs on the lights were shattered and the towers fell out of the collective cloud rocketing downwards towards the massive crater below.

"See, I knew you could fly!" Jitters shouted.

Standing before Abbadon was a man with three large, white question marks in place of a head. The third question mark was reversed and leaning slightly to the back. The metal pipes connecting the question mark heads ran down into an oddly closed, forest-green leather longcoat with streaks of some other murky colors; and strips of black leather, which rose up from all over the coat. He had long, pointy leather shoes of a blackish-brown-- similar to his skin and fingers. And a dog tag hung around the stranger's neck inscribed, "???"

"Marthreek." Abbadon murmured with

command. A couple hundred medieval weapons of endless design began raining down from the sky, metal blades meeting steel platforms or nothing at all.

"Tut, tut. Tisk, tisk." Marthreek said before vanishing. His body was in a blur as he knocked the remaining specters off of Abbadon into a fall. Then '???' grabbed Gald. Marthreek resumed the place on the platform where he was originally standing, smoke rising from his shoes due to their friction. He dropped Gald in front of his smoking feet before the last of the raining weaponry had landed on or passed the seemingly endless gridwork.

Gald grabbed his black and orange 'stache and went sprinting away.

"And manilla folders." Marthreek pulled a singed, slightly-manilla paper-holder out of his coat, holding it up in the air.

"The fourth?"

"It wants to stop traditions. Says it's in control." Marthreek commented, dropping the barely-manilla folder, its papers falling with it down into a gas-covered void.

There was a remote group of four people stumbling around. Two had on thin, shabby cloth of green, dark red and brown, with mixed, alien furs over top. Another was wearing a kind of futuristic helmet with a cut-up, shaggy ensemble and similar murky color. Three picked up one of the weapons lying on the ground-- the third picked up two. Each of the three placed them in hilts they already had. The fourth person was hard to see, traced behind the far-away four.

Abbadon raised his wings readying to take a flight in some equal measure of grace and force, despite his ugly head.

"Headed towards a mechanical conglomerate? You'll be fixed wrongly and longly." Marthreek said with a dry, cheeky chuckle-- his third question mark temporary turning the right way before spinning back.

It was only moments before Marthreek's paperwork returned, and in blowing back upwards, was lost to a higher darkness.

* * *

Diego was seated at the table of a restaurant which appeared to be predominantly serving Chinese dishes from a spanning, centered buffet. The bottom halves of his sunglasses had been diagonally cut from a prior meeting with his prey. A doppelganger of Diego was repeatedly walking through the double doors, vanishing, and re-emerging which caused one of the workers to swat at the ghostly pattern with a broom, to no avail.

Half of the room was awash in dim, golden lighting that brightened the surfaces of close, shadowy tables while the larger portion of the restaurant was a bright white and much more spacious; with the corners of the restaurant all full of sand deposits.

The material of ceiling tiles ranged from extravagant to shoddy. One of the tables was attached to the ceiling from its top, stuck there in limbo between dinner and breakfast, with glass and gunk oozing from its sides. A patch of ceiling tiles that were glass had a poorly-dressed, gaunt man peering down at Diego's table with wide eyes as if trapped in the ceiling, the soles of his feet most visible. The man in the ceiling was in a ball and without movement.

Between the difference in lights, some of the floor formed into spiral staircases leading downwards to doorways or dead ends. These spiral, zigzaggery ramps would vanish and appear upside-down from the ceiling or rarely sideways and coming off of a wall, like a material flicker, before re-establishing their exact circular descent in the floor-- sometimes just barely verging upon the tray-filled buffet tables as a result of their teleporting tenacity.

A Chinese lady with a menu came up to Diego.

"Seated or coming in?" She asked.

The high-pitched voice of a male rang out, "Seated!"

The word came from a pot-bellied Mexican man in his fifties dubbed by most as Jose Suervo-- it was on his shirt. He looked between a real-life man and an archaic, hand-drawn cartoon. A living rooster rotated around his upper torso, scrambling around as if the poor bird had no choice. The man grinned hugely and cheekily as he put a scoop of something on his plate from the buffet line.

Around the restaurant were two clusters of age-varied people missing faces, their entire bodies and slight surrounding space were blurs of color like moving watercolor paintings. Some of them exuded red around their heads like blunt trauma, or black spots around their eyes. Occasionally their bodily segments would slip into the detail of reality before returning to a blur. They went about getting food or eating, but their conversing was inaudible, like cut-up reverberations of intimately-sized crowds.

On one wall, where pots of boiling water lined the edges, Diego noticed a glossy portrait of a sunflower with a toy bulldozer on a shelf next to it. The portrait had the emboldened words underneath, "Nature as a metaphor for life’s challenges."

Diego leaned over his food. He grasped

a butter knife reflecting light like the lenses of his aviator glasses, "You said, this character, Malluso?"

"Why.. yes!" Jose nabbed a bite of some meat from one of the buffet trays before turning around with an over-emphasis of facial expression as the bulging-eyed rooster crowed and struggled in orbit around him. "You two have a playdate?"

The blue-and-red-haired hunter stuck the blade through his plate and into the table, "Something like that."

At once the heaviest of the glass ceiling tiles shattered, and the shoddily dressed, thin man broke out. He began running around the restaurant like a bouncy, frightened animal--and would've played the part of a frightening man, had there been an audience for it.

Diego noticed a non-watercolor person, a kid, sitting at a dimly-lit table near a corner filled with sand. He had on a beret and a bushy fake mustache that was drenched from the glass mug of root beer he was sipping on. The boy had been watching the spiral ramp switch places with a sense of pseudo-drunken awe, but this emotion was soon to be replaced.

"No running inside, asshole!" The child scorned the desperate sprinting man; the frightened man ran into Jose; and the frightened rooster broke free from orbit.

Chapter 19

Lacie and Mr. Greary found themselves back in Black Stock, the sleek machines they were buckled into had overheated and were filling with smoke. The two coughed hard as they quickly scavenged for the levers which would let them out of the murky contraptions. They got out of the machines as soon as the glassy faces raised and still coughing, began fanning off the smoke.

Mr. Greary took off his glasses. Then, he pulled the red cape out from underneath his gravy-colored spectacles. If the glass in Greary's frames might've been tinted rose, that color was gone now. He and Lacie silently noted that the order of the machines were all the same, but they were off to the side of what seemed to be somewhere further down in Black Stock's side hall, and the dead end their machines once occupied was covered in shadow and ice with leaking liquid nitrogen tanks.

"That worked? Oh cool." Lacie said with a whisper, referring to the cape warping with Greary's glasses as the smoke cleared enough for her to see. But she was also disappointed, as the almost two hundred pounds of weight she had acquired remained.

Not to mention she was still covered in black guck.

The hall was still long and twisted, luminescent with poetic words, too lighted with blue on one end and too dark with shadow on the other. Coffee makers littered the blue path ahead. Most appliances were knocked around, while some were plugged in and running as if taking electricity from wires in the wall-- a rare selection of these were steaming. The smell of coffee beans penetrated the air, subsiding in hints with gusts of wind blowing back and forth from large rooms on the fringe.

"This is only one half to the recipe of our ticket out of here." Mr. Greary explained looking at the long red fabric, "There is a secred way to make the ceiling open up ahead."

From behind the two, the boy named Midnight appeared like a piece of origami craft unfolding. He held the golden wall clock of numeral reform that read '11:15', and he stared out blankly without drawing attention to himself. The Black Stock walls around Midnight gave testament that few 'attentions' were wrote, while no attention was drawn.

"Secred?" Lacie was barely able to voice.

Mr. Greary ran his hand down the wall,

"Somewhere around here."

Lacie spotted a red Eggola Cola machine that stood some feet ahead with an LED display that showed it had no power. There was a small AA battery on the floor in front of the broken, mechanical merchant, but not yet under. The battery was graced with the scattered chaos of the coffee pots, with its tiny outward cylinder of positivity pointing towards the left. A paper was posted on the Eggola cola machine reading: "Dlhbfbpwubf."

"Oh it's this giant button." My Greary asserted. A large green button had appeared hanging down off a pipe covering its wiring, over the push switch were the words, "This is a button, it does something if you press it.. Don't press it twice."

"Where did that button come from?" Lacie whiffed.

Mr. Greary pressed the green push switch once without pause. The switch rose back up towards the ceiling and folded into it, disappearing with other actual pipes. Black Stock instantly began cycles of shaking like it was under an earthquake, stopping, and then continuing its shaking; while this happened, the blue-lighted end of the hall began raising upwards, and the dark end lowered downwards, while loud beeps hit the start of so many seconds like the sonic mark of a spacecraft's emergency.

With effort, Mr. Greary ripped the cape in half and placed the halves on the floor.

"What are you doing?" Lacie asked, completely confused by the action.

"It's no good this way." Mr Greary said, speedily pulling some beef gravy out of his pocket. He opened the can, tossed the lid, and poured the liquid topping on top of each piece of fabric. The gravy began bubbling and something formed under the fabric with harsh sound and a great deal of flightless brown bubbles.

Meanwhile the shaking, twisted hall continued to inch towards becoming a pit. Lacie and Greary leaned forward with the changing difference in gravity as coffee-makers, cleaning supplies, and food returns started to roll down the hall. Both of them understood that if they didn't get out in time, they would be taking a lethal fall.

"Grab them!" Mr. Greary yelled as he grasped what looked like a bulky strap underneath his cape scrap.

Lacie leaned over and picked up a strap attached to something heavy and metal underneath the other cape scrap. She made enormous effort to pick the contraption up, and as she did the extra one-hundred-and-eighty pounds of weight on her began shedding off into unknown flying insects that immediately took retreat. The half of a cape fell off the bubble-covered object-- and with her weight and her clothing shrinking back to normal, she saw that she was holding onto a jetpack covered in bubbling beef gravy.

"Just put it on." Mr. Greary said, picking up and pocketing the halves of red cloth. He then quickly began pressing buttons while looking at the jetpack display coming off of a connected rounded pad that was at the back of his head. After Lacie got her jetpack on, Greary, who was now profusely sweating, pounded in a bunch of codes on the instrument's keypad.

"Oh no." Greary said, thinking something to himself.

"What?"

"I left my eggs.. We'll have to fly to the Farmer's Market." Mr. Greary almost said to himself in exasperation.

"How do I fly this thing?" Lacie asked, a happiness arising halfway in her phrase as her voice and weight returned to normal-- though she was still drenched in something that seemed between water and tar. The jets of both flying instruments turned on, answering her question, and the two began moving forward-- as something with human weight grabbed Lacie's foot.

"I've programmed it to will itself." Mr. Greary explained as they jetted upwards through the blue-lighted end of Black Stock.

The hall was almost vertical as the blue bulbs passed by, and the exit only displayed the mixed color of the sky. When Lacie came shooting out of the ground she kicked at the weight on her right foot, which suddenly felt like two hands slipping away. The weight subsided and she heard a young male screaming exactly as though falling from below her. Though she saw nobody to accompany the sound. And when the scream diminished she heard no crash.

They jolted towards the pale white shreds of the smoking moon while commotion and play made beelines below. The exit Lacie and Greary took rotated towards invisibility, their exit into the outside was part of a great, roughly-formed wheel in and of the ground.

With panning and zooming, Lacie noticed All-Mart had become a mix of green garages, orange window shields, and outer walls painted in crimson, dingy yellow and brown. In the parking lot there was a crying woman looking down into her hands and walking in the middle of a group of people whose heads were fixed upwards, half of the people twirling-- the other half standing on upside-down floating umbrellas. The tower of pink hats had fallen, and there was no sign of the trailer underneath it, or man who once stood by it so triumphantly-- and in so much fear.

Other adults: colorful, bleak, sober, and drunk-- were sprinting to electronic music; the music was coming from speakers on the crooked posts for power lines-- while some lines were unconnected, down, and uninspected.

More trees, large and small, had uprooted themselves and were crashing into buildings-- like missiles, never missing. Some of the buildings were retaliating, forming mouths at their halves or limbs with which to swat at the trees.

Architectural debris and splinters stormed the air from the war between buildings and trees, causing some grounded individuals to take shelter. Others were hit, which somehow resulted in them falling into the sky. Unaffected by this were a group of multi-colored cats on strike and a singing llama that was dancing (albeit abnormally on four legs), who was of different breed than his underground, melodic ally. Over the storm of aerial conflict, a group of birds and stranger flying objects traveled off towards a donut shop.

A group of police officers focused

sternly or with quizzical analysis on the events around them. However the group's attention was mostly drawn towards the moon and how to get to it. Their outfits ranged from official to imposter, and here to there. Differently sized ladders from futile to dangerous, stood or laid on either sides of the collective cops. One lawman was climbing down a ladder shaking his head.

Shivering from the air as it grew colder, Lacie took in no less of a lensful when she looked over her head at a moon, which seemed far too close to N'Quevna than she had originally perceived. Beyond the smoke was a bulbous grey and white rock full of raggedy-edged craters and huge, specially lit patches of dirt; the patches were farmland that had been lit on fire, hidden from afar by billowing smoke. As she and Greary got closer they heard the resonating of some catchy mixture of reggae, jazz, and Arabic folk music.

As the two passed through the smoke they noticed its composition had a sweeter and more complex smell differing totally from that of the machines they were trapped in earlier. They flew into a clearing with a fairly-sized collection of curious vendors set up below. As they landed on the rock, the two were immediately met by a dreadheaded man with a multi-racial patchwork skin-tone, a smiley paper-plate mask, and skeletal cardboard wings.

Chapter 20

Elizabeth was preparing dough. The red tips dangling from her black and now tied-up hair had mostly darkened against her volition. The left half of the store ceiling had instinctively sagged from a water leak as it always did around 11:24; though the clock in Mr. Bagel's Donut Shop was always stuck around that time. An apple fritter with gravity applied to it (more then those pastries which could float) hopped down into the linoleum desert of therapeutic light browns and classic white floor tiles. The sole employee saw this, stopped what she was doing, and went after the rolling 'ponchy' pastry.

Just before Elizabeth grabbed the donut, the door swung open in front of her.

A young woman in her mid-twenties stepped through the door with a long make-shift skirt of drooping dark rags shifting underneath a corset, with a collar of bones curving 'round the back of her white-haired head. The woman sat down at the corner table where Lacie had woken up hours ago, giving off a sweet, yet unpleasant smell, that was strong enough to cut through the freshly-made sweets.

An old radio in the back turned on for a

second accompanied by a mysterious voice, "Anyone with a distinct lack of ideas for absurdities would most definitely place a lot things upside-down."

On the next table up there was a man in a white labcoat with a row of upright vials in different volumes of concoctions and sheets of formulas strewn about under his meticulous focus. His hair was a greying mess, the uppermost parts of his fingers occasionally appeared and then were gone. He had no discernible ties to the outside world. Nor did he have any discernible ties.

The theorist cursed under his breath and scratched his head with the stubs of his two first fingers.

"Hello." Elizabeth greeted.

Mona offered no reply.

"If you don't mind me asking, how did you get through that door?"

"It was unlocked." Mona said.

The English book Lacie had left on the table of Mr. Bagel's Donut Shop had been charred to a near-blackness. Mona rested her arms behind it looking over the book with a curious gaze. She gently opened the cover which was falling apart, and turned a crackly and smoldered page as if expecting to read something.

"You know.. usually people come in

here to buy food."

"Quiet! I'm here to protect you, stupid girl!" Mona replied.

The scientist ignored them as he poured two vials, one full of light purple liquid, and another glowing with yellow-orange, into a large green-filled beaker on the table. The glass cracked as a chocolate-frosted donut materialized within. The scientist raised his hands in excitement, his fingers all back, his eyes fixed on the tasty circular treat, "One donut becomes a whole new donut reversing itself and switching dimensions with its kin donut!"

There was a giant moth on top of a decommissioned, jumbo-magnet-covered microwave in the back of the store; the insect flew high towards the store lights as the outside dark birthed a hoarse roar. The sound shook the long store bulbs along with the glass panes. The right half of the ceiling had its tiles crumble into pieces which fell onto Mona and the scientist. Mona shielded herself with her arms; the scientific stranger shielded his vials and newfound donut with his fingers all stubbed.

An old radio in the back turned on for a second accompanied by a mysterious voice, "The moths are getting bigger and fluttering towards the light."

Mona closed the charred textbook and stood up with a look of vindictive concern on her forehead, her lenses retracted to a shortness: a wider view. Elizabeth had hid behind the front desk of the restaurant but leaned in curiously towards a window. The theorist had his excitement drained from him.

Mona, Elizabeth, and the scientific man peered from their places at the desolate outside, the colored sky that glowed slightly less than that of orange and yellow street light arrays. Changed from their prior normalcy, the vivid lights were also hoisted by radically bent, calligraphic poles-- where seldom white fires surrounded, or mysterious, broken power lines occasionally drooped off dangerously.

The lids on nearby dumpsters were all open and emptied, and something resembling a crooked human being had formed from the trash. It was made from styrofoam, plastic, metal, paper and cloth; containers, clothes, broken appliances, and a rubber Halloween hand. With egg-shell eyes and a body from the charitable consumer, the putrid human shape came ready to consume and concoct itself.

Mona went to the door as the demon made of waste, now in view from the window, trudged across the pavement from its fenced origins. The demon turned its head unnaturally, and stared at the scientific man through the window, an eggshell eye falling off of its face to reveal what was the literary section of a dirty magazine in its eye socket. The scientist got up, left his vials, and bolted towards the door. He weaved around Mona and reached for the doorknob.

Dumpsters flung open all around the block and trash traveled in grotesque, midair streams to pack itself upon the demon. The scientist ran out through the door to Mona's dismay-- she had forgotten to snap her fingers in the commotion. She sneered at the loss of a good decoy, and crouched down to begin drawing some complex sigil on the floor as quickly as she could without mistakes.

The side of the building with the saggy ceiling tiles rose up a few feet, as though it was under a giant tire jack.

"What's going on? What is that thing?" Elizabeth asked.

The demon outside grew till its back twisted and bent to the ground, its hands like grounded maces; its face became a hateful, grinning collage of shifting junk.

"It's an S.U.V." Mona said.

The anti-aging witch kept drawing. She turned her head but barely looked at Elizabeth, "Don't go anywhere. We're leaving."

Mona continued a slow line on the complex, outer square that compromised her artwork. What she was drawing with was unknown. At one of her line changes, the donut shop burst from its foundations and rocketed into the air.

* * *

Malluso was investigating a small, blue and white sea-food restaurant that had went out of business; the location was close to a four-way with a wrecked, fenced-in car; the tail-end of the vehicle was now covered in a vast colorful array of different awareness ribbons. The neon-blue lights once surrounding the building were stolen or off, its windows boarded up with the light brown of cheap, processed trees. The area and space around the building was untouched with broken bookshelves on the corner. And there was no longer any smell of fried fish in the air; but would a marble-headed man have smelled it?

By the stop sign at the four-way was a creature in a wide, eight-foot tall cage. The enclosure had a dented sign marking the monster's name in some language from the East: "Lotus."

The Lotus was covered in dark, leathery skin with streaks of violet, green, and red across its body, across its head. It had vicious eyes glaring over a long mouth, full of teeth that appeared as jagged, black shards. Six, long wings stretched across its back like that of an infernal insect, each appendage jutting out from the gaps of rusted bars.

Diego stood on the opposite end of the restaurant in a parking-lot akin to larger businesses. He was looking at his aerial reflection in a puddle, like footage from a still drone.. and he saw the black-clad stranger on the other side.

Malluso noticed bizarre reflections in the puddles as well, as if they were coming from cameras in the ground.. in one puddle was the image of a man with arm warmers covered with swirling lines of jewels trailing off towards his ringed fingers. The man's left arm warmer had blue jewels and metal plates; a similar hue as the left side of his blue hair and its grown untidiness at the top. The right arm warmer had red jewels on glass plates encasing some sort of liquid metal, as sleek as the left red side of his long hairdo.

Diego raised his head and stared towards the boarded-up place in front of him.

"What do you want?" Malluso asked, backing up with his hand on the hilt of his blade, knowledgeable that someone was on the other side of the building.

"Your Black Cloud franchise, blocks out

the the rest of my sky." The hunter replied.

Malluso unsheathed his sword and flashed it downwards with so much energy that the abandoned restaurant cracked and parted down the center, giving view of Diego.

Diego had raised his arms above his waist, with his palms facing the vacant-looking building; the left palm faced down to the left, the right palm faced up to the right, as if occupying an invisible cube. As he rotated his ringed hands, the blue and red jewels on his arms began breaking, one after another towards his elbows.

In response, the black clouds, perpetually remaining at a much lower elevations than their enormous, colorful counterparts, shifted speedily, becoming more scattered. Where no clouds were, of any variety, there appeared violet-outlined curlicues and squiggly loops, both hollowed with starless black. And unlike the stationary stars, most of the shooting stars, in their short appearances, were now all falling. The world, or some part of it, it seemed, was meeting its other side, and turning upside-down.

Chapter 21

Jeffrey ventured from the ladder of a manhole, into a parking lot with a broken-down mini-mall; with Geoffery tailing behind. The mini-mall businesses had names like Video-Tech Reseller, Italian's Food, Vehement Clinic, and Laughing Old Dude. Long, yellow blossoms were growing out of the edges of the cement towards the grass. Not too far ahead were some large, fermented fish lying in some weaved bowls on the segmented, paved ground; their scales glimmering under high and twisted streetlights in the night.

The pavement of most of this parking lot, and the earthen composite underneath, were split up in crooked and more circular segments, with small gaps in between. The segments of ground moved in organized ripples whenever something touched one, as evident by a terrified Italian greyhound that had bells tied to it, which rung constantly as the dog barked loudly at the ground he had just tried to step on. This field of segments was growing as the ground slowly cracked more and more. The segmented pavement slowly traveled to normal parking lot and a version of All-Mart now almost entirely marked with the neon splatter of nineties rainbows.

The two young men could hear a stranger's voice from inside one of the small stores beside them. "I've been trying too hard you know, and it's definitely getting to me."

"Trwy wrotin in a Colwa." An abnormally high-pitched voice replied.

Geoffery jogged up to Jeffrey and tapped him on the shoulder, "Hey man I think there's cola in there."

Jeffrey looked up at the colorful night sky in curiosity, seeing its growing black clouds, fluctuations, and shortage of shooting stars as dangerous omens. Those victims who had been hit by tree and building debris, conscious or not, and falling upwards-- began drifting back towards the ground-- though they were barely visible to Jeff. The steel door behind Jeffrey and his friend was shut and the only way was forward. And as Jeffrey looked nearer towards the ground, he saw someone who looked familiar on the fringe towards the road..

After spotting Ratty, Jeffrey turned to notice an oddly-shaped, truck-sized wagon covered in differently-sized theatrical masks. It rolled down the far-off road from behind the yellow blossoms, in a kind of half-silhouette. Towards the front of the misshapen wagon the masks grew larger in appearance. Hidden behind the masks were shifting, painted faces, and some of the masks had voices which rang out in garbles in an abnormal, creepy symphony.

From behind the wagon appeared two genetically-identical teenagers out on the horizon. They had grey clothes, white hair, and grey skin; sullen eyes, normal shadows, and expressionless faces. Each of the strangers had on a slightly layered, gray long coat with the ends sewn together orderly.

A mutual bad feeling came over Jeffrey and Geoffery upon seeing the children or young teens as they looked across the distance between the wagon and the mini-mall-- across garbage-covered grass wet with paint, riddled with large holes, and covered in pizza boxes and silly string, and of course, the dandelions.

The shorter of the grey twins peered around, "This is unacceptable."

The caravan of masks swerved to the side of the road by some unknown force. The makeshift vehicle collapsed with a raggedy crackling of timber and crafted faces, ceasing all movement. Neither of the grey-swathed individuals paid attention to the incident.

"Do you see those church windows?" His taller brother mimicked him with a slightly higher chin, spotting a walking church. One of the men holding a stained-glass window lost his footing, and the window on his side fell, shattering across the pavement.

"Colors are gay." The shorter, grey-faced brother said.

"Maybe next time he'll learn how to disassemble a window appropriately." The older brother sneered.

Back across the long, littered gap, Jeffrey decided to attempt to cross the obstacles before him. Early in his footsteps, baskets of fish were lost to the earth. Jeffrey found that running was not applicable, that the radical leans of each segment were constant and unnerving.

"Are you coming!?" Jeffrey yelled to his friend.

Geoffery stayed behind for fear of harming himself trying to cross the weird pavement.

On the other side of the segments, Ratty paced further away towards the mess of pink hats, her arms crossed to keep the unstable breeze from bugging her.

* * *

On the smoking moon, the man with a patchwork skin tone introduced the others rather than himself, "Hello, this is Lacie Tilde and Brian Greary."

Around the moon were fragments of

mirrors that seemed to float entirely around it, reflecting the colorful sky and moon in a stunning and alien sight; the shards of reflective glass individually shifted underneath and over the top of the dust, and soil, and body of the smoking moon, with a broad view of the city behind the field of glass.

"How did you know our names?" Lacie asked, dumbfounded.

"Memory." The multi-racial man bellowed, unbeknownst to Brian and Ms. Tilde, speaking his name.

Lacie and Mr. Greary both noticed that Memory twiddled with something in his left pocket, and then took his hand out as though it was unimportant.

Lacie also glimpsed a brown, furry, long-limbed thing with half of its body hidden by red and indigo smoke, coming from the ground; it talked into a cup attached to a string, which traveled off a great distance into N'Quevna.

Then Lacie looked down at the display of one of their jetpacks that was laying on the ground, it appeared to be electronically dead, and gave off a burnt smell.

"That's quite different." Mr. Greary added. "..from a formal introduction."

Behind Memory were painted, wooden stalls with crops for sale and crafters making “techno-country art”. The small shops were amongst gold and silver strands of grass or alchemical hay. Other than fruits and vegetables for sale, there was a mixed aroma of sweetness not limited to the smoke in the fields; the smells of fudge, bread, pies, cookies, and other unhealthy treasures. People eyed the products up close in analysis or unwelcome, unwarranted sampling-- which led some to learn that they could not eat crafts.

There was a lost-looking young man apart from the handful of shoppers and the vendors at their stations. He had a metal bucket over his long-haired head, with little wide, rectangular eyeholes in the metal, and with a strapped longsword leaning against his shoulder. Half the blade was covered in foam while the other half was extremely sharp; half of the sword's handle was metal, the other half was covered in foam and cloth. He had baggy, handmade black pants, and a similar shirt with an emblem on the front underneath chain-mail.

The swordsman kept looking at Lacie like he was waiting for the right time to say something, though she had noticed only once in her preoccupation.

Lacie glimpsed up, and to her surprise, saw that she was looking down on the city. She zoomed in on a group of disgruntled out-of-work felines with picket signs. These mostly male cats rallied their strike to the sound of a singing, dancing llama as the world around them made its rounds-- but seemingly did not in space.

Among the cats, Lacie noticed an eccentric fellow with crooked whiskers, with his eyes bulging and his fur upright like it had been hit by voltage. One of his front legs was in a medical cast, and both were guarding a small pile of catnip. Lacie was surprised and bothered that she could hear this particular cat from so far away and so high above him-- to any bystander who came near, to any bystander who could hear, he spoke with a wide smile and sad eyes, "Won't you write your name on my caste?"

She zoomed out to see radical changes in the architecture over her head, modern apartment buildings had sprung up, rising out of the ground with asphalt or earth and its greenery over top. What looked like a wide one-story mall had a taller, more contemporary mall ascend from its center in a show of brilliant steel. Smaller buildings that looked like Japanese storefronts popped up, built themselves, or switched places with other businesses.

Lacie returned her consciousness to the moon upon the sound of some vendor, "I also enjoy cutting onions. I'm going to have to do a thorough look-through of this band's discography."

Someone in a suit that looked like a train-conductor ran out of sight across the fields shouting at Greary and Lacie. "Watch out, the end is just another beginning!"

"It's a bit high up here." Mr. Greary said.

There was a vendor in his fifties with brown overalls and a snow white beard. He was whispering gently to a tomato, "Lack of acceptance for victimless change is lack of education; and all of which are the repeated thoughts and actions of people posing as vegetables."

Over in a tilled field in a spot where the was no smoke, a smiling scarecrow with an antenna had left his post. He had a stand set up, and was unboxing and selling robotic farmers.

"You came here for that?" Memory pointed to a space suit laying in a field where there was no smoke and fire, while the sound of giddy, foreign music relayed under his voice. "Ms. Tilde?"

"I'm terribly sorry, I have to go buy eggs." Mr. Greary interrupted.

Memory obliged with a friendly open hand, "Of course."

Mr. Greary went off, not far, to a stout egg saleswoman. In the process Greary noticed a squash of a man next to the egg-seller. This man was surrounded by squashes and his body was proportioned in such a way that one side was frail, while the other he kept weighted. The squash man had covered himself in more layers of old clothes than ever necessary; worn hats on his head followed the same principle-- though his headgear also gradually spun, at snail's pace.

The squash man's somewhat nasally voice approached all who would hear him, "All people are insane and I'm one of the sane ones. I'm going to go glue carpet to my obese, naked body and walk backwards to Indiana.."

"No, I don't have any desire for a space suit." Lacie said, the horrible feeling subsiding at a snail's pace in her stomach that Mr. Greary was not meant to buy eggs. On the subject of suits, she also wished that she could find different clothes, her's had dried off but were stained with black guck.

"I'll take a dozen eggs." Mr. Greary said to an unenthused woman, forced to listen to the nearby squash vendor.

"In India Nana they sell bananas." The squash man spake while holding a yellow squash.

"Then you don't remember?" Memory asked. "The tailor failure in Black Stock?"

Lacie rose an eyebrow over her ocular-metal protrusion, “The shouting naked guy? He was a tailor?”

Memory made an open gesture with both his hands, a smile fixated on a paper plate. “Well my memory isn't perfect, I'm just taking a guess.”

“It's not what it looks like, motor-squash.” The squash man said while holding a stainless-steel cyber-squash, with turning gears on either side.

Lacie paused. “I should probably take it back to him, if I'm ever going..”

“To get out of here. You feel guilty about it.” Memory completed. There was a buzzing sound, and Memory pulled a cell phone out of his pocket, walking away and answering the cell before Lacie could ask to use it without anxiety creeping up on her. Having neglected the chance for communication when underneath All-Mart, Lacie was unsure if fate or bad memory was conspiring against her.

Mr. Greary put his eggs down. He gave a broad, inquisitive look at the plants for sale, followed by a broad, inquisitive look at the inside of his wallet. Then he picked the chicken eggs back up and ventured over to Lacie with an idea in mind.

Lacie watched as the young swordsman approached her as Mr. Greary looked behind her like he expected something.

The train-conductor reappeared on the opposite side of the moon far behind Lacie. He had stopped, squatting in sweat, and breathing heavily, “Like a maze!”

Near the train-conductor, there was a large wooden sign that read, “I am made of cheese, if you believe I am made of cheese.”

The bucket-headed swordsman now close, plead his case to Lacie and Greary despairingly, “Hello, I am a medieval futurist and I find myself stuck on the moon. I couldn't help but notice that you are not from here, can you help me get away from here?”

Mr. Greary nodded.

“We can help you Mr. Bucket-Head.” Lacie added, her scope-eyes zooming out.

“Where are you headed?” Dreary-Gravy asked.

“The Kingdom of Wanderers.” The swordsman said.

Chapter 22

Diego rose one of his ringed hands in the air and turned it. In response, the halves of the sea-food restaurant broke from the ground and rushed towards Malluso. But the hunter may have twisted his hand a little too far, breaking off a water vein which caused a gushing stream to rise from the site.

In response, the marble-headed man pulled out a tray of brownies, shielding the mass of dinner-scented cement that came at him. Chocolate crumbs hit the ground as cement crumbled and metal dented against leather and marble, pushing Malluso so far back that he lost his hat as he crashed into the Lotus's cage, bending the bars, and causing the top of the cage to pop off. A pile of rubble covered the marble-headed man near the stop-light and left him looking like a demolition site.

A group of Japanese men and women in fresh white suits watched from some distance away hearing the crash. Almost all of them had torches, while a couple had flamethrowers, one of which was wearing nothing but a diamond-studded mawashi-- like padded underwear, the sumo wrestler's outerwear.

A calm-eyed Asian women looked to a

heavily-clothed man wielding a flamethrower, "How is your daughter Okiku?"

The man raised one of his stern, skeptical eyebrows, "Well.."

The Japanese h'ragon hunters quickly went on their way downtown as a frightened nun-raver quickly got out of the way, glow sticks and glowing rosaries on strings, trailing.

The Lotus flew out of its cage with a dubstep flutter while Malluso's slightly ticked-off voice came from the debris, "That was.. my only batch."

A young man in a hoodie was running out of a convenience store with a forty while being chased by the clerk. He was spotted by those among the police officers who weren't carrying ladders back to the station. One American-looking, foreign cop bolted after the young man.

Some of the sprinters around decided to see the ladders cops were holding as hurdles. Most runners jumped them, while some crawled under them. A middle-aged woman with mini-flashlights on her spectacles, and handfuls of half-full shot glasses hit a ladder; she skidded into the pavement, shattering glass and spilling booze everywhere.

Diego barely paid attention to the weather and surroundings as they changed around him, his eyes fixed on the oncoming

Lotus. Sky-colored snowflakes, in pink, red, indigo, violet, midnight blue, and black, floated down from the sky to melt into the summer night-- but other colors of snow might've appeared, hidden among their contemporaries. Some of the outer darkness surrounding the city had thinned to reveal enormous mountains under the moonlight. Pieces of buildings still in the air found their way under the people who had fallen up and were now rising back down, as if in some magical sense, under Diego's fingers.

"So the seasons are combining; and the whole thing might just break apart." Diego calmly stated.

Malluso stood up, pushing the heavy pieces of wreckage off of his tattered longcoat where rips revealed abysmal marble. He picked up his wide-brimmed and dusty fedora, plopping it back on with one gloved hand. Then Monsieur nodded to the Lotus creeping out of its cage on all fours, "Mr. Bagel's brother I presume, it seems like it's time for you to go and be culinary."

The Lotus somehow screeched and laughed all at once with a multitude of vocal chords, charging forwards at the hunter.

Malluso yanked his rapier from under a thick cement wall and found that his blade had bent to a square angle. He swiftly marched to the stop sign, pulling it off its stand with great force, and somehow attached it to the end of his blade. Malluso's blade began to spin the large, red stop sign in a counter-clockwise motion, "Before all of this over, you'll have faith in something other than yourself."

Diego had raised his right hand; his left hand behind his back, facing up, safely dropping off the collateral victims. Malluso noticed one of the Japanese storefronts had broken from its foundations and was running through the air like a spinning missile, a trail of foreign products being littered behind it. The convenience store soared vicariously towards the Lotus, and the Lotus charged viciously towards the hunter.

* * *

Meanwhile, in front of a closed bookstore, an American-looking, foreign police officer came up to a British "Chief Constable" with a mustache made from whole-wheat pasta. A blond-haired female officer behind the constable rambled on about how much she hated donuts.

"They don't even have any nutritional value." She said.

The American-looking, foreign officer had handcuffed the young man with the hoodie who had stolen the forty. “We've got him.”

A Russian officer approached in short shorts and cowboy boots. Despite this appearance, he remained unnoticed.

“Who?” The constable tasted some of the colorful snow pouring down and made a face of disgust.

“The man who stole the alcoholic--”

“You stole my heart.” The Russian officer interrupted.

“Roy, is this true?” The constable asked.

Roy gave no reply except a facial visual as though he had tasted the snow.

The constable pulled Roy away and gave him to the female officer, “Ecila, take this man in.”

Ecila handcuffed Roy as the constable spoke to him, “You are under arrest.. you have the right.. to join the military.”

* * *

The Lotus had opened its long mouth in front of Diego Caprice and regurgitated pocket-sized boxes at his dodging feet. In the split seconds before they exploded, Diego could see the different flavors of the dangerous delicacies. Hovering with a vicious expulsion of deadly, boxed pies, the Lotus barely caught attention of the Japanese convenience store which slammed into it with a bone-crushing force.

The lotus put up its bony, black arms and turned as the store's first wall smacked against it, pushing the insect-monster through. The second wall smashed through the Lotus a split-second later with a horrific symphony of childlike laughs and boiling teapots. The insect monster met the pavement and ceased movement.

A round-faced, Japanese merchant who had temporarily left his store slowly made his way towards its ruins as he tried to pick up the trail of his products. The merchant's stocky arms were practically full, with two police behind him, one American and one Japanese, helping pick up the slack.

Malluso charged towards the hunter, his sword still rotating off of the hilt.

Diego had backed away considerably. He rose both his arms at once to rip an entire apartment building behind him from its ground-laid foundation. He was now standing on the mall parking-lot far from the mall's towering combination of stores. A red car raced by him veering across the grass and onto the road. The car faded out of site as Diego moved the now-leaning apartment complex with great telekinetic force.

Diego saw that the Lotus was slowly

getting back up. The instant he needed to crash the apartments into Malluso would be lost in order to fend off the Lotus. He dropped the building, letting it crash into the ground; Malluso was halfway to him.

Diego got down on his stomach as pieces of the apartment building came barreling everywhere. With the hunter's arms covered with thick dust and thin color, he had an outstretched ringed hand in the air, pulling out a grey jet plane from the sky, from behind Malluso and the Lotus, and seemingly out of nowhere.

As the Lotus approached, the jet plane plowed into it with an ear-splitting blur followed by a brilliant, shocking explosion. Malluso was in reach of Diego seconds later, the force of the blast only serving his attacking swing from the air. The marble-headed man hit the hunter with the stop sign sword at just the right angle.. while a stainless-steel squash with turning gears on either side, came down with the bad-tasting blizzard, clanked and rolled nearby.

Chapter 23

Elizabeth tightly grasped the edge of the desk at the back of the rocketing store while the now frigid air thinned and chips of paint fell from the walls. The donut shop employee had a look of fearful recognition towards the hunched-over, twenty-something white-haired girl who blocked the front door. Elizabeth's voice strained, "I remember you now. I know what you've done."

"I don't think you do." Mona turned around and grinned capriciously. "But if you don't shut up, I'll show you."

"I saw you turn him into that." Elizabeth froze after her words, along with everything else in the contemporary store. Donuts motionless.

The donut shop cracked down the middle, splitting in half by invisible force, and dividing Elizabeth and Mona to the building's new, wide-open contours in the sky.

Mona was also froze in place with her hand on some strange, fountain pen stabbing into the floor, the building halves flailing downwards.

Elizabeth regained her movement. She looked down to see Monsieur Malluso holding a crooked stop sign and riding a caravan with a camera on it's head; packaged ground chuck dangled from the giant bat-dog's black smog-gushing mouth. The caravan dive-bombed into the tilted side of the building where Elizabeth was.

She was now holding the ledge of an upside-down desk, eyes wide and heart pounding. The donut shop employee reluctantly dropped down onto the back of the caravan while cookies, pies, and donuts scattered downwards in a rain. The three left behind the falling architecture while a flock of birds and flyers made their escape in the opposite direction..

"I've rescued you." The caravan said in a rash voice, raising its head and eyes to the side to focus on the girl on its back, the thin trails of ash from its eyes blowing away from her with the wind.

Elizabeth looked down at the beast with raised eyebrows, wide eyes, and a closed mouth, "..."

The caravan flew towards the desserts that had fallen from the donut shop, gobbling them up.. forgetting that there was anyone on his back.

"You're going to raise my blood sugar if you crash into the ground!" Malluso yelled.

When the caravan started flying normally, Elizabeth looked back on the dark and distant traces of the frantic flock. Her heart rate beginning to lower, "She's evil. Why did she help me?"

"We're being hunted." Malluso replied.

"For what reason?" Elizabeth held onto the tufts of the caravan's fur sticking out from calloused skin; the caravan didn't seem to mind.

"With certain action comes a greater chance of suffering." Pieces of Malluso's invincible jaw crumbled and fell onto the caravan, bits of black gas forming around his mouth to put the mandible back together. "We have acted near the reach of our dreams, and have thus been bound to the full effect of our intentions."

* * *

James ran his fingers over the fretboard in a blur, a metal solo blasting through the back of Null-Mart. Mycroft sat behind the employee desk, banging his bony head and throwing up devil horns.. while Ecila merely banged the back of her noggin' against the glass where more video games had once been; her mannerism in a show that her eardrums might be about to pop. Some of the game cases fell off the shelves from her play of self-injury.

James's hand went to the bottom of the fretboard, in a frenzy of high notes that started busting the television sets in the store one by one, glass shattering and insides blowing out.

The end of the metal song came with the end of the television sets.

Mycroft looked around at the smoking destruction with his gummy eyes. He looked at James who stared back at him with impressed shock. The skeleton's most conjoined thought was voiced-out calmly, "This can't be good."

* * *

Jeffrey was only a few platforms away from Ratty, he had crawled, jumped, and balanced his way across the now colorful snowy segments of rippling parking lot. Geoffery watched from the other side, hearing that familiar moisture-sucking-sound from his straw. The stocky geek remembered he had borrowed the money for the drink from Jeffrey, and it was his third time doing so.

Jeffrey's theatrical boots obtained solid ground, and he began running towards Ratty. She was walking towards the turned-over pile of pink hats (though there had to be a red hat in there.. somewhere). It was most deducible to Jeffrey from her behavior that she was looking for answers, revenge, or both-- after what happened with the last hat she had put on.

Ratty stood and looked over the tipped-over tower of head tops. She began to turn as Jeffrey came to the side, both of them suddenly stopping.

The bodies of Ratty and Jeffrey duplicated to fives, each body growing more ghostly with its distance from the center. The orange pipe cleaners sticking out of Ratty's hair mostly changed to different colors. Their far-off transformation appeared to a panicked Geoffery, each image of them moving sporadically, and each image confused by all others.

"I.. I thought.. you'd thought.. I you.. never I.." Four Jeffrey's uttered.

"No one appreciates the concept of clones." The fifth and center Jeff replied.

"Concentrate on.. look for.. concentration.. the hidden colored hats." Images of Ratty replied.

Across the cracked cement, Geoffery was silent. Holding his empty slushie, he decided not to litter for once and looked around.

Geoffery went behind the mini-mall where he found a dumpster, sprawled on it in paint, the words, "Someone Here."

Near the big metal trash-bin there was a silent woman with a beret covering her face, long blond hair, and a half-drunk fifth of clear alcohol next to her. As Geoffery dropped his empty container into the empty dumpster, he decided upon himself what he had to do to save his friend.

"Look at you, I bet that's all you drink. Classless." The woman said condescendingly, she sat up, her top revealing some of her sizeable cleavage. Geoffery just stared. The woman looked at her perfectly manicured nails, "I'm too pure to be near someone as a disgusting as you."

The volume of liquor seemed to wane if only slightly, if only half an inch.

The woman looked like she wanted to get up, and was trying with her hands. Instead, she leaned over, away from Geoffery towards the back of the dumpster; and began puking.

* * *

Malluso, Elizabeth, and the caravan underneath them landed in front of a Japanese pastry shop, somewhere downtown between an out-of-business bookstore and a nutrition outlet missing a door. Long, green push-pop popsicles littered the ground. The marble-headed man found one under the sole of his boot as he got off the bat-dog. Elizabeth was more careful. As soon as the young woman was off the caravan, it jolted into the air-- no hamburger left.

Malluso and Elizabeth noticed a terrifying creature made out of trash, the S.U.V., pounding its limbs forward from a football field away.

"This is another shop in the chain, a backup if something were to happen. Which it has." Malluso explained.

"Is that thing after me?" Elizabeth asked with a tremble in her voice.

The mace-like formations which made up the ends of the demon's limbs, pounded the cement with a slimy trail. The S.U.V. was closer now.

A malformed, deep-pitched voice boomed from a speaker inside the S.U.V. "Act with who and what you are, I am sick of who and what I am."

Malluso unsheathed his sword, "Get inside."

Elizabeth grabbed the entryway handle, "The door's locked.."

"Act with who and what I am, I am sick of who and what you are." The speaker garbled.

Chapter 24

“Thanks for letting me use your catapult.” Lacie said to the medieval futurist. The space suit flew through the air towards the kingdom to which they all were planning to head to. Lacie supposed she might soon find herself in a castle of some sort, but didn't look forward to the journey there by the appearance of the thing Greary had been working on. The town above and below bustled with confusion and certainty, in each blackened and colored entity; and the scope-eyed girl noticed some odd entities in particular who were bricklaying across the road she had first walked down with Elizabeth, building what looked like a wall.

The bucket-headed swordsman began untwisting a bolt from his large wooden contraption, “Now I just have to fit it back in my pocket.”

Greary kicked around moon-dust as he nailed pasture pumpkins, painted squash, and other produce together into an onion-shaped escape pod.. along with the help of two old men who sold young produce, and a “squarecrow” who came out of nowhere and also volunteered. The squarecrow was different from a scarecrow: dressy clothes, glasses, not meant for the crucifixion pose of his former stock.

Lacie looked around for Memory, but he had disappeared. The patchwork man was the type to wander as he talked on the phone, and though the moon was small, if the train conductor was to be believed, Lacie sensed that Memory had, maybe.. entirely left the porous rock.

"A copy machine." The squarecrow smiled and repeated, his straw limbs stuck to the outer layer of the escape pod. He had a combination between a pickaxe and an umbrella stuck in his shoulder, with the umbrella unfolded and facing outward.

"Yes. I'm sure there's one down there." Mr. Greary said, trying to feel innocent about the beaming squarecrow's request.

The scarecrow merchant, who had just sold a robotic farmer, shook his head in disapproval at the nailed-down squarecrow.

"So are you sure about taking the kingdom's way back into Black Stock? Even after you almost perished?" The bucket-headed swordsman asked.

"There's something I want to do there, just quickly." Lacie replied, one scope-eye further than the other, looking for Memory. "And then I have to look for Ecila, and someone else who thinks she's a bird.. and Elizabeth. Or I'll.."

“Let's get in and waste no more time.” Mr. Greary used the umbrella-pickaxe as a door knob to swing open the squarecrow door, as two old farmer-looking men, who'd helped with the contraption, backed away with blades towards the pressurized vines that were holding it down.

The three got in; the swordsman was last, and bumped his metal head against the top; how he had gotten an entire catapult into his pants pocket.. remained unknown.

The two helpers cut the vines, and something in the produce made the contraption leave the moon with rocketing might.

The force of the ugly escape pod's movement was such that it caused much screaming from its squished together comrades who had neglected the idea of seatbelts in their hurry to build and use it. Their momentum was faster than their ability to react with nausea as they crashed through the roof of The Kingdom of Wanderers; and the escape pod bashed and bounced against the ground.

* * *

The door wouldn't open at first, until some mysterious force began pushing the escape pod over.

When the door opened much of the

escape pod's produce seemed to detach and get squished by invisible force, as though breaking apart late from its incredible impact with the floor. The first thing Lacie saw was a tall, scruffy, and hefty man in his late-twenties, holding the compartment's door open with one hand and holding a half-gallon of liquor in the other. A large crossbow was strapped around his back with a quiver of arrows whose heads were half foam. He stared blankly at the trio with small eyes, green paint around his face, and a long, lit cigarette dangling from his mouth.

The door spoke in its upbeat voice from out of view, "A copy machine."

"Ridderack!" The medieval futurist tried to stand in his excitement and bumped his helmet against the top of the escape pod, "Ow.."

Since he was closest, Greary got out of the onion-shaped pod with smashed and rolling produce all around. Then he helped Lacie out, followed by the bucket-headed swordsman-- who once again, banged his metal head against the top of the contraption.

Lacie was disappointed and surprised to see nothing castle-like in sight, instead she took in what looked like a former grocery store.. with a short trail of craters in the tiled floor, courtesy of the moon. The black and glass automatic doors of the store were locked and barricaded with an entire aisle division pulled towards it; the entrance to the realm was also covered to the top of the doors with a pile of strange canned goods, and stacked boxes of normal canned beverages like beer and soda. Metal bars had been welded over the nearby large glass windows in the front; while two of the windows were shattered, and covered with taped-down plastic that fluctuated with the night's breeze.

"You made it back, Russ, brotha." The tall man puffed.

Russel rubbed the top of the bucket like it was his head. "Thanks to these people."

Lacie noticed two girls around her age talking. The taller girl had an eyepatch and a steel halberd (a combination of spear and axe) where the half with the axe jutting out was real and the back half was foam. The other girl had on a knight helmet, and two short swords: one sword was painted yellow, white and black.. the other sword was yellow and orange, each with blades similarly half covered in impenetrable foam.

The girl with the knight helmet rose the mouthpiece of the helmet which covered her face, "Did you hear about those lost teenagers that are supposed to be at All-Mart walking into walls?"

“The ones at the Lawn and Garden Department? I heard they were all in their twenties, not teenagers.” The girl with eyepatch replied.

The escape pod rolled over and the squarecrow got up, glasses missing; he made his way to some other medieval-dressed people who were standing next to an open armory.

“How do we get on the roof?” Lacie asked Mr. Greary with intentional loudness, in reference to the space suit she wished to give out of curiosity and guilt to the nude and possibly homeless man who resided in Black Stock.. if he was still alive.

* * *

In another aisle in the kingdom with cluttered food next to and inside cages, Midnight stealthily unfolded like origami from out of thin air; shaping from and into a real person. He had a single crutch under his arm--it was just for show, he flicked it to the ground. Then he grabbed some Vietnamese salad dressing off the far back of a nearby shelf, and poured out a decently-sized, “Nobody Was Here”.

* * *

Greary turned to Ridderack who flicked his cigarette butt to the ground, “Is there a way? We need to get a space suit.”

“Well with the spamurai, it's too dangerous to go outside.” Ridderack explained.

“There's a stairway in the back.” The girl with the halberd cut-in.

Some average-built guy was leaning against the aisle shelving with a couple sheathed swords on his back and his head down under a brass fedora; he rang out into the discussion like a telephone with bad news while pointing to something hard to see. “The steps are full'a pissed-off strays.. Not to mention some lethargic band of familiars, barely keeping their eyes open-- thinking they own where they rise, and just as moreso where they collapse.”

“Strays and familiars?” Lacie asked.. following his gesture to see an oddly placed staircase that blended with the wall in back, rising towards a closed patch of metal roof. “There's no-one there.”

“Used ta be.” The stranger replied. “..used ta be.”

Greary's curiosity got the best of him while he was staring at the weapon on Ridderack's back, “Pardon me, are you an archer?"

"Oh hell no. I'm a Crossbowist." Ridderack replied, a glossy look in his eyes.

The wide window to a higher room for employees only, showed a half Caucasian, half Japanese girl, with a grey suit and non-grey skin, smoking weed in an opium pipe, and talking to a portrait of an anime schoolgirl. "There's high spirits in my pipe telling me about your oppression Sana Chan. Or is it mine?"

Her voice echoed through the speaker system, which she quickly turned off with embarrassment; though from inside of the room, the window to the side of her was black, and she could not see through it.

Something clashed loudly against the front doors followed by the sound of glass shattering.

"I'm going to go grab that thing." Lacie said, reverting her attention back to the chameleon stairway, now mysteriously lit with black light edges, badly shining in the brightness of the realm.

Lacie made her way to the stairway, passing aisles half-full or scattered with food. The temperature in the store would go from normal to colder or hotter, like hidden thermostats jesting anything nearby. To the left of the stairway, a phrase had been scrawled out with the medium of rotted fruit and rotted vegetables, "POISON IN THE SUPERMARKET."

When Lacie saw the rotten produce her head itched and she scratched her hair.

From the front of the stairway, the steps and their lighted ends were all crooked, like they had changed in the time it took Lacie to make her way there. She decided to stay in the center of the steps; save the two steps where there was a hole in their center, a pit that couldn't easily be climbed out of. At the top of the steps and hunched over, she tried to lift the patch of roof, but it was far too heavy for her.

Luckily something else lifted the roof up for her.. like a spring, the tower of top hats on Lacie's head stuck to the ceiling and pushed upward. The hats forced the hatch open and it all crashed against the roof outside, leaving her head hatless. While inside the former grocery store, Lacie had forgotten the hats were even on her head.

"This place is so strange." Lacie said to herself, feeling more sane since her quick visit to the moon.

The snow had stopped falling; it had melted into puddles of water that looked like leaked anti-freeze, over-reactive with color and reflecting the vivid sky. In one of these puddles the space suit rested. Further off, the multiracial girl was walking along the roof towards the furthest edge, with square envelopes in-hand.

"Wait!.. where are you going?" Lacie yelled to the courier girl.

"Crater Park." The girl replied, standing on the edge of the building with the thin pipe dangling out of her mouth, and then disappearing down what appeared to be an outdoors escalator..

Lacie left the hats underneath the heavy hatch. She took the suit, dragging the bulky outfit as she made her way back inside.

Down the steps Mr. Greary and the bucket-headed swordsman were waiting.

Mr. Greary motioned frantically, "You have to get out now, the spamurai have raided!"

"Where will you guys go?" Lacie asked.

"To help the others and buy you time.. since apparently you need it, since he says a clock was pulled out of your head." Russel said, unsheathing his sword.

"He would know, he's a futurist." Mr. Greary added, with his egg carton missing from his person.

Lacie made her way down the stairs, hugging the side of the store she hadn't yet traversed.

When Lacie got to the opposite corner

of the kingdom she discovered an array of refrigerated furniture on her left which was disproportionately displayed to anything edible. She arrived to dented, metal-sheeted, double doors-- with a metal plaque above pronouncing the weird, “Stifferent Apartment Dore's Black Stock*!*”

“Don't look at me.” A woman's voice rang out from behind the doors.

“Who are you?” Lacie inquired.

“Something like Imagiption.”

“Wha--”

“They destroyed my caravan. They destroyed my masks.”

“Who?”

“Malicious grey kids! That's who. Oh, don't come in here. I don't have a solid face..”

“But I need in there!” Lacie put her hand on the door and inched it out. Meanwhile, metal clashed with war cries over the kingdom's food supply, near the automatic doors at the entrance.

“Well I guess I could wait in the restroom while you pass by.” The woman changed her tone to misunderstood paranoia, “I'll be holding the door shut.”

Lacie looked behind into the easiest-to-see aisle-way, where frozen foods were. She saw the squarecrow with a sword and shield. He was dueling someone in samurai armor who was holding a hockey stick instead of a sword, and wearing a mask made of meat. Not far from Lacie's feet was the umbrella-pickaxe that had been stuck in the squarecrow's straw clavicle. She thought it dually useful, picked it up, and folded it.

The woman in the restroom was slightly muffled as she whined to herself, “Oh where is their father to discipline them!?”

With the heavy space suit in her left hand, and umbrella-pickaxe in her right, Lacie opened the metal door with her boot, and ventured away from the fight.

Chapter 25

Malluso cut into the S.U.V. repeatedly but there was no reaction, no incentive in the creature other than to repair itself with the heaps of trash connected to it. A kid and a teen dressed in different shades of red were walking along the sidewalk nearby-- they were redheads to boot. The younger redhead was talking to his much older accomplice, and didn't notice the marble-headed man slashing at the malicious, animated dump.

"Rocket, TO THE MOON!" The eleven-year-old redhead with natural orange follicles shouted exuberantly, pumping his fist in the air.

"You can't get on the moon, Ralphie." The seventeen-year-old redhead said, scratching the top of his maroon hair.

Malluso thought he would try speaking back to the S.U.V., that it must have hearers since it had speakers. His jaw crackled open, "Who and what are you?"

The S.U.V. ignored Monsieur's words, attacking him with a swipe of one of its massive limbs. The marble-headed man dodged and swiped back with his rapier, papers, containers, and spoiled food going all over the place. From the speakers in the garbage, "Act with what and who they are, I am sick of what and who they were."

Elizabeth tried to stop the monster, "*Goopy Goopy Fried Gumdrops!*"

The donut girl noticed that the door to the Japanese pastry shop seemed to open on its own, but the living trash was hostile as ever.

"It's no use." A moving Malluso replied. "You should get inside there."

The redheads had noticed by now, and seeing her dialogue did nothing, decided to try to speak to the S.U.V.

"Rocket, TO THE MOON!" The orangehead tried to no avail, as the S.U.V. attacked the marble-headed man again. Malluso got out of the way and cut off another small part of the versatile, reconstructive monster. This time the S.U.V. stuck its limb into the trash it had lost and instantly reconnected it.

The tall maroonhead was calmer, "Still different."

The S.U.V.'s speakers shut off and it suddenly rumbled like being shook from the inside of its coreless being; the creature's face collapsed and disappeared, and its form exploded, scattering trash everywhere into a great formless storm, made neurotic as it met the undecided breeze.

As the trash flew everywhere, Elizabeth

entered the shop, the door shutting behind her.

One of the people who had been hit by building debris, who had been thrown and saved by Diego Caprice, stumbled by. His clothes were baggy and cut-up below a mess of blond hair. He was obsessively looking down for detail, “I'm not going to fall yet.”

“Looks like you got it, Mikey. RED SQUAD!” Ralphie cheered, giving the peace sign like there was a camera in front of him.

“Do you even know what those hand gestures mean?” Mikey asked.

Ralphie flicked Mikey off.

“Right.” Mike replied, looking away uninterested. “Not many customers down here.. I guess they're all shoppin' uptown.”

“*Goopy goopy fried gumdrops,*” Elizabeth was now trying the door handle without success to see if she could get out, “*Goopy goopy fried gumdrops..*”

Malluso walked up to the front of the glass where she waited, his jaw breaking open, “Set up shop like the other place and wait. Don't worry, the donut shop closes fairly soon; you'll know when it does.. I'm sorry to have to put you through this.”

Elizabeth's eyes widened and Malluso watched with a prescience as the store twirled in a circle and then sunk into the ground, replacing itself with a square of red-painted cement.

* * *

Beyond five warped bathrooms, three of which were not for humans, Lacie found herself in a twisted, crooked tunnel-- its contours cast in cold cement with left-behind pieces of ripped-up arcade carpetting. The large tunnel ceiling, wall, or floor was always missing, twisting along then jutting down in segments like stairs for a giant child; and these empty spaces shed view to a plain black and starry sky, with whiteish clouds occasionally coming in.

The astronaut suit felt so much heavier, and at a second glance, Lacie found the entrance she had taken to be metal boundaries rather than doors. For a second Lacie was afraid that maybe the exact opposite had happened upon returning to Black Stock, and that she had became extraordinarily frail.

Lacie peered down.. Her arms were normal, it was all paranoia, and the unnatural heaviness of the space suit subsided. Though her balance was off, as if the mixed stretch of painted white brick walls-- similar to her dorm room, and the cut grey slab of the floor and ceiling, were dangling on wires and rocked by the indecisive wind. She wondered if this was even the same Black Stock, and took a deep breath before taking another step towards fancy, white double doors with golden handles that were far out of reach.

Before Lacie reached the first gap where the rotations began, she found rectangular holes above her to the left and right, like giant paneless windows. Seeing them as a potentially safer path, she struggled to climb up the right ledge, eventually pulling up her space suit and umbrella-pickaxe. She saw a handful of adults in different shades of red ahead who paid no attention to her.

At this new corridor, the scope-eyed girl found her pass through Black Stock to turn into another debilitating, moving portrait--where a single grey, worn door with amateur graffiti would totally disappear behind moving segments of the hallway, and where she would still have to walk on the borders of gaps to keep from falling through them; but where the exit remained forward and feasible. The glow of stars had all mostly been exchanged for darker, grey, and stormy clouds, that peered through the gaps in the new, giant red hall.. while frigid colors of light in ribbon-shapes covered the edges of Lacie's visibility, like tiny, floating debris in her mechanical eyes.

“I don't know if there's glass there or not.” A woman in dark pink and sunglasses said, kicking at the sky as it appeared through the floor.

The five adults in red gave Lacie nasty looks as she traveled forward slowly, dragging the space suit behind her. A man spoke from spite and Burgundy, "Are you with him? The enemy?"

Lacie looked around her and saw Midnight on her right, gawking at the spacesuit with some unopened, stout vinaigrette dressing in his hand. Upon being seen by the college student, Midnight saw the Red Squad and backed away, disappearing in his usual convention.

"Well I guess he's gone now." The man's tone immediately changed. "Never mind."

The Red Squad went back to their casual conversation and Lacie passed them down the wide zig-zag of sloping hallway.

Climbing and treading around while avoiding the stretches of cloud and stars, Lacie heard a familiar old woman's voice, as if from the speakers of a far-away concert, "You got.. ta.. too choppy.. find me."

Red Squad trailed behind Lacie in a nature difficult to tell whether programmed or willed.

The hall had moved into a more rapid zig-zag, sinking a couple feet diagonally down and left where the ugly exit had originally appeared, but the banged-up door and its dingy metal handle also grew close to Lacie, enticing her mechanical vision.

Before Lacie got to the final downwards zig, her vision turned black and white again, with the cold ribbon borders disappearing. Familiar disfigured figures rose from the grey ground and surrounded her, though without burning papers. And the sign "Aisle 9" reappeared above her.

Midnight's voice rang out. "Won't hurt they of anything.. bad economists.. Just figurines, from the speeches.."

Lacie took what she could understand of Midnight's advice. The girl shut one of her shutters with a fearful facial grimace and clenched teeth. She passed by the figures with her bulky things and focused her one-eyed vision as much as she could on the exit at the zag. The figures melted back into the ground as she passed by them. And when she had passed them all, color returned to Lacie's vision, and the "Aisle 9" sign behind her disappeared.

After this, for a few seconds at most, there were all these different makes of cell phones ringing on the ground behind Lacie--she felt too much fear to look backwards or answer them, and she didn't look back until there was silence and they had all disappeared.

Lacie turned back around and murmured to Midnight, “Thanks for helping me, but I can't have you following me. Please go away.”

“Up is ahead, the mall.” Midnight whispered. “Nobody is here.”

Chapter 26

The new hallway Lacie found herself in was smaller since it belonged to what was apparently the mall. This black and neon corridor only twisted a little compared to its larger counterpart.. while scattered screens looking into Null-Mart, lined the walls. Most projections gave show of more chaos in the store then Lacie had previously seen. One screen showed a clock on the wall, the Second Midnight clearly approaching. But the clock face shattered from a baseball, and both objects fell out of sight.

The theme in the hall seemed to drain into or pour out from a medium-sized arcade. Lacie only caught a glimpse of the arcade as she walked by. The lights around this room flickered and exploded at random intervals, though the explosions were illusory and the lights were fine. Some of the video game machines were standing on the ceiling or wall, or taped-up with busted screens, or had things trying to get out.. banging on the windows, so-to-speak.

One of the screens suddenly shattered and something got out, which triggered Lacie to move faster.

The food court at the end of the hall had

a high portion of tables knocked on their sides, or totally upturned, mostly thrown into a pile in a corner; the pile of furniture was freshly stained with green and black shades of paint. A sleek surrounding balcony overlooked closed-down restaurants, one of which once served rocks and grass. A pizza restaurant is where the old man was who had been naked in the shadows of Black Stock, now hiding from something or someone with only his head popping out from the counter. Lacie caught sight of his face from behind the cash register.

Near the center of the expanse, a middle-aged Caucasian man sat at a bolted-down table alone. He was talking in a low voice, like the chair in front of him was occupied by someone close. His sunglasses reflected tinted fingers, sprinkling sugar in a cup of coffee to some tune with brass and guitar that droned on in a dream-state.

Otherworldly sweet,
tries to pull you out of your body,
and you see someone down sayin',
just don't mind me,
don't mind me..

Lace heard laughing coming from a group of girls on the balcony; some of them were in dresses-- while all of them were dressed up, with buckles. At first Lacie thought the girls might've been laughing at her; then it appeared more likely that they were giggling at the policewoman who was shining a flashlight into a vacant store on that same second floor.

The song came to its tail end and Lacie could suddenly hear the ringing of pay phones or a pay phone in the entryway. She turned to the upper half of an aged face behind the Pizza Plaza's counter, "Are you the old man from Black Stock?"

"..no." The old man lied.

"Okay."

"Wait!" The senior citizen said, seeing the space suit. "You brought me that suit?"

She lifted the space suit forcefully and pushed it over the counter.

"Hmm.." The skinny old man shifted around behind the desk talking to himself. "This suit smells abnormally sweet."

"Hey!" The female cop said, shining her flashlight on Lacie (with poor effect). "What's going on there?"

"Nothing." Lacie turned to the officer; and then turned again, looking on into slanting halls that must've been mostly full of closed or empty stores.

A flatscreen peering into Null-Mart on the food-court wall, showed a man in his seventies with patterned cotton clothes from the early-Industrial age. Full of life, he had saddled a male deer, and was riding around the store on it. "Catch me breaking eggs on my boot and laughing at their windows! Two pence, half past six."

Minutes later the old man at the Pizza Plaza stood up covered head to toe, “Now I am an em-per-or.”

“I thought you were a tailor.” Lacie replied.

“Quiet alien.” The man said, and turned to the small kitchen. Talking to himself again, “At least here there's sugar and..”

The creamer near the old man floated over a mug at the corner of the Pizza Plaza's kitchen table and poured out.

The wanderer with a brass fedora from The Kingdom of Wanderers, came out of the black and neon hall with brisk pace, tiny shards of glass shining off of his hat. “Ecila!”

The blonde policewoman turned around, “What?”

“There's a fight going on in Kingdom Market.”

Lacie watched as the cop paused for a moment in thought. Then with one hand on the railing, “Hey, get back to the library.”

“I ain't a book!” He swiped most of the glass off of his hat.

"That's littering!" Ecila scorned.

"Aliens, all of them.. aliens in-- human form." The man in the space suit murmured from the floor of the Pizza Plaza; he fanned himself with red money he had plucked out of the cash register.

A mug of coffee floated over the center table with the man in shades, and the other chair shuffled out and then in.

The history book or historian, had taken out one of his swords, spinning his brass fedora on it. "Well if you arrest me are ya gonna to take me ta jail or the library?"

Lacie shifted her scope-eyes to zoom in on the police officer, "You're.. Ecila?"

"I'm not Frank if that's what you're asking." Ecila replied.

"Someone from the past is looking for you, he says you're his daughter."

"He's confused, has a television problem." The officer said. "His daughter is named Fry; thinks she's a bird."

"What?"

"Looks like you can find her in the Automobile Department in All-Mart." Ecila pointed to a moving image near the once-laughing group of girls, now talking in whispers. "See here, this flickering screen made by.. 'Mechanical Convenience.'"

Lacie zoomed in on the screen on the

wall; her lenses reflected the sight of an African-N'quevnan lass masked & in her late twenties, her arms folded like chicken wings; her head jerked in the stares of a bird towards a portion of some sort of advanced tank under construction.

Lacie was jolted as parts of the roof on the second floor flew off as if they had only been patches like with The Kingdom of Wanderers. She thought she might go and answer the phone, the eternal ringing that droned from what was now the blurred glass of the lobby. “Thank you for the information.”

The historian with a brass hat had booked it, back towards the arcade, where he hoped he couldn't be mistaken as something he found so trite.

“It's no-- where did he go!?” Ecila broke.

* * *

Lacie went towards the lobby with her metal eyestalks retracted back to normal, opening the door to find two Middle-Eastern punk rock guys who had not previously appeared from behind the glass. The black-haired guy was dressed in all one shade of red, trapped in a large rock, blocking some of the doors; some of his head, upper torso, arms, and a shoe-d foot popped out of the grey mass. His free, blond-haired acquaintance taunted him, "People aren't fixed in stone. Except for you. People can change, sometimes.. Except for you."

"What's going on here?" Lacie asked, confused that no-one had picked up the phone; it was just one phone ringing, and hard to tell which. On the right, across from the telephones, there was a shape popping out from the wall in a blotch of a person with an over-sized head.

"Leave me alone." The black-haired guy wriggled in the stone. "I'm fine."

"Woah, wait a minute. Is.. that an umbrella-pickaxe?" The taunter asked.

"Yes it is. Why haven't either of you picked up the phone?" Lacie asked.

The blond taunter leaned against the rock with one hand, the wide-trapped-eye of his acquaintance gawked at him as he raised his eyebrow. "Maybe it's for you."

Lacie went over to the payphone.

"Ow!" Lacie was shocked, as if by static electricity.

"Wrong phone." The young man in stone said.

Even though the phone she had touched was the one that seemed to be ringing, Lacie picked up the one beside it and the ringing stopped.

"Before I get drunk, disorderly, and discursive, give blondie the pickaxe and tell him to get cracking." said Herbert's suave voice on the other end of the line.

"Herbert! How did you know I'd be here?" The scope-eyed girl asked.

"There's a camera in the corner.. Now miss, you'll have to get the ball rolling because there's not much time at all."

Lacie handed the umbrella-pickaxe to the taunter, who in some redeeming state, had no reluctance to take it. He started chipping away the rock with it.

"Hey be careful!" The punk in the stone said.

"This is all insane.. and so are you." Lacie's voice dropped realizing the two others in the room were overhearing her, "I.."

"Maybe I'm immune to insanity and leaking class for the hell of it. You're not my niece or I might say that's your opposite."

"What do I do?"

"Only you know what to do, before The Second Midnight." Offended and at the end of his words, Herbert hung up.

"What niece!?" Lacie said out loud to herself, before putting the phone on the hook.

Lacie turned and zoomed in, seeing Ecila come down a stairway and head towards the arcade; and then the former student zoomed her vision out and in again, looking past the food court at the quiet halls of the aging mall with more resistance in her than resolve.

Chapter 27

At the peaks of towering lights, illegible to most of their denizens, above the crater of Crater Park and floating with its floating isle, Marthreek squatted atop a two or three story house; the structure was crafted like a dome amongst the calculated ruins of the black cloud. The wingless red mirk mirks dived in and out of the darkness, their bodies, if not ghostly, were thinner than before, with a pallor. At this height of Above, the dragon-worms were scattered, barely showing, and all the caravans were nowhere to be found. Glowing materials on the sides of the dome kept back the black cloud that crept across everywhere else, save a nearby tower of foreign machinery going up five stories with closed entry.

The towering mechanism, chiseled with the pieces of its function, put out smog in all directions from the horizontal border of each of its cube-layers. Masses of thick, black cables connected to the tall mechanical building and traveled out of visibility. Underneath the cables, cloaked figures with long white and violet claws stirred around the tower like working zombies, as if they were stuck halfway in some dream-state.

Marthreek's voice came from the three twitching question marks which served as his head, "Wrongly.. and longly."

One of the cloaked workers poured some green liquid out of a bucket into a nearby valve; steam immediately followed with creaks and what sounded like oven timers with low batteries, the machine emitting some fragile admission of its age. Colored sand poured out from the bottom edges of the machine; falling in reds, golds, and greens like Christmas for the abyss. One of the violet-clawed workers knelt down, grasping at the falling sand in futility-- while another worker had caught a wingless red bird in its claw and inspected it.

Abbadon's voice bellowed through the machine, "I don't trust Malluso anymore."

"Do you think I care?" Marthreek said cheekily with a chuckle. "You can do nothing to me right now."

"Your existence hinges on him, so he must've done as he was supposed to." The h'ragon's voice shook the tower.

"It doesn't matter much to me either way." Marthreek stared at his pointy leather shoes, with three points on each of them now, instead of one. The strange man formed a compass with his feet.

"When I get out of here.. I'm going to eat you!" Abbadon howled.

"We'll see if it leaves you with a mouth." Marthreek stood up and laughed, and then backflipped into the surrounding black fog.

* * *

Lacie looked outside at the mall's aged parking-lot underneath a black and starry sky. The fading makeup of the wrinkled gravel gave view to a distant bent-up shopping cart, further from that, the mysterious ruins of some building's foundation. The outside was more ordinary though, and she hoped it might be an exit or lead to one. So the girl decided to leave the weird and wild mall behind, saying no goodbye to the two punk rockers, and heading through the doorway.

None of the buildings in the landscape had animation like before, nor were they mixed with Japanese buildings like before. Nor did the breeze move in different directions, rather just bursts of one direction in the silence. And rather than the sounds of so many things, the silence of the night covered all visible terrain. The darkness was simply lit by plain streetlights, and a crescent moon, without smoke, that felt cold and out of reach.

Lacie wondered if this empty stretch of gravel, or what was beyond it, could take her home. But then the girl recalled something said to her earlier. Water started to form in her eyes, distorting her vision, and then dripping out somehow at the bottom of the lenses. But the sky did not respond to her tears and the pavement stayed dry.

The scope-eyed girl wiped the tears away with her shirt and blinked her shutters a few times. Then she looked back at the mall, through the foyer windows, the punk still hacking at the rock stuck around his acquaintance. Strangely, there was a dock built less than a foot above the cement, coming off of the mall's exterior.

Lacie took a deep breath. Then she spoke softly to herself, "..curiosity and guilt."

_

The former student made her way out of a cool and ordinary summer night, back into the foyer, and heard the doors click and lock behind her.

The guy with the pickaxe stopped picking, "Can I ask you something?"

"Yes?" Lacie asked in reply.

The blonde punk let the umbrella-pickaxe slide down to rest on his hand like a cane, "Why the change of heart?"

"I could ask you the same." Lacie said.

Lacie thought that instead of trying to

call home, she could try to call an operator, and get Mr. Bagel's Donut Shop. But instead she found herself disappointed. The phone buttons weren't there anymore.

Jagged pebbles flew up as the punk continued, some hitting Lacie and her lenses as a slightly cracked monitor above the back of the foyer caught her mechanical eye. She backed away from the debris, the other punk almost out of his rock. The imagery had a bird's eye view of a Null-Mart manager; she was standing behind one of the registers talking to a man in paint and plaid who was twitching around a dirty floor. From the manager, "Uhh, um, so.."

Lacie turned to see the returning translucence of the glass and an almost materialized and younger Mona, at the end of the food-court, with the last few flyers forming the back piece of her white-haired head.

Mona smiled a wicked smile that lasted only as long as the rotation of her scope-eyes. A man crawled behind her coughing up grey blood, long ponytails coming off his head; he was wearing some coat with misplaced coat-tails, with two extra-sleeves like a modified, off-white straight-jacket. A woman with shoulder-length blonde and white hair also came stumbling into view with similar garments, but her face was more beaten and grimaced; she fell to the ground and began acting like a bird with clipped wings. The man looked at her, "Oh no! Yes.. No.."

The phone in front of Lacie fell off the hook and then started ringing; with her sight fixed on Mona, Lacie put the glossy speaker up to her ear.

The blotchy, human-shaped part of the foyer wall crumbled into pieces, like most of the rock in the center of the room had.

A well-dressed man with white gloves, a black vest, and a red tie emerged, however, his head was a big rabbit head with an unlit cigarette and a familiar face.

"I assume you needed more advice." Herbert puffed.

The black-haired punk was now free from the rock that bound him, "Holy shit, a rabbit man!"

"What the..? Why do you look like that?" Lacie was still holding the payphone up to her ear for no reason other than shock.

"This is how I've always looked." Herbert replied, pulling one of his gloves down over his wrist.

The younger Mona picked up one of the food-court tables with one arm and threw it across the room, past the green and black pile of them, "I'm not walking away this time little girl!"

The pixelated manager in the foyer flatscreen continued with hair in her face, "Alright. Uhh.."

"I'm.. sorry." Lacie found herself growing tense and gently let go of the telephone as Mona approached. "What should I do?"

"I would recommend.. that you run in the direction that she came." Herbert said in high regard of his logical faculties.

"But--" Lacie was interrupted as a chair shattered a pane of glass next to her, and she instinctively ducked down. The chair had flown over the middle-aged man in the center of the food-court who was minding his own business drinking coffee. He ducked underneath the table in response.

"Holy shit!" The black-haired punk said.

"Damn." The blonde punk found he couldn't open the door, thought quick, and used the pickaxe to break the window to the outside. Clutching the umbrella with a face-full of metal-- which was better than glass piercings. "Let's get out of here."

"Okay, so.." The manager in the Null-Mart feed leaned over the twitching man as he began grasping at candies.

Given the opportunity to leave in two directions, Lacie looked outside.. but the punks were gone, and in place of any parking-lot there was a blackness, like an enormous pit. She thought she didn't really want to go back that way if she could've, nor anger Herbert, and had no logical choice but to go forward into the mall. Before she stepped out of the foyer she noticed something new, scratched into the paint near the phones,

"Recycle The Code.
- c10ck7hr0w3r".

Chapter 28

With her heart pounding, Lacie stepped through the broken glass door over the jagged shards it had left.

"Curiousity and guilt." Herbert said, as she made her way into the food court.

Lacie grabbed the nearest chair to shield herself. Mona had turned back into a swarm of mostly angry birds. As the swarm charged at Lacie she whacked two or three, one hit the ground while another hit a table and slid across its surface onto the floor. There was a radical parrot in patterns of winter blue on white, perched over the sprawling, second-story balcony; the bird seemed to dance quite rhythmically to the radio, rather than fight.

"Space fight!" The muffled voice of the old man in the Pizza Plaza rang out. "Alien parrot!"

Lacie found herself losing gravity and balance. She looked at her feet which felt as though they were standing on invisible moving platforms.

"What the.." She mumbled to herself.

Many of the birds had trouble flying and flapped their wings towards each other as if they were underwater or submerged in crumbled jello.

Lacie noticed the dancing parrot-- who now had nun-raver-rosaries with glow sticks dangling off of its wings. The comical bird was unintentionally doing a forward barrel roll through the air, intentionally moving its wings in unison to the beat of the food-court music.

All that was left in Lacie's view of the two hunters at the end of the food-court-- which Mona had nearly incapacitated, was the woman's upper torso, the rest of her hidden as the crawling man dragged her along and away.. farther from the pizza that could've saved them.

Lacie swung the heavy chair again at birds trying to flee from her; the couple which were hit made noises in pain, but they all made their way back into a humanoid form, as gravity returned to Mona, Lacie, and the dancing parrot.

Mona snapped her fingers, and at first Lacie could notice no difference to her surroundings.

Then Lacie noticed that the group of giggling girls on the balcony had all changed. They had balloons with drawn-on faces tied to their arms and wrists, and all of them were wearing wooden masks similar to the faces on the balloon sets. They jumped off the balcony in single-file, landing like carnivorous extraterrestrials, searching for a meal in the near-abandoned and nocturnal food-court.

The sound of a gunshot went off and one of the evil girls' balloons popped, her hand dropping down to her side as half of her wooden mask fell off. What showed of the young girl's human face was in surprise and conflict as she looked in the hallway leading to the arcade, where a policewoman held a clear handgun pointed at Mona.

"I think I saw her in magazine." The astronautly-dressed man in the Pizza Plaza exclaimed, it was not known to Lacie who he exactly was rambling about.

"Well this should be interesting." Herbert took a sip of his cocktail that he was now holding, some hard concoction in a snifter glass; the bottle had been on a hidden shelf in the man-sized hole his mutant form had broken out of.

"Run, girl." Ecila said to Lacie with a tense voice.

The floor began flickering with intense, white light, and most of the walls seemed to push out at the width of a road. The pile of painted tables behind Mona slid and fell over, blocking most of the way to the end of the food-court. The U.V. Road appeared, fully glowing, and ran down the food court hall to where the hall split like a four-way.

Lacie ran down the left side of the

glowing food court away from the masked girls, all but one of the girls laughing again-- this time at her, and with violent intent; Lacie ducked as she moved forward-- a chair barely missing her head that one of the masked girls threw.

Still hiding under his table, the middle-aged man in shades who had been sipping his beverage and keeping to himself, grasped the top of the table with his fingers and began walking like a crab, animating the furniture with a slow pace towards the non-glowing end of the hall outside the court. It seemed as though the man had unbolted all fifteen bolts between the table and floor, though he could've had help, and as to where he got the tools remained unknown.

Ecila's translucent glock went off again, straight into Mona, who turned back into a flock of flyers and birds; a bird and a shoe lied dead on the floor, both with holes, no blood.

"Oh that reminds me." Herbert remembered in his half-drunken stupor of near-perfect balance.

Lacie made a run for it through the angry flock, swatting and yelling at the birds as they pecked at her. Little could be seen of the girl's boots from the intense light shining on the floor as she made her way around the mess of tables, the moving one in the background.

"I guess I won't be able to tell her where she got those lenses from." The rabbit-man somehow puffed. With a cigar now, instead of a cigarette, between two gloved and yellowing fingers, Herbert's empty glass felt as though it looked back at him. "This is dreadful."

At the end of the food court Lacie stopped abruptly, and then ran around a different cop, and a Japanese shop owner in flannel holding a brand new ladder. The UV Road turned both into a glowing escalator on the right, while the hall on the right also continued to glow. Only the escalator gave off small rainbows, though with many of the colors out of order, similar to some vending machines on the second floor. Meanwhile, the hall to the right only gave off graybows.

Going past the escalator, the right of the hall flickered back and forth at random, in and out of existence, even the glass doors at the end.

The broad hall went completely missing for good as Lacie made her first step on the escalator. It was as though this section of the first floor had been ripped from its very foundations-- jagged metal just jutting out into the night.. and then everything returning again with a stretch of stores with doors half-closed. At the end or entrance of the hallway when it flickered into existence, were strange kids or teenagers that appeared to Lacie in blur.

Lacie noticed the left of the first floor hallway was a maze of walls mostly four feet high in all directions, both on the ground and on the high-up ceiling above. An upside-down group of people were standing and talking at an entrance to the maze on the ceiling, while an old woman sat right-side-up and asleep on a bench, on the ground, near a shoe store. Raising out from these maze's segments of clinical whites were giant puppets that resembled parading Chinese dragons, specimens which popped in and out with the utmost rarity or uniqueness-- not shared so much in aesthetic by the nearby, and mostly upside-down shoppers.

Lacie stopped momentarily to look around in wonderment at the mall as the mechanical stairs rose her up. But the angry storm of peckish airborne creatures were still trailing, and Lacie started running up the stairs even though they were already automated to move upward.

When the girl reached the second floor, she saw sleeker, cleaner stores, some marked in vertical English, some in horizontal Japanese.

A calm and knowledgeable voice rang out from one of the stores while smoke poured from the ragged entrance, "I've looked into it and it seemed too full of risks. Better to stick to a malfunctioning time-machine headed for the future."

By the time Lacie got in front of the store with a smoke cloud coming out of it, she was starting to lose her breath. Her vision changed like earlier in the night before she had first lost Mr. Dreary-Gravy, with rips and scratches like old film filling her eyesight, like tiny cracks in her cold glass eyes. The unwelcome and angry sounds of birds were inching closer. She thought fast as though without thinking, looked for a nearby screen with a picturesque view of Null-Mart that appeared on one of the walls. Scared, and trying to catch her breath, Lacie reached out her hand to gamble with the world again.

Chapter 29

Cuithbeart sipped a frothy, glass mug of beer, "Sometimes you have to improvise to improve, to excel, to succeed."

Televisions were all on the right of the old Scotsman, and on the left of the Scotsman. It was a room made of televisions, even the door. In Mr. Cobalt's back pocket was an unopened bottle of olive oil. It was evident to Geoffery that they were outside, as the ceiling was the sky, and the young man had no idea how to perceive the parts of the sky which were painted-- or the left edge which looked sketched.

Geoffery looked down, blank and confused as he stared at the ten blue plastic cups on the ping-pong table in front of him. Ten blue cups grouped on each side, formed like triangles. They looked to be full of just beer--

"These blue cups are full of lager that is a little under the proof of wine." Cuithbeart retorted, as though reading Geoffery's thought.

Geoffery noticed a brown beast that looked like a cross between a bear, human, and cat, standing six-feet-tall in a corner behind Cuithbeart; the creature was listening to a cheesy song in Spanish, headphones on one once-pointed ear. The animal moved its large, bloodshot eyes, red veins and amber-yellow scanning the room. Then the beast went to punch the side of a television without known cause, and was radically sucked into the screen like sand chasing itself down an hourglass; the t.v. screen went brown.

"What does this have to do with repairing televisions?" The husky geek asked.

"Neverything!" Cuithbeart spit and spilled beer, arcing his arms with the alcoholic seriousness of his botched or brilliant answer.

The room responded in a frightening rumble. The cold spit beer sizzled and fried against a couple TV's it hit when it shouldn't have. Cuithbeart puked breakfast all over the side of the ping-pong table and spilled some more of his glass mug, his remaining booze less than an inch in the glass. The Scotsman had narrowed his eyes as he looked down at his expulsion, "Maybe I'll give you a handicap."

"But you just puked.." Geoffery's face shifted towards disgust as he covered his nose with his hand.

"Ohhh.. Right."

Cuithbeart took a ball from a white and blue basket glued to a television behind him. He dipped the sparkly-blue ping-pong ball into a cup of water off to the side of his triangle of lager. When the ball emerged from its involuntary dive, a lot of the paint had come off of the plastic, but not all of it.

"Well I guess I should've let it dry." Cuithbeart slurred smugly, before throwing the more-white-than-blue sphere into a cup in front of Geoffery.

"Drink.. it."

Geoffery adjusted his glasses, "I'm not drinking that, it's got paint in it."

"Drunk.. it."

"..you're a real S.O.B." Geoffery replied, with some fumes of his own.

"If you don't.. my mother was.. an ugly lesbian." Cuithbeart lied, maybe, with glossy eyes.

Geoffery pounded down the cup and gagged. He scrunched his face from the burn and stared at the floor with anticipation from his stomach. When he looked up again his voice was less fuming, metaphorically. "I don't think you know anything about repairing TV's."

Cuithbeart stumbled as he temporarily took his hands off the table, "I forgot that some of the cups had rum."

"Which ones?" The theatrically-dressed geek asked, taking the ball out, and dipping off the last of the paint in a cup of water.

"Mostly yours!" Cuithbeart Cobalt

chuckled while the tiny, distracting blue lights that were wrapped around his loosening suit randomly blinked on and off.

* * *

Geoffery had lost the game. He had only made Cuithbeart drink two cups-- who was now drinking anyways due to a hidden tap between two t.v.'s in back of him. The husky geek found himself drinking his last cup, barely able to stand in a warm haze that was not the colder room. He noticed seldom colored fragments of paper hovering into the area like snowflakes, as if there was a celebration around him he didn't know about.

"I don't know anything about fixing televisions." Cuithbeart confessed, which followed with the room of televisions, boxy and flatscreen, breaking apart and collapsing.

Surrounding the wreckage of tellies, boob tubes, idiot boxes, or what-have-you's was a wide-open basketball court on a small hill; it was silent, dark, and moonlit with only one whole basketball hoop, dark houses in the distance. Confetti poured out of the few, towering dead light fixtures, while the streetlights farther away acted like they had a payroll, brightening the roads with an absolute efficiency. There were box fans in the cement of the basketball court with deep holes to nowhere or somewhere, blowing the confetti back up as it tried to drop down from the busted illuminations.

Underneath the basketball court's one hoop was what appeared to be a wooden, beverage stand; the whole front of the stand had childlike handwriting in violet paint, 'Purple Lemonade - 50 cents.'

From the stand came the boisterous sound of a man, "Mirk! Mairk! Mackin!"

Cuithbeart went stumbling to investigate the sound but stopped abruptly at the sound of a cooler, more elegant voice from behind him, "Have you come to browse my collection?"

Geoffery turned with his surroundings in a drunken blur to see a man with a pony-tail made of indigo yarn, ripped-up dress clothes with black cloth underneath, and a monocle with monocles welded to it. This wash of gold and glass went around one half of the gentleman's flat, cardboard head, an oval with a doodled, distinguished face that had giant, plastic, googly eyes. The man's expensive footwear was hard to see, and he stood on a broken basketball hoop pole with one knee pointing out to the side without the least bit of wobbling in his balance. The scribble of a mouth moved with the gentleman's words, "Mwehehar! Teetee."

Suddenly time sped up, but not quite to a traditional fast forward status.

Cuithbeart was too drunk to want to turn around.

"Who are you?" Geoffery asked. – The cardboard head jostled in the wind, "The very rare, the very exotic, Backstory Curator." – Cuithbeart looked behind the lemonade stand, his head in a crouch overneath the desk-like table and its higher, wordless sign. He saw two little men with enormous facial hair and small eyes. – The basketball-sized man behind the lemonade stand with a whiteish-red beard spoke, "We're gonna make plenty of gald, Gald."

The flow of time went back to a normalcy as Gald's great white mustache twitched.

Cuithbeart searched his pockets for change, "I'll take a purple drink little man!"

Jitters flung his beard up into the air, and it formed like two arms, grasping a pungent, purple beverage.

Normal-sized suit ties and ribbons on the two small vendors shifted at their ends with the slightness of the wind, catching the Scotsman's drunk eye.

Across faded lines and the technicolour vomit of paper projectiles going up and down on the basketball court, the Backstory Curator spoke out of turn, "A bald, dark-skinned man named Jupiter was launched into these very skies not long ago: wriggling his robotic limbs and screaming with a deep-pitched tongue, before the catalyst of this event brought him a land-loving return.

Jupiter found himself in front of grocery store windows, all broken and full of war. A battle raged over a floor scattered with edible products and refrigerated furniture. There were clashes between an intrusion of ancient warriors who looked like samurai with meat fetishes, and medieval wanderers protecting their fortress of food.

A sweaty husky black man with nerdy clothes and glasses named Mr. Greary, was running next to a much smaller teenager named Russel. A metal bucket with two black eye-holes was stuck over Russel's head. The two were headed towards the armory, but a tall menace now guarded it; this spamurai was armored in metal-studded meat, and meat-studded metal, a handless katana in an iron grasp.

They ran past a scarecrow in a white-dress shirt with similar glasses to Greary, he was laying still, missing an arm; but then again, just being a scarecrow, this was probably less problematic for him."

"How does those monocles stay on your

head?" Geoffery broke up cardboard face's story.

"How do they, indeed." The Backstory Curator returned, googly, ready to return to his retelling..

"Rather than unsheathing the sword that was on his back, Russel headbutted the spamurai in the abdomen. Greary couldn't fight, as he only had an egg carton, changing randomly between yellow, baby blue, and green, every time he looked at it; but Russel had bought Mr. Greary time to get to the remains of the armory by distracting the spamurai.

The armory was made up of aisle divisions that had been smashed in half by some monster and pushed into a square by people; inside Greary found medieval weapons and shields, part real and part foam. Mr. Greary would leave his eggs here, light green, to grab a rather odd flail and an enormous shield.

A tall, blond wanderer named Renegald--"

"Ya got some gald in ya, where'd ya pocket it ya Pied Piper!?" Gald screamed from behind the lemonade stand.

The curator cleared his throat, "A blond wanderer named Renegald--"

"Ya got some gald, why don't you bring

it ova here ya big goo--" Jitters shut Gald's mouth.

Geoffery unfolded a lawn chair that he had acquired from nowhere and sat down in it to think about how he wished Jeffrey could buy him a lemonade.

The Backstory Curator had an unenthused line acting as his present mouth, wandering strands of indigo yarn-hair blowing over his googly corneas; he began again. "A blond wanderer was near a spamurai with spare rib across his chest by the name of Spare Rib. They were near the armory as well."

The curator waited in silence, for any reaction, while his face remained comically unenthused..

Nothing.

The curator began again. "..both were in battle position, moving back and forth without having attacked.

The blond man spit out his mouth-guard looking at the other spamurai who had lost his katana blade after being hit in the abdomen, 'That's not much of an attack.'

'Who are you to judge your own comrade's attack?' Spare Rib replied, holding a tower of unopened beer and pop cans duct-taped to a rather menacing spatula."

"I'm really drunk right now." Geoffery mumbled, looking down at a broken watch that was pointing back at him. He peered behind him at a couple houses playing leap frog with massive crashing noises. Then he noticed Cuithbeart was stumbling around groaning from a hangover, while attempting to meticulously pour olive oil out onto the pavement.

The curator had different pitches of voice for each character, some that maybe didn't fit-- in a high pitch, "'Maybe he's not my teammate, maybe I'm a mercenary.' The blond man paced back and forth, menacingly. 'You should take that weapon apart and hand me a soda.'

The battle raged on. In some aisle-way in another part of the store, a girl named Sue with an eyepatch and a unique halberd brought down a spamurai who had a helmet made of ground chuck on his noggin. She had whapped him in the leg with the foam half. The spamurai instantly knelt down as if he had lost a leg. There were other wanderers and spamurai like this, kneeling down, while some were actually laying down as though they were dead.

'Your egg carton reminds me of the Eggola.' Reneg-- the blond-haired man stated, glancing at Mr. Greary who was hesitant to rush into battle.

Russel pulled off his helmet, the

spamurai that he had hit was rolling around in pain behind him. The sword-wielding wanderer had strands of greasy blond and black hair accompanied with grey face-paint, 'Eggola?'

'I've heard of him.' Spare Rib said in battle stance. 'Supposed to be an egg that came to life, drags a mountain of soda behind him in All-Mart.'

'I must say, it sounds like a product worth investing in.' Mr. Greary had dropped his flail down to his knees, and pulled out his wallet to check his funds. His egg carton in the armory had changed colors once again (blue). Tortilla chips and sharpened metal dangled off the chains of his unused weapon.

Jupiter, the faller, did not hear any of this, but witnessed enough of it. He walked away from the grocery store and decided to try another place for dinner.."

"I'd burn the midnight oil, if it was covered by insurance!" Cuithbeart guffawed, staring at his writing, standing proud with his hands on his hips like he had partially sobered up in superhuman time.

The curator pulled an envelope off of the back of his head, half underneath the yarn, scotch tape pulling at the cardboard; he jumped down from the broken basketball hoop pole and stood normally, "Cuithbeart Cobalt?"

Cuithbeart looked over at the cardboard-headed man, standing over a clear phrase involving nobody in particular.

"This envelope is addressed to you, from someone named Midnight."

Geoffery got up and went to the rubble of televisions. In his drunken state, he decided to try fixing them. Whether or not what the young man was doing worked, he began piecing them together, finding tools within the ruins, and avoiding the electrical charges. As the geek got into the groove of this, Cuithbeart opened and scanned the letter addressed to him; the urgency in the words spreading to his face overneath blue and white facial hair.

Chapter 30

Lacie materialized in the air, halfway between the floor and the ceiling of Null-Mart's Automotive Department. She fell onto something metal, but was able to bend her knees to absorb most of the shock. A bird had followed her teleportation-like travel, though it seemed to have lost its link of intelligence with Mona; the avian now flew like a spaceship with no flap of its wings, and busted through the metal roof as if it was harder.

"Glad I didn't get attacked by that." Lacie thought.

The place was dismal, littered with empty booze containers, though brightly-lit in more ways than one. There was a unique doll collection with each doll hanging from the ceiling. Underneath of that, a birthday clown (well it's assumed he or she did birthdays) lied dead-- or they were just drunk. Coloring books were scattered around the entertainer on the warm, dry cement.

There were musical instruments set up in a corner, a drum set, a knocked-over microphone, two electric pianos— one broken; and three guitars, one bass. And a fish. There were also amplifiers, most turned off, one or two turned on with the volume way down. A man in his seventies with over two-hundred pounds of muscle and a white head of hair sat on the drummer's seat; he was staring at himself and his surroundings through a rather large shard of a mirror that he clutched in his hand.

A Mexican Null-Mart employee covered heavily in variously-sized sheets of blank paper gave a curious look at the lost girl on top of the broken machine. Lacie also noticed him. She stood up straight, her lenses expanded forward barely to see the glimmering wrench in the employee's greasy, paper-covered hold.

"What is this?" She asked, pointing downward.

"It's a giant, heavily-armored tank. Why are you standing on a retractable turret?" The employee dryly replied.

Lacie made her way down from the half-conical-like front of the vehicle, like sliding down a metal slide; she hadn't noticed that there was a metal ladder behind her while she was standing.

There was another worker who was younger, in his twenties, he had on a normal work uniform and four or five faux antlers. His nametag said "K'vin." K'vin was looking over the giant tank with an upside-down clipboard and a feathery pen.

K'vin glared at a black girl with two-inches or so of a jet-black mohawk, gold irises, & heavy make-up; she was sitting near the corner drinking a beer; and Lacie thought that a decent amount of the nearby empty cans had to have been hers, along with a bird mask that had ended up on the floor.

Lacie went over to the girl, "Are you.. Fry?"

"Hey!" K'vin shouted at Lacie. "We take ourselves seriously around here, and we don't care too much for pretty polly-annas who play dress-up against our rules.. so why don't you take your friend and get the hell out?"

Fry's shirt and pants were patches of dark greens and dark blues, with random sewing patterns, and mostly covered in small variations of zippers, studs, and stranger metal fastenings. She stood up and folded her arms with an angry look on her face.

The man covered in paper, Jifftural, blew his nose on his arm and went into the small office off to the side.

"BLOW IT OUT YOUR ASS K'VIN!" Fry blasted the antlered man.

"Shut up!" K'vin yelled at the air while spinning like a graceless ballerina, hitting the tank with a wrench in his rotations.

Afterwards K'vin motioned to two other guys in grease-stained Null-Mart uniforms who were working on the other side of the tank, and they went about their business.

"What do you want with me?" Fry turned to Lacie with a critical stare.

One of Lacie's boots were pointing towards the door, "You don't know me, but I need to ask you something."

"Lost souls, lost seeds.." The muscle-bound man behind the drumset spoke at his reflection in the glass he held before looking up at everyone. "If you shatter the mirror, it can cut you. But if you know the shards are still the mirror, they can grow you."

Everybody heard him, but nobody said anything for a few seconds.

"Do you know your father is looking for you, the guy with eyes like mine?" Lacie finally asked.

Fry pointed forward with a new can in her hand, "Let's walk."

"Okay."

Lacie and Fry crossed into the automotive lobby and then further into the rest of Null-Mart.

Suddenly the whole store shook, causing Lacie and Fry to grab and hold onto nearby shelving. The ground separated about a foot from the entrance to the auto department, with a dark and dangerous gap appearing behind the two frightened girls. Lacie looked around and saw another distant gap that had formed some distance away; All-Mart or Null-Mart, it was starting to come down, just like The Man In Pink had told her. And the familiar fear in her that had waned somewhat began to well up again.

The girls composed themselves as much as they could and stood up straight.

"That guy.. He's confused, has a television problem." Fry explained. "His daughter is a girl named Ratty, she's gone violent because earlier tonight he called her a cactus."

Lacie's lenses rotated with slight involution, "Why?"

"Something about furry spines I guess." Fry took the last sip of a can that was half-soda and half-liquor then threw it into the foyer of the automatic department, in front of an empty desk half-covered in stickers.

Lacie thought that furry spines might be the pipe cleaners in Ratty's hair, but her thought was interrupted when she noticed Thee Chaotician nearby. He had his hand atop an invisible staff the same height as his real one; the real staff or cane was on an aisle shelf behind him, on sale for twenty-three dollars.

"With the top semantic I have some fear, the last time I recall it disappeared." The Chaotician mumbled.

There was an eccentric woman, professionally dressed and drugged, in a housewares aisle with dishes sporadically shattering.. "Look around you at the dishes you haven't washed. We're on the edge of danger!"

Thee Chaotician cleaned some grease off of the lenses of his sunglasses with his shirt as the housewares lady went on.. "The movements of post-modernism threaten absolute expense at any mismanagement of practicality-- and any practical movement on the part of humanity. May such actions be confined to something more than lesser states, and may the residue of that confinement be washed away by superior textures-- regardless of their susceptibility to rust!"

"What is her pro--" Lacie began.

"Carry on, dish soap, Devilspeed!" The woman threw a bowl at the ground but it bounced, then she picked up an excessively large floor tile, and disappeared underneath of it.

"..we need to get out of here, this place is going to collapse tonight.. very soon." Lacie said. She and Fry heard a loud rain of thuds and some cursing: the creepy and antique dolls that lined the ceiling in automotive had all fell down.

Some Japanese man in a suit and glasses

had come out of the Automotive office to scream at Jifftural who had returned to the workroom, "My collection! You've ruined my collection!"

K'vin ignored them and went underneath the tank to have a sandwich.

The suited Japanese man pulled out a pen as if waiting for a checkbook, "Give me compensation!"

Then, the Japanese higher-up shook Jifftural by the shoulders, the fountain pen between his fingers. The Null-Mart employee covered his reddening face with canvas-blanketed arms and hands, "You'll have to draw on me first!"

Fry grabbed a skateboard off of the bottom shelf on the right wall along a plethora of other sporting goods, it was already unpackaged with wear and tear.

“I need to find my friend before we leave. You should follow me if you want to get out of here the fastest way.”

"You skate?" Lacie asked.

"Yeah." Fry dropped the board in front of her and jumped on.

"I used to.."

“Then follow me.” The black punk asserted.

“But there's holes in the floor.” The former student complained.

Fry seemed confident, “I've never walked over holes, but I've skated over them.”

Lacie hid her anxiety of falling to her death as best as she could, grabbed a skateboard off of the shelf, and started unpacking it.

"I hope it's okay to borrow this.." Lacie mumbled to herself.

Thee Chaotician intervened, "Looking here and there for your friend, what eyes would you care to lend?"

Lacie paused with a weird expression, then took off one of her lenses instinctively, surprised afterward that it had came off. As a result of this, half of her glasses had reappeared, barely holding to her face. Before she could take off the other scope-eye, Fry took a couple eyeball gumballs out of her pocket.

"I'll cover it." Fry replied confidently, and handed the eyes to the Chaotician who grinned over his profit.

"I propose you follow me to the Lawn and Garden Center.." The black-clad youth stated. Behind him, strangers and animals were evacuating the store, while armored military men and rednecks ran around together shooting at the flying bat-dogs amidst an old grey van driving around at a crawl.

"So that's where she is, with those lost

people.. your friend." Lacie looked at Fry, who gave her a colder stare back.

"I suppose if it had a landlord he'd pawn off every renter." Thee Chaotician had propped up a much closer giant floor tile that looked like a bunch of normal sized squares, he was using it to lean on while chewing gum.

"Crunk Punk" was scrawled off in gaudy cursive on the underside of the oversized floor piece.

From Automotive the Japanese suit-and-tie was heard, "I hold a prominent title!"

"Ahhh! Evil drawer!" Jifftural screamed as Kanji he couldn't read was written on him.

Lacie and Fry, who was now taller than Lacie because of her skateboard, watched as the Japanese salaryman ran out towards them, a black cloud swirling around the suit-and-tie's head and quickly dissipating into a black dresser drawer.

"Oni! Oni!" The Japanese man exclaimed in terror, tripping over the gap in the floor, getting up, and running out of view with the evil drawer on his head.

"This place is fucking crazy." Lacie murmured, tossing the skateboard packaging on the bottom of the shelf she had got it from.

"Who the hell was in my bedroom?" Fry mumbled after seeing the black dresser drawer.

Odis was heading frantically towards the

store exit from an aisle-way away; he had the long-haired clock-thrower collapsed and nearly unconscious in a shopping cart, a victim from his own clock-barrage. A light above dropped a tupperware container full of some alfredo casserole and it crashed onto the long-haired man who moaned angrily in response. Odis made tired eye contact with Lacie and Fry without losing pace, and then looked back at the man in the cart, slipping a pair of swimming goggles over his face with one hand, "Let's go cracker-jack."

Lacie looked down at the scope-like apparatus in the palm of her hand. She placed it back over her eye and it attached, and the remaining half of her glasses disappeared. She looked up and saw the lights on the ceiling which were all passing food towards the exits with invisible limbs, save “the flickering” and “the out”.

Chapter 31

Elizabeth was nervous and chewed on the tips of her hair that had now turned purple. She found herself in a Japanese version of Mr. Bagel's Donut Shop, nearly identical to it. The flooring was a tolerable brown, and large windows gave view to the location of the old store, where she met Lacie, across and down the road. However, the space was filled with renegade desserts, floating and flying at their leisure. The ceiling appeared in twitching shades of black; it left her with an uneasiness, soon to be forgotten, when she noticed a water-damaged, and closed Science textbook in the left corner of the establishment, followed with a sound.

The bells on the door rang as a guy in his twenties, older than Elizabeth, came through the entry-way. He had conditioned brown hair, a calm face, and a comfortable-looking, dark grey longcoat which was cutting off a bit past the knees-- although it is to be noted that his skin and other clothes were not grey. He was carrying a walking stick over his shoulder, and he flipped it around into an umbrella-pickaxe holder next to his right leg.

"Hey sis, I came in here to buy some food." He said mid-walk to the counter, swatting a floating cinnamon donut-hole in his way.

"Glorge!?"

"Yes, it's me, Glorge." He scratched his head at the menu. "It's all in Cheananese.."

"Then she's gone? The silver birtch that turned you into a.."

"Yeah. Maybe someone broke the right record." He pointed to food. "I'll have two of those and a multi-glazed, chocolate-filled, long-john necklace."

Elizabeth pulled her hair out of her mouth and let the strands drop to her shoulder. "Glorge, to tell you the truth, I don't think I work here."

"It's late but, I think I'll have a coffee too." Glorge's stomach replied.

Elizabeth grabbed his ordered donuts without putting on gloves, "I don't remember filling out an application."

Glorge hesitated.. "Ya know what sis? Neither do I."

Elizabeth gave him a puzzled look.

Glorge put on his pastry bling. Concern formed on his face and he stared at the countertop, "Ya know, I feel something in my gut, like something impending is going to happen.."

"Stop ignoring the nightmares!" Some Japanese rock song on the radio ended.

Elizabeth poured her brother his coffee and put in creamer and sugar. She went to hand the cup to him when something black dive-bombed into the cup from the ceiling. Coffee splashed everywhere. Elizabeth retracted her hand and both her and Glorge jumped, startled by the blur of what looked like a black bat without a head; she wiped her hand on the side of her clothing instinctively from the heat of the coffee; and the winged creature flew back up into the twitching black of the ceiling.

"I got to go somewhere.. I gotta go." Glorge took a bite of one of the donuts on the counter.

"Glorge wait." Elizabeth raised her hand, her tone of voice lifting out of fear. But she failed to get the attention of her brother Glorge, whom was adamant about leaving for some unknown reason. He grabbed his cane and put it over his shoulder, a fixation of worry across his face, his spilt coffee and donuts left on the counter-- save a shiny pastry necklace marking his rise from the streets.

The exterior of the donut shop appeared relatively calm under the colored sky, though the windows were blind with the rest of the building. The shop was mostly covered in green shapes and grey lines on a black canvas which somehow left Elizabeth's brother uneasy. Glorge took a brisk pace down the side of the road, leaving view of a storefront that almost appeared tame..

* * *

It wasn't much longer when the doors of the donut shop burst open on their own, with the store unilluminated from inside. The headless ceiling fragments flew around an expressionless young woman in the doorway and swarmed the night air. Both doors, upon hitting the outer wall of the donut shop, busted off of their hinges and began moving across the building in animated half-circle rotations.

The woman in the doorway had on a trenchcoat-dress covered in two-dimensional illusions like mirrors or camera feeds with shifting localities, fleeting images never to achieve any definition beyond the darkest greys. Her hair was up in similar anti-hues, with a wide-eyed snapping turtle hanging off the back of it. Some sort of tape in black and green strands formed X's over her eyes. She was.. She.

Three and a half helicopters covered in splatters of grim color circled around the pastry company. The flying machines were full of books, navigating the heavens with no evidence of pilots. Occasionally books would fall out and reign downwards. The 'copters shone spotlights in reds and violets coming close to She, but due to some error of judgment or momentum, these spotlights failed to stay on target of the moving black figure.

From out of anti-corners, cats with strike signs and off-color fur came through the orange and yellow luminescence of the street to follow She. Some felines stood on two feet, one with crutches, while all of them had cactus hats or plant-occupied flower pots atop their noggins. Maybe they were following the package of Goopy Goopy Fried Gumdrops in her pocket, made overseas in oft abusive jobs that were the best of confining activities on offer.

Sitting cross-legged on the ground some ways away, a man with dirty and overgrown hair on his face and head went through strange spasms. “She” traversed left, across the odd glow of Main street-- away from the jerky fellow and the far-off All-Mart.

"The ethereal of greens. Stringy celery and the Peanut Butter Savior.." The long-haired man murmured with bloodshot eyes, his voice drowned out by an endless chorus of large bells chiming in unison from shifty and shoddy buildings, which had started noising since She had appeared.

Creatures who were a cross between a

whale and dolphin came up out of the roads and sidewalks in a dozen or so, destructively. Course cement from the road served as skin where skin was present, while their eyes and organs were made of dirt. They went a few feet into the air before burrowing back down to breathe the breathless air. One of the 'dhalefins' flew up over She and propelled some dirt clods in her direction which she paid no heed to, while the colorful felines behind dropped protest signs, and made temporarily retreats.

* * *

Geoffery and Cuithbeart were lounging on springy chairs, sipping purple lemonades in the second story of a classily furnished house. The Victorian house was in mid-air and about to crash into the ground. Luckily, the structure's giant springs kept its leap-frog activity from being harmful, albeit jarring. They piloted it using a retro video-game controller that was plugged into the floor.

Geoffery had a white and brown bulldog mask over his face. Fake furs and plastic doodads made his Elizabethan appearance more alien; while he had received a tie around his left arm and another around his right-- for bad and good luck, from esteemed local salesmen. Suddenly well-educated in the field of technical miracles, he had changed his name permanently or temporarily to Repairgoddog!

"Hopefully we don't run into a jumping police station!" Cuithbeart laughed.

The Scotsman's expression went stern, "Because I think there's something in this lemonade."

"Well there's nothing in mine and they can't arrest us for drunk gaming." Repairgoddog replied. He looked left to the mini-mall parking lot that was still in unstable segments; then he looked forward to All-Mart and its parking lot which the jumping house was going to land on again.

Ahead lied the shifting images of Jeffery and Ratty losing consciousness next to a pile of a pink hats that someone had set on fire (there was a purple one in there somewhere); the pile was burning white. While an excited Swedish man with blinding, metallic footwear attempted to converse with the crowd of two.

"If you jump once more, you'll hit them!" Cuithbeart jarred.

Repairgoddog pressed the 'SELECT' button and the house fell, and the house stopped.

Chapter 32

Cuithbeart and Geoffery went down the steps of the once-jumping house. When they got to the kitchen on the first floor (well-kept at that), they dropped the structure's exit ramp with a lever (which was the handle of the sink cabinet). The metal slope clashed against the cement, across giant and slightly-rusted springs. And the duo-who-were-not-a-duo, ventured out into the night.

The five images of Ratty and four of Jeffrey (the fifth one was trying to sleep) flickered more often, and acted more individually than previously.

"The store.. owes.. me money.. new sneakers.. my money.. to me.." The outer Jeffrey's said. The center Jeffrey kept dozing off while trying to stand, like a looping hologram.

"Not sneakers, shoe-boots!" The Swede replied, kicking up his shiny shoe-boot in the air.

"Ha!" Cuithbeart found the conversation to his liking.

"There's more there.." The second Ratty to the right tried to say, pointing at the pile of hats now half-burned with a greenish-white flame.

The Ratty on the far left delusively retorted to her clones, "I'll kill you all!"

"Get a.. therapist," The center Jeffrey mumbled to the Ratty, before sitting down abruptly for a deeper sleep.

The excited Swede accented the city's remote mountain range with his excitement, "You've told me many things about your shoe-boots, but now I will tell you about my shoe-boots."

"Shoe-booty?" Repairgoddog verbally tripped, the vehicular two-story house behind him.

Cuithbeart kicked Geoffery in the ass. Repairgoddog gave him eyes full of daggers for it.

"NooOOOoo." The swede replied; and with that, he jumped onto a large, oncoming, paper airplane and surfed off into the air.

"Well.." Cuithbeart said as him and Geoffery stood and stared awkwardly. After the paper plane became a tiny sight the two men went on their separate ways; Geoffery to repair televisions, while Cuithbeart went to save his brigade.

Repairgoddog entered All-Mart through a hole in the brick. He noticed a portrait containing a quote on the side of the store's busted brick. The portrait was made up of small lights in primary colors, save the quote itself that was between blue and green, "'The classless are not assless.' - Spear Shakes".

Cuithbeart decided to enter All-Mart a different way, and made his way back inside the vehicular two-story house..

Repairgoddog found a man who was eating ceiling casserole from the floor while in a musical note costume like that of two notes connected together. His face was painted red like the attire, while the person in the connected music note was not moving, eyes shut, and feet dragging. With cheesy casserole on the conscious man's face, his eyes seemed to drift off into space as he talked to the latex dog, "If you aren't having fun, you'll never survive."

A plaque ahead on the floor narrated itself, "'Most young people get bored and then complain about it. I take my shirt off and start screaming at the top of my lungs about Brorange little men with Gred hair, I throw my cacti-cats through the window, peacers come around on scooters and find me DRiZUNK, an empty bottle of mouthwash near my feet while I hold a stick of deodorant at a swamp monster that frilly-nilly boop-bots are confiding in me is a fire-breathing Desk Lamp.' - George Washington II".

As the plaque narrated itself a particularly fierce caravan landed on it and

spoke in the loud, gaseous rasp of their kind..
"A general?"

Repairgoddog motioned in correction, "General television repair."

"My name is Poposhi. In a strange alternate universe.. I forgot I was alive. But I have been renewed as a pizza thief." Black gas bellowed from the mouths of the caravan-- but he had innocence and bits of vegetables in the black sclera of his ashless and whiteless eyes.

"Very well, I have to get to the tele--"

"All meats and fruits but pepperoni. I'm allergic to red dots you see."

"That's all fine and well." Repairgoddog stated, with more hand gesturing.

"Oh don't get me wrong.." The giant dog had height and size over dog-mask, "There was a time when I thought about it. That and extra cheese, I mean, it sounds like a good idea. But only if--"

"I DO NOT HAVE TIME.. for this." Geoffery realized Poposhi's menacing size mid-sentence.

Poposhi dropped his nightmare-head over half a foot in embarrassment; with a murmur, "..I had immunity to constipation.."

The ceiling ahead waned with a massive crash and the dents of giant springs.

Even Poposhi winced at the sound of the impact, "The hybrids made a bigger weapon?"

"No Poposhi. That's just an unarmed drunk piloting a jumping house." Repairgoddog replied.

A man who looked to be over one hundred if not older, was manning a sample table of miniature cobs of corn. He had on an All-Mart employee uniform, but with a style as though it had come from the early 1900's. He was forty feet from Poposhi, talking to a small creature that looked like a mix between a hermit crab and a squirrel. The animal was cyan and violet save a more colorful shell.

"Johnny Denven works in a supply store with his own fort built out of plywood, and old man Juniper draws pictures on the walls." The ancient employee explained.

The 'crabrel' cocked its head to the side, fixed eyestalks in confusion.

The ancient man had a cob in his hand and banged it against the table, "You don't know enough to pound samples."

The worn, grey van that had followed the bat-dogs into battle crawled through a large stretch of space between aisles. Bullet holes riddled the vehicle, and what was probably a ninja-with-a-fruitcake-on-her-head opened the sliding door.

"We will take you to the televisions, but you might not get out in time." Poposhi explained before flinching as gunfire rang out, the ninja woman nodding while she held the door to the van open.

* * *

Malluso happened to be sitting in the furniture section of the store on a couch. He was reading The Nightly Paper when he noticed the massive denting of the ceiling. There were still customers, squatters, and stranger strangers in the process of evacuating the store around the marble-headed man; while some were faster paced, others took their time shopping, lounging, and attacking each other.

"Equations!" A tall, frail woman with dirty, blond-ginger pony-tails tripped over the vacant side of the couch dropping a boxed blender. "Screaming about equations!"

The woman got up and went running towards the exit with her dicer, while Monsieur moaned with annoyance and put his paper down. Malluso got up and pushed the couch, about half the furniture's length, further from the dented ceiling. Then he sat on the other side of the couch and resumed reading.

"If I scare myself, am I doing a good job?" One of the mechanical suns asked another in Japanese, after the collision.

An aqua and turquoise Jack-O-Lantern on top of an aisle divider had a raspy reply, "It depends on the spices."

Nearby on a small, oak table was the foundation of a bust, but the head was missing; in dotless, seamless lines, the black and gold label read, "Monsieur Malluso of the Presiding Manor."

"Faxiom!" A tall, frail woman with dirty, ginger-blond pony-tails ran past the couch towards the exit in the gap where the sofa had once been. She only had a brown cardboard box, "Faxiom an axiom for our transfinite function!"

There was another crash which caused enough of the ceiling to collapse and give way to the Victorian house on springs. Malluso jumped off the couch at the massive springy collision. He threw his newspaper in the air which, in contrast to his cry of sheer terror, made a yawning sound.

Then, upon standing with tremendous, instinctual gusto, Monsieur picked up the couch and threw it at the house: this did little. A jumbo-sized gummy worm under the couch caused the marble-headed man to jump back in trepidation again. And the candy reptile squirmed away, back into the wild commerce, dentures and all.

The exit ramp of the springy house clanged as it hit the store floor; Cuithbeart Cobalt walked out with his hair a bit more messy, and some lights on his suit no longer flashing.

Cuithbeart stood apprehensively on the ramp, leaning on its rails; and upon seeing the marble-headed man, "I didn't land on anyone who was dressed in blue, did I?"

Chapter 33

Lacie and Fry skateboarded towards the Lawn and Garden department. They left Thee Chaotician in the storedust. They skateboarded past children in blue, they skateboarded past jumbo cans of low-sodium soup, Lacie ducked from the sound of misplaced gunfire, while Fry noticed a caravan-- flying wired. They past a road sign in the store, it read, "IF YOU'RE NOT WEIRD YOU'RE NOT TRYING HARD ENOUGH TO RELAX IN SITUATIONS YOU MADE UNCOMFORTABLE."

"It's all these cheap shots taking you where?" A hybrid man incoherently replied to some prior sound, he was in a SWAT outfit, taking cover behind Halloween decor. He had the name 'Captain Bubblegum' embroidered in small print on his outfit.

"Whose day isn't made by new underwear?" His caravan rival replied from an aisle or more away, a terrifying grin on its face.. man's best enemy, apparently.

"I'm fed up and sick of you and your hobby." Captain Bubblegum replied. There was poppy music coming from the store, but: the captain did not dance.

"I took up two boxes of them today!"

The monstrous dog replied, ash trailing from the ducts of his four aging eyes.

Someone contacted Captain Bubblegum on his radio, "Are they playing a song at you?"

The captain picked up his radio.

"Know the difference between mp3's and mp5's, it could save your life." Captain Bubblegum replied, then he holstered his radio and shot an industrial song at the caravan; the percussion sounded close to gunfire, and the great demonic dog toppled over dramatically from the placebo effect-- spitting out a live chicken in the process.

"They got married backwards drunk and run a website where people send in artwork of obese superheroes!" A short well-dressed man in a top hat said; this stranger ran past the Chaotician, toilet paper dragging from the man's dress shoes as his height changed up and down sporadically-- the Chaotician pretended to still be walking with a cane, which made his right hand almost look like it was measuring his own height inaccurately.

Up ahead Lacie tried to keep up.

"Why are you going so fast?" Lacie yelled.

"Your hair smells like rotten fruit!" Fry replied.

In the corner of Lacie's lens, within a gap in the store ceiling, someone's house flew downwards across the pink-and-red-tinged indigo and dark blue, and black of the sky, followed by the loud sound of metal crashing.

* * *

Thee Chaotician passed by Victor who was in an alleyway checking all of his pockets frantically. There were five carts around Victor's right side, all of which were full of different forms of cheese.

"Where did I leave my wallet?" Victor talked to himself before he noticed the Chaotician.

In cheekiness Thee Chaotician spoke, "How many years pass in a universe of chaos, before the prior wears thin? And then amongst the changing racket, where and whom begins?"

* * *

Lacie found the nearest entrance to Lawn and Garden had its walls covered in dark red paint, with green liquorice plants with black and red liquorice in their pots, and over-grown green vines and redhead hair falls hanging between two small Roman pillars that were mostly yellowing white and chipping away; and between these two ruinous pillars, there was a legless skeleton on the floor, its jaw detached as it clutched at its neck while wearing a college graduation cap. Lacie was thoroughly freaked out as she stepped around the bones; but Fry had already made her way inside without being bothered.

Inside Lawn and Garden were some 'late age teenagers', mostly people in their twenties, each running, walking, or crawling into one sole direction. Some of the group had hanging glow sticks, and a few had glowing rosaries, with tank tops and t-shirts tattered and new. Some of them had neon paint on their arms and faces, edges of bras showing, or their pants drooping past their underwear; one guy posing as a girl had on a bra, however it was to be noted that it was not the guy in blue overalls.

Among the lost youths, Lacie heard her roommate's voice, “Things get mixed up sometimes.”

Lacie peered around everywhere but her roommate was nowhere in sight.

"When my artwork is finished my pride will be offset by the feeling that I have survived something." Said the young man in overalls; he additionally wore a straw hat, knee pads, and a painted hockey mask. The countryman kept banging into a shelf, occasionally he'd step on the bottom layer, but it was only a staircase in his mind. Fry watched and found it comical.

A husky white fellow with a beard sat on the top of this shaking shelf; he utilized his fake Irish accent in the mannerism of a strange, Irish drinking tune, "Shatter my fifth on the road, and I'll drink from the liquor I poured in my trunk.."

Lacie noticed that Same was in the large room, across from a couple large sinkholes. The mannequin was still sparkling with shades of blue, though it was the first time Lacie had seen it; and Same was in a stationary pose as though she had lost sentience.

A scantily-clad girl who kept sprinting into a wall gave the mannequin a quick, tense hand gesture. "Shh!"

Upon closer inspection with her ocular zoom function, Lacie noticed that Same had been keyed with the words: "Straight people are taking back the rainbow."

Syll and Dave were also there, though it was only happenstance. Syll was sitting in a corner with her arms and legs crossed, as though waiting for someone. Dave was in another area and occupied with graphing the lost youths. Syll and Lacie caught view of each other.

Syll motioned to Lacie, "Hey, Lacie, over here!"

Lacie walked over, looking around at the young people bumping into things with a general expression of confusion. This expression turned to concern when Lacie noticed that Syll had a bandage wrapped around her head that wasn't there before, covering the top half of one of the Asian lady's brown eyes.

"Did the spider do that to you?" The young woman asked.

"No, a programmer threw a clock at me." Syll stated.

Dave began printing out graphs on a guy in a Null-Mart employee uniform who had dyed his hair and beard black, and who was covered in splatters of neon paint. He was drunk and crawling towards the exit to the outer part of Lawn and Garden, but the automatic doors weren't opening and so his head simply hit the glass repeatedly. A half-eaten cheesecake was next to him, still fresh.

Lacie looked behind to see Thee Chaotician and Victor appearing at the entrance to the department. Victor had more carts than before, his three four-wheeled containers in a successive line. The Chaotician helped him with the other two, making five carts stock full of cheese; and with his hands busy, the black-clad young man had stopped pretending to still have one cane.

An expressionless girl with grey skin had on a longcoat similar to her two grey brothers who were not present. She stood in front of a young Japanese man, tattooed and pierced, who was crawling into a wall head first.

"Maybe that's your fate." The grey girl spoke with cold on her breath. "To be old, grey, and white. To bang your head around the young.. Maybe you won't even get that far."

Syll immediately eyed her cheese-lover as he entered the room, "Vic!"

"Syllable!" Victor let go of his carts of cheese near the entrance, the Chaotician followed the older man's lead.

"My head.." The young Japanese man mumbled; the grey girl standing next to him unenthused.

"How is your head?" Victor asked Syll; though the Asian fellow thought someone was asking him and moaned in reply.

"Well the bandages there aren't as interesting." Syll replied with a friendly smile.

Dave had begun graphing Fry who was trying to talk to her friend, he caught some sort of glitch in the computerized base which helped him float around in the air; with the word 'ERROR' lighting up on his base, the technacle sporadically spoke, "LaShawnda get yo cheesy bread!"

Fry gave Dave an eyeliner-tinged death-stare, "..."

"..I have graphs on the subject." Dave stated as math-filled papers piled around the front of him.

"Are you sure five carts is enough?" Syll asked, quickly having to dodge as a barefoot young man sprinted towards the shelving, soil was all around the floor which the lost youth had knocked over.

"I actually think it's too much." Victor scratched the back of his head with his cane.

Syll pulled out Victor's wallet from the side of her mummy-like outfit white strips dangling off her arms and fading off into warm colors. "We should ring it up before the store collapses on us."

"My wallet, you had it."

"Yes, remember?" Syll and Victor were walking towards the exit as she spoke. "You gave it to me because you had pockets."

Lacie waved to Victor and Syll and they said their goodbyes.

"Ah hah." Victor smirked, turning around three of his carts before a tangent of curiosity overtook him. "I never asked you, what's under all those bandages?"

"Just underwear." Syll said deceptively.

Lacie noticed some gross dark blue liquid that had landed on her foot.

Midnight appeared like unfolding paper, he had salad dressing-- dressed in dark blues, the label on it said 'Morning After Midnight'.

The teenager mocked Lacie, "Your foot is most covered in the delicious of all salad dressings! If only your footwear was made from assorted raw vegetables, well, you just might be popular more and not such a big, stinky loser."

"Uhh.." Lacie was at a loss for words as Midnight went and wrote on the floor with the dressing.

After Midnight had finished his familiar writing Thee Chaotician spoke broadly. “Rising to occasion, I will forever retire my identity and give those lost one for the moment. With great elation, ‘Nobody Was Here’ will be mad entities’ final atonement.”

The lost youths stopped banging into walls, windows, and shelves, but not all of the plants in the store stopped their trembling. Having regained their composure, the young people looked to their peer, Thee Chaotician as having the most recognition and blame. Fry found this behavior to be too conformist for her to look upon favorably, and continued flicking a shaking potted plant.

"To make this quick, to not get hoarse, I dub them the Super Sexy Task Force!"

Having secretly and publicly stated his

real-time strategy gamertag, the black-clad poet took his trenchcoat off and put it on a shelf, and blended in with the crowd before him.

Chapter 34

Repairgoddog got out of the slow-moving, creeper van with a briefcase kit full of screwdrivers, sand and desserts. The female ninja closed the sliding door behind him while balancing a pumpkin pie on her head. The stocky youth found himself in an increasingly vacant store-- even a tumbleweed wearing a cowboy hat was headed towards the exit. A carrera had slipped into Null-Mart and was chasing two children in blue that hadn't made it out yet. The young repairman noticed a washing machine through the giant, flying worm's golden, translucent skin.

The technology department had mostly damaged products lining the floor in pieces and cords. There were strange pod-like machines on the right, overturned and smoking like they could explode-- and one or two of the human-sized devices already had. A guitar amp was left on with the instrument on a stand close by, a subtle, endless tone pouring from them. Two stained-glass windows had been left leaning against the counter and register; there was a hole in the bottom of one the colorful plates of glass, but no-one around boasted about it.

Repairgoddog saw a skeleton with

missing ribs. The skeleton lied stationary, on the floor, over top of an enormous compass-looking device; and a grody slice of bologna with some strands of hair on it covered the face of the skull. While standing over the remains, Geoffery noticed two odd television sets with solid colors over their screens.

Mycroft pulled the lunch meat from his face to reveal his gummy eyeballs, and then lowered his mandible in a shriek, "Ah!"

"Holy shit!" Geoffery jumped and threw his toolkit at Mycroft's head. The toolkit bounced off the bone with Mycroft raising his phalanges in futility and placebo pain. The kit opened up and sand came out from it and onto the floor while the tools and treats stayed strapped down.

Geoffery went and picked up his kit, "..are you okay?"

"My life flashed before my eyes.. and I denied it." Mycroft said, still holding his bony fingers over his face.

"Alright then.." Repairgoddog replied, and went straight to the t.v.'s.

Mycroft pulled his hand off of his face and talked to himself, “Was this a true near death experience, or bologna?”

Some television sets had solid colors over their screens while most were in bad shape, some even showing giant vegetables golfing. Repairgoddog began sniffing the televisions and came upon two which he would attempt to fix; one was a large high definition screen in constant yellow, while the other looked more like something approaching antiquity in flashes of blue and cyan.

Repairgoddog digged around his kit for the right tool and found a miniature souvenir baseball bat.

Mycroft sat up on his pelvis and leg bones, and quizzically raised his absent eyebrow, "What do you intend to do Sir Canine?"

The dog-masked repairman beat the old television's screen in with a couple swift swings of his novelty sports gear. As the crazy repairman withdrew, a ball of electricity came out of the screen. Then Repairgoddog reached into the television with both hands and pulled out a fuzzy yellow creature that looked kind of like monkey with a baby octopus for a head..

The fuzzy yellow creature enthusiastically widened its eyes in a high-pitched, "Woohoo!"

"That's one down; that's probably Jeffrey." Geoffery said.

A woman with a face full of matted blond hair struggled to walk in a hunch along the edge of the technology department. She had thick rectangular glasses, dark bags under her eyes, and plastic bags under those.

Mycroft looked at the woman quizzically, using two small pieces of licorice to act as imbalanced eyebrows with his hands, which the skeletal philosopher must've attained from the floor.

"Breathing too deeply or too little are both disorders." The stooping woman blurted. A steady breeze moved the plastic bags taped to her face. Her legs buckled from the slight wind current, and she collapsed into multi-colored dust.

Mycroft fashioned his red candy into a cross and placed it in the stranger's pixy stick remains.

* * *

With his movements losing convolution, Jeffrey began regaining his sense of self, while the night had claimed something of fall in its chilling air. He wondered if he had dreamed of the two strangers and the giant jumping house they had emerged from..

"Hey.." Jeffrey said to Ratty, finding himself to be one person.

"The dancing hats.. burning." The second Ratty to the right coughed as the smoke traveled through her.

Jeffrey realized she was both split-up

and unavailable; her see-through clones had different styles and colors of pipe-cleaners sticking up out of odd short hair.

Jeffrey turned to see dozens of smoking hats next to mounds of ash.. red, violet, orange, yellow and green headwear-- everything but pink. The pile started rustling, but the 'play-er' didn't dare get closer to it.

The second Ratty on the left began laughing at the yellow-lined black pavement.

* * *

Repairgoddog opened up his kit, focusing his attention on the high-definition television. This time he unplugged it-- but the screen only flickered and stayed on. Near the fringe technician, 'Nobody Was Here' was starting to dry.

The fuzzy yellow creature could not contain its estranged excitement, "Hoohoo!"

"Odd." Mycroft commented as he stood up.

Repairgoddog untwisted one screw, then hammered in a nail, and repeated.. this caused a round yellow cake with cyan frosting to squeeze its contours through the modern television in a neon glow.

“Weird.” The hefty geek said.

"Hoowoooo!" The fuzzy yellow octo-head blinded Repairgoddog with its tentacles.

"Shut up." Geoffery jarred in his concentration and pushed the furry limbs away.

An enormous amount of flooring, with the amplifier and neo-lute, collapsed into technacle territory. Televisions and a piece of aisle with unwanted video games on sale went pouring down hundreds of feet.

Repairgoddog lost his balance slightly and changed his footing to compensate while holding the television back that he was working on; the 'cup full of cake' was right in his latex-covered face.

"I think its time for me to get out of here, sir." Mycroft explicitly stated.

"Woooohoooo!" The furry yellow creature jumped on the living skeleton, piggy-back style with eyes popping out. The underweight philosopher grunted as the 'thing' landed on him, following with its furry limbs wrapping around his neck-spine in some parasitic or symbiotic embrace.

The skeleton looked at the fuzzy puppet-like creature and then at the collapsed floor. He put his hand up to his chin, "How strange that moments in time can be perceived, and remembered, as eternal, and as a consequence of that, their participants are perceived to be immortal.."

Mycroft paused for a moment but did not voice his further thoughts, if he even had any present.

"I'll see you on the other side, dawg." Mycroft's gummy tongue flapped as he lifted his hand in a stationary wave at the masked repairman.

When the pastry came out of the television it appeared as an unwrapped and over-frosted cupcake, with grooves suddenly forming at its base; and it landed frosting-first on the floor; and the telly had started smoking so intensely that Repairgoddog had to back away.

Store lights swiveled with the confusing breeze that had made its way from the outside, but the lights had lost their personalities. The pile of flavored sugar that once was a tired, old woman was blowing away. The vacant-looking, out-of-order store had sections of aisles and flooring crumbling and coming down violently into the underground. Geoffery knew he didn't have much time; he took his mask off, threw it into the massive nearby hole that had formed behind him, and ran.

* * *

Jeffrey looked at Ratty, whose bodies

were flickering, inching closer and closer together until they became one cohesive person. Strangers bolted around him as he heard the crashes from the store collapsing, his stomach filling with uneasiness.

Jeff had thought over his predicament and the trouble he had gotten himself into; the chance that his good friend could be dead, and that it was because he had left him behind. The young man finally had his chance to say something to the girl standing before him, “I.. I think I hate you.”

All-Mart's dark asphalt around the smoldering pile of hats had its potholes filled with splashing glowing liquids and stationary rainbow puddles. Further off.. ancient leaves ventured higher than their resting places, both mysteriously and naturally, from deep in bulky sewage vents and along the shallow pits of empty roads. While scattered, seldom bats without heads flew off in the distant, multi-colored sky, past the far-off shadow of a stranger drifting under an open parachute.

“I'd thought you'd never ask.” Ratty smiled, hearing what she wanted to.

Walking across the sidewalk lining the store was a malnourished stick-man with a heart-attack shout, "You kids looking for a fight!?"

Chapter 35

Mr. Dreary-Gravy saw the Eggola coming towards him on the way to the Null-Mart exit. The animated breakfast was now holding a red marker and was still dragging a block of Eggola Cola behind it. Milk-chocolate and coffee-bean floors dipped into colored tiles that were even darker, with occasional bright squares underneath the tread of the aging yolk.

At the top of the cube of cardboard, aluminum, and wet sugar was a woman in dark red with a fake or real mustache shaped like a blimp, and hair in giant, punk-rock spikes. Her one oversized scope-eye twitterpated at any red it saw. Two Japanese businessmen sat beside the mustache art sipping sake, while the trio's presence was ignored or unseen.

"Hold it!" Greary held up his hand. In his other hand was an egg carton striped between dark violet, light violet, and orangeish-red. And the two pieces of cape that had once hung out of his back pockets were now missing-- likely by accident.

The Eggola stopped with a high-pitched grunt, followed by a low-pitch, "Huh?"

Greary could now spot black stick arms coming off of the animated egg; three fingers protruded from one arm with the marker in hand, the other hand on a paint-chipped handle.

"Surely, you cannot get out of this store on your own as that would be theft. You will need someone to launder you." Mr. Greary stated.

The Eggola gave off another high-pitched "Eh."

This was followed by a low-pitch, "Oh?"

And with that, on the Second Midnight in a dilapidated superstore, the "first draft" of the Dreary-Egg Treaty was verbally formed.

Victor and Syll were at a Null-Mart register, the green paper holder's surroundings were covered by water balloons filled with unknown beverages. Mr. Greary spotted them and soon after, one or one and a half of the registers crumbled with a splotch of floor, falling into Rock knows where. But the cash holder near the couple remained.

Syll and Victor collected themselves after the collapse, grateful that their carts had not been taken.

Syll held Victor's hand to her nose, "You smell like mothballs."

"Oh.. that." Victor fidgeted with his silver lion's head cane, unenthused, "How will we pay for this? There is no one here."

Syll started unwrapping the bandages that were not around her head.

"What are you doing?" Victor asked.

"Securing our cheese." The Japanese woman replied, as warm colored tips and tinted white gave way to blue and brown, revealing a Null-Mart uniform.

"That's a very uncomfortable choice." Victor said, continuing some past conversation, and not realizing that his tailored black suit under his fluffy yellow bathrobe counteracted his statement.

Mr. Greary smiled faintly but warmly, "So there is someone to ring us-- I mean.. ring my eggs up."

"Just so long as you are quick." Syll said with sleek glasses suddenly appearing, hiding her large brown eyes with a glare.

Some part of the store floor could be heard crumbling from an invisible catalyst; in the same shape as the floor, a piece of the ceiling decided to go with it.

Syll had got behind the counter and started throwing water balloons away from the checkout area to make space. The latex broke into splashes of tea and hot chocolate, spoiled milkshakes and inedible concoctions. Victor was keeping his head low while laying cheese on the not-so-black consumer conveyer.

Mr. Greary turned around to look at the

block of cardboard, aluminum, and acid behind him, "That sure is a lot of soda, I hope it's cheap."

The Eggola was nowhere to be found, hidden out of sight.

* * *

Lacie started to make her way towards the Lawn and Garden exit to the outside and found her own scope-eyed sight in a temporary blur, the bricks around the double doors collapsed violently through the ground, forming a large hole and giving view of an unreachable outside.

Lacie gasped, backing away. She would have to find a new exit, but she had very little time. She kept hold of her skateboard but found herself too afraid to use it. Herbert's three words repeated themselves in her brain, guiding her forward. “Curiosity and guilt, curiosity and guilt..”

She wasn't sure which feeling she felt stronger, but fear overpowered them both. For a moment, it seemed the store had stopped collapsing. But the sudden peace was ominous.

After getting out of Lawn and Garden, the young woman passed by an aisle with what looked like giant out-stretched nerves mixed with pop bottles and disconnected wires giving off electrical charges. Because of massive gaps and fissures in the Null-Mart floor, Lacie found that the only path forward was to cut through another aisle, an aisle of mirrors.

The floor in this aisle creaked like thin ice and Lacie walked carefully. She came across an antique, oval-shaped mirror with a chipping frame, and a label that read: "The Life Wrecker".

There was a humanoid walrus in a jester outfit who tightrope walked along the edge of one of the aisle shelves like gravity was sideways for him. His sudden appearance scared Lacie and she backed up a few steps as the grey thing talked, "I could feel your energy-- and I knew you were the duck I was looking for.. Let me gamble with your follicles, Larcie."

Lacie blinked her shutters and the flubbery creature was gone.

The former student forgot about how bad her situation was and laughed before noticing her reflection in one of the mirrors: pearly white teeth under jutting, ocular metal protrusions. Before it could sink in that she had become somewhat willingly abnormal, she was interrupted by a change in her appearance that she hadn't noticed before, the white cursive on her green shirt-- stained with thin black sludge.. now read, "Out of Business."

Lacie felt a new surge of fear as distant parts of aisle shelving started collapsing with the floor underneath of them. She only saw this, but did not hear it anymore. What she did hear was an abnormally calm Midwestern American voice, coming from the store's public address speakers.. "This is the Null-Mart story technacle Anthony with a story for you all. Since the store is falling apart, we are not responsible for what happens to you if you listen to this story. Please get out of the store for your own safety."

"What's going on?" Lacie said to herself, with the strange muteness in her ears, apart from the store speakers, as if she was coping with a former explosion without the warzone ring tone.

A Jamaican voice came through the PA system, "Yo, this is the other Anthony, dis da story! So a little boy goes to a different universe than his own 'n' shit, and he tinks he can become anyting he wants to be."

Lacie was jolted as a two-story Victorian house rocketed up out of the store from the giant hole it had previously made in the patchy metal ceiling.

"At first, he becomes a superhero with a red cape." The Jaimacan voice continued, "But a tall, evil monster called Mr. Bagel takes his cape, throws him into a wall, and threatens to eat him if he come close."

Lacie's heart jumped and she fell backwards as a part of the aisle of mirrors crashed down into the technacle catacombs like the floor was melting ice. She let go of the skateboard and it rolled down the tiles, and into the darkness.

“Looks like Fry was lying.” Lacie thought.. “Or something changed.”

"So to get he revenge, da boy ventures into Black Stock, tinking of a monster he could become."

Lacie crawled backwards, and turned to notice she was blocked off, a gaping hole leading hundreds of feet downwards was also now behind her at the aisle exit she was closer to.

"As the boy grows and the night wanes endlessly into itself, the legend of a new monster appears, but the boy is never heard from again."

In her panic, Lacie noticed that The Life Wrecker was no longer reflecting its surroundings, and instead was acting as if the mirror gazed perfectly upon the dimensions of some sort of adorned violet door with the girl completely out of view, like a window to a completely different room.

Other mirrors that were left were

spontaneously cracking, shattering into reflective pieces that rustled in their doomed slide down the slanted floor, inviting a lethal fall.

"And so the boy's fear of a monster eating him.. becomes someone else's.. Or sometin' like dat." The voice concluded.

The calmer Anthony came back on the PA system, "Good job other Anthony, I appreciate your help, but I locked the door for a reason and I'd like to know how you got past the security system."

"Oh dat's easy bruddah." The second Anthony said, "I was livin' in da closet while you installed it."

Out of curiosity Lacie reached out to see if she could open the door that appeared in The Life Wrecker, finding that the mirror now acted like a window. She couldn't reach the doorknob and panicked, so she quickly crawled into mirror and accidentally banged her scope-eyes and forehead on its door inside, which caused her lenses to fall onto the now carpeted floor. From her hearing, hopefully fully returned to normal, she heard the echo of an old woman. "Watch your head, young man."

* * *

Jeffrey witnessed a giant rabbit in a shiny vest hopping out of All-Mart. A large cloud of water vapor poured from Herbert's mouth, with strange golden and silver squiggles in the mist.. and he had some little machine in his fluffy paw appearing to be the source of the puff. A fair amount of the bunny's backside also blended with the shadow as some rock and roll'er in All-Mart had tried to paint him black.

Jeffrey's face went to surprise when Herbert dryly talked to him, "It's getting dangerous in there."

A high-pitched scream came from the smoking pile of hats. The man in shoulder straps broke free from his burnt collection of hattery and stood tall and visible. His pink fedora had also survived the fall and discoloration of the other cranial accessories, remaining on his head.

"The Fifty are upon us!" The man warned as he pointed at Herbert.

Also watching the department store was the United Queendom Chief Constable with his whole-wheat mustache and his partner Ecila. Near the officers was a mostly blue and giant tomato on a far smaller wheeled platform, it acted as a police carriage with a jail cell carved in its back. The vehicle had no horses in front, just a couple wheeled recliners, each with a motor and a steering wheel; and one of the comfy chairs was stained pretty badly with hot sauce.

"What an excitable man, it's just a little rabbit." The constable's wheatstache ruffled. He continued to listen to the All-Mart collapses with a pleasant acceptance in his face.. "It's all coming down like cold clockwork."

Ecila had handcuffed Ratty, "Under Act 339 of 1919, you are under arrest."

The policewoman pulled off Ratty's scope-eyes to reveal Ratty's bright orange irises; Ecila put the mechanical eye-coverings in an evidence bag. Then the police officer pulled the multi-colored pipe-cleaners out of Ratty's hair and threw them on the ground.

"Why are you taking my pipe-cleaners?"

"No cactus heads." Ecila said.

An almost homicidal expression came across Ratty's face as Ecila dragged her towards the giant blue tomato. The policewoman opened the cell door of the police carriage while holding Ratty with her other hand. Then she put Ratty inside the police tomato carriage as a house on springs blasted through the roof of All-Mart and off into the sky.

"You.." The hat lover sweated and pointed to Herbert, "Are.. are you going to send them to trample me? Or are you going to do it yourself!?"

Herbert only replied silently, pulling one of his long feet out of a colorful puddle as he eyed the house on springs. When the Victorian house finally came down and smashed its metal foundations across the pavement behind the two males, its sound and shockwave was startling. Holding onto his hot pink fedora with his eyes bulging, the man in suspenders screamed again, jumping backwards as far as his legs could take him-- which was above the two-story house and across the horizon.

Chapter 36

Lacie picked her scope-eyes up off the floor, got up off of her knees, and turned around to find herself on a wide, dimly-lit and contorted balcony. The sides of the balcony went in twisted strips of wood up through the ceiling, and then down to the ground floor of what looked to be an old theater for plays. There were sporadically-placed, glossy wooden seats everywhere. Chairs below were randomly ripped out, and the floor was like fixed waves, like a picture of a storm at sea, but with old wood instead of water.

"I'm not a young man, and my name is Lacie." Lacie said, looking at an empty picture frame leaning against the railing.

"I'm sorry. I've loaned out my spectacles so I can only see through this telescope."

There was an X made with masking tape near the center edge of the balcony, on the ground, in front of the largest gap in the railing.

"Your voice, it sounds familiar." Lacie scratched her nose. "Wait.. you mean these microscope eye things?"

"Don't walk anywhere but towards that 'Z' I made with masking tape."

Lacie took a step and then stopped for a second. She looked around before cupping her hands on the sides of her mouth to shout, "There's only an X!"

"Well just step on that." The old woman's voice echoed.

Lacie walked towards the X. Two big cameras on tall tripods on either side of the tape stared towards the walls at nothing in particular. Lacie couldn't tell if either of the recording devices worked.

The old woman was covered in shadow, completely hunched over, and looking through a large telescope combined with a sewing machine. The opera house stage had its back wall busted out, a sky with scattered nocturnal clouds of a normal grey gave way to a burning field of lights; some stars closer than others, and a floating white laundry bin on wheels with donuts painted on it. The woman looking at the dark heavens was so still, it was as if she might be a mannequin. Her outfit had excessive shoulders, triangular tidal waves made of plastic and felt, almost like wings. Curiouser, she could almost be taken for someone Lacie knew, maybe older.

"No one introduces themselves around here." The astronomer said, her words caught by a microphone duct-taped to the side of the telescope in the empty building. "My name is

Verga, young lady."

"So you're the person that gave me these." Lacie stared at the scope-eyes in her hands; the cameras on the sides turned to film her and then fell over the railing.

"Put them down on the X please." Verga said, unbothered.

Wood was always creaking from different places, like something in the place wanted to reform; it could've been the faint voices and whispers coming from rock knows where, craving to play with the shape of the opera house.

Lacie did as she was asked and noticed that the tape was now in the shape of a Y.

"Your boyfriend doesn't make milkshakes like my boyfriend does. You are at your happiest when you're no longer attached to circumstances, and you rise above them like the steam above fallen empires. I was once a flatulent ducktopus fishtick." Verga muttered to herself.

Lacie decided to ignore this remembering why she was there. Her voice followed suit, "Where is She with a capital S?"

Verga chuckled before she spoke, "Hardly anyone knows of that troubled soul. She migrates from the donut shop around now to go towards An Abandoned Apartment."

"How do I stop her!?" Lacie yelled.

"Nobody knows of any way to stop her. She is the reason skeletons litter that street.."

Lacie rubbed her nose.

"I'm all out of tissues so go ahead and just pick it."

Lacie hesitated and then covered her nose with her hand..

"Not in front of me! Have some decency, please." The old woman said, though her back had been turned from Lacie the entire time.

Lacie turned around, greeted by Kanji labels on the glossy wooden chairs around the balcony. She took a step towards her right which caused familiar rips in her vision of the world around her. Her one misstep seem to alter reality into something more alive but discolored, as though her surroundings were trying to fade into self-destructive vintage film. The girl returned her feet near the line towards the Y.

When Lacie was done picking her nose, she put the booger in her pocket to be polite, then she turned back towards the woman.

"I've been entertaining caves for 3,000 years. You will never match my randrum. Beepita bobipita Disco-Italia." Verga said to herself.

"What?"

"..."

"What's the sewing machine for?" Lacie asked.

"The cape on the tape, don't break it since it's late. I am a giver. The golden technacle told me to give it to the one who thinks he can eat leather."

Lacie looked down, remembering the voice she had recently heard in All-Mart and the story of the little boy's cape. She took the cape in front of her. It looked familiar. It had been mended by fishing string and its red had mostly been painted over in blues.

"Can you take me to She?"

Verga straightened her back as she turned around with Lacie's mechanical lenses on her withered face. The astronomer motioned with her left palm up, fingers pointing, "I'll do what I can. If you'll just step to the right."

* * *

In the living room of the house on springs, Geoffrey had fully reverted to his old self, a bottle of bleach next to his foot.

"I can pay you back." Geoffrey said.

Jeffrey sat down on the recliner in front of three screens displaying the outside, "Man.. you saved my life!"

Jeffrey was ecstatic, "So just get me

some pizza."

On the left television, The Midnight Brigade traveled with dripping blue paint towards a red department store. On the right screen, the Super Sexy Task Force casually wandered in a different direction with a strange looking tank in front of them and a handful of them sitting on it. One of the guys on the tank had a boombox playing loud, he was shredded and wearing pink.

"Sounds good dude." Geoffery replied, looking at the center screen, which faced 'All-Mart' or what letters had not fallen off the sign.

Jeffrey flipped through an instruction manual he had found in the cushion crack of the recliner, "..and then you can buy me a 30 pack of beer."

Geoffery hesitated for a second. "Okay."

"And a cybernetic ninja suit." Jeffrey pressed a button which caused the house springs to shrink down in tension.. "And we'll be good."

Geoffery checked his wallet.

Chapter 37

The four-eyed nose-picker with her normal glasses back, ran out of the Men's room, its blockade wracked. The snow trenches had melted off their benches with new signs that were quaint. Further behind though, the store felt blank, with ceiling bereft and shivering walls, nothing was left untouched, from storeroom to bathroom, not even the stalls! As Lacie exited in or out from the cold, from out of the restroom hovered a technacle.. of gold.

Lacie saw the house on springs. She looked for a way to get inside but she saw no entry. The brunette was jolted by the force of the home as it left the ground, spewing out a shockwave from its curved metal springs.

She turned around at the sound of cement cracking and a bold set of orchestral strings further off. All-Mart's structure deteriorated all at once into grounded up tobacco, covering the sprawl of cement rather than falling further-- as though the technacles' underground dominion did not exist or was now suddenly closed to the public.

In the distance were murky floating lights around an hours-old Shadow Orchestra. This time Lacie saw their faces and did not while the conductor waved and weaved his melody of madness. They were masked and masquerading like strange animals; and their dress lied half-tattered like some forgotten socialite club from the 1940's possessed with and poorly hiding the evil spirits of some mysterious tribal culture.

A man in gauntlets named Phil let the tobacco sift through his fingers and then with tears in his eyes, banged his hands on the ground, "Now I'm stuck here forever.. why, why, why.. why, why? Why couldn't it be menthol!?"

The gargoyle came running across the tobacco, towards the man crying out with gauntlets. In the background, the orchestra disappeared into the woodlands, as though on a giant conveyor belt. In the middle of the mass piles of tobacco, a plump Japanese man with a Western accent was running a food booth.

Through a multi-colored drizzle of raindrops, the gargoyle ran past the Asian merchant who held his spatula with pride, "Haut dogs! Get ya' haut dogs here!"

Lacie thought maybe she could talk to the sprinting statue, to ride it towards She. So she went towards the distressed man; the gargoyle was coming straight for them from the other side.

"Please, stop!" Lacie pleaded, adjusting her glasses. But the statue did not hear, and was going to hit her.

The man in gauntlets with his crusty hair, did hear. He charged at Lacie with a toothbrush, "You'll taste minty!"

Lacie bolted. The gargoyle's arm clipped the man with gauntlets, forcing him into the ground of dried brown.

After making some distance between her and her assailant, Lacie recalled she had the blue cape. She tried wearing it.. jumped up and down, even raised her arms, but nothing happened. Then Lacie looked up for the shooting stars that had once sprinkled the sky, but there were none left to wish on, and she only saw the stationary glowing dots, unresponsive to her wishes amidst darkness and under the surreal and colorful streaks of cloud. It seemed like the young woman would have no way to get to Elizabeth in time.

Then Lacie heard an engine. It came from a spacious bus with childlike colors, Japanese lettering, large windows, and an excess of out-of-place mirrors. There were also seven street lights on the top of the bus.. and a defunct technacle base rested at the top between some of the mirrors and a couple of the street lights. On top of the bus was a banner of LED lights, “Next destination:

Clay's Historical Brownies".

When the bus pulled up next to Lacie it stopped and the door folded open with a squeak.

A Japanese man with adequate hair and an unnecessary comb-over was driving and seemed wired. "We! WE should find Mizaki in time.. You! Can replace the tobacco in his cigarettes.. with dried tea!"

"O..kay." Lacie replied.

Lacie got on the bus and sat down near the front. The driver handed her a tiny ticket and a large quarter. She skipped the seat directly behind the driver because there was a hole above it where the metal had rusted badly.

The bus passed on through the All-Mart parking-lot. The man in gauntlets looked angry and chased the bus with his toothbrush until he ran out of breath.

Turning into the road, Lacie noticed what looked like two black and grey squirrels, each with slim streaks of two bright colors, and reddish-black eyes, one jumping head-first off a tree and clawing supernaturally fast into the ground, the other grounded shadow-squirrel following it down the hole.

As the bus neared the intersection between "You Is Twenty-Three" and some main road, something dropped in front of it, the driver swerved violently but found time to put his baseball cap on. Lacie clutched the seat in front of her as the bus driver pulled out an electronic apparatus with a white cartoon cloud on the screen and different colored rectangles coming out of it. Lacie noticed that a sea-food restaurant she had walked past with Elizabeth was in ruins, but not the formally problematic one-- and there was a middle-aged Mexican man with long red and blue hair who was frozen like a statue nearby.

"What the hell is going on?" Lacie mostly said to herself, while the traffic lights in back flashed black and white like inappropriate strobe-lights.

A red blur plummeted through the rusty cavity in the bus ceiling. Lacie moved to the right a little where she couldn't get touched by anything that might come through from the gap, and looked over the seat. She saw a crimson cinderblock, now laying in the bus, painted on it in another shade of red were the words.. "Throw at blue people."

"I drive through walls!" The bus driver madly exclaimed.

Scattered cinderblocks rained in trails of colors, some of which thudded on the bulky Asian bus. Lacie looked through the windshield to see a tall brick wall that had only been in its infancy when she was on the smoking moon. The most notable of graffiti on the wall was a word that was too hard to read.

"Please stop!" Lacie pleaded with the driver.

The bus came to a screeching halt with rubber smoking from the back wheels and mirrors busting off as the vehicle turned hard with its side coming inches from the brick. And somewhere, in that frantic pace of things, Lacie found herself able to read the painted word on the brick blockade which spelled out 'FEAR'. The man opened the door for Lacie, and she made her way out of the luxury vehicle a little shaken up, leaving her tiny ticket and giant quarter behind.

Lacie looked behind her and saw a fierce black dragon soaring into view, though it had giant skeletal hands like that of a human. There was a brown, leathery, and seemingly headless man, being chased by the monster; Marthreek hopped from the tops of street lights and under the smoky moonlight across the otherwise dark road.

Lacie looked left and right but the wall stretched on too far, was too high, impossible to climb with hand and foot.. or dig under.

A frosted sweet-roll with eyeballs and a mouth passed by Lacie with its tongue hanging out. The pastry hopped along the edge of wall, dodged a cinderblock from the last of them coming down, and was hit by an arrow from the sky.

"Wahoowa!" The edible critter flapped sporadically before its eyes closed and it rolled to a stop.

The h'ragon was close now and grabbed Marthreek with its giant black and green bone-hand. The leathery victim's question-mark heads were all bent far back from fear or wind, or one force or another.

"I taste horrible." Marthreek pleaded, holding his open palms out in front of his chest. "I really do. Ask the last monster that ate me.. I've got its address."

Abbadon leaned his head forward and clasped Marthreek in his jaws while still flapping his wings. Tasting how horrid the question mark man was, the h'ragon spit him out with incredible speed at the giant brick wall. Lacie was between the two and the wall, she was cradling her head with her hands and kneeling down low as Marthreek's body flew over her.

Marthreek smashed through the wall, and hit the ground on the other side with bricks all around him, appearing unconscious; and Abbadon flew over Lacie; and landed with its demonic, spiny back and tail facing her.

Lacie stood up, determined to get past Abbadon, with her hands trembling and her heart pounding out of her chest. She took out the more-blue-than-red cape hanging out of her pocket and walked slowly towards the black-scaled dragon who stood in front of the hole Marthreek had made in the wall. The monster was on all fours and turned like a winged lion to face Lacie, towering over her with an angry and horrifying face, toxic swirls of green gas in his black eyes.

The Japanese hot-dog vendor had reappeared, and held the limp sweet-roll with his spatula. The merchant had a broad scooter at his side with a truck engine awkwardly attached to it, the smell said that he had just turned it off.

"We'll always remember him as hard worker, big talker.. go-getter, and to be honest.. a foodie and a ladies man with an allergy to gluten." The Japanese vendor put the sweet-roll into a sweet-roll-sized earth box.. he had to use some finesse with the spatula to get its tongue off the container's edge and inside. Lacie would've laughed at the absurdity of the scene if circumstances were different, but was completely preoccupied with the giant evil-looking thing staring at her like she was a mozzarella stick.

"This is your cape. I think." Lacie said, holding the blue fabric out.

There was a pause before the boom and

breeze, "My cape was red!"

Luckily for the girl, while the vocal gusts were strong, the black air from the monster was no longer toxic after its mechanical reformation.

Lacie shut her eyes waiting for the black cloud to clear, and then she spoke assertively, trying to push her fear away, "It was painted.. probably just by kids."

"Hmmm.." The massive dragon paused again, and then with bony fore-finger and thumb, picked up his old cape. "This makes me feel like saying something poetic."

Marthreek was now alert and scared. He sprung up with his heads on straight, save the inverted one; he hopped onto the nearest streetlight, and left in a leaping rush.

The h'ragon held out one of its skeletal hands theatrically.

"She, the 'She,'

is like a scooter engine."

With Abbadon distracted, Lacie cautiously walked around the h'ragon through the blocky finality of fear. In semi-distant view from her was a one-floor apartment building that would appear and disappear in the center of the road, its lights flickering on and off. Sections of the apartment door would open, but there was just blackness and strange flashes of color inside. A black clad stranger, followed by cactus-headed cats and helicopter spotlights, and possibly in a dress, was walking towards the doorway.

"She.." Lacie thought, ignoring the loud poetry.

The four-eyed girl started running as fast as she could. The wind seemed more noticeable, its game of direction growing blunt.

"Only She moves on random gears,

causing laughter and tears.."

"Elizabeth!" Lacie yelled. There was no response. 'She' continued walking towards the shifting doorway.

"..towards An Abandoned Apartment,

a historical compartment!"

There was a great gust of air with Abbadon's last line. He looked around. By this time the hot-dog merchant and bus-driver were gone. He stared at the tiny red, and mostly blue cape; something seemed more and more different, like he was shrinking and changing, becoming more sane.

Lacie remembered the most sensible words of Herbert and Verga. She zig-zagged around plant-head picketers, avoided the spot-lights of mechanical searchers, and ran past h'ragon hunters in all white, who were high-tailing it in the opposite direction with their weapons.

The donut girl in the trenchcoat-dress went through the unstable apartment doorway; and Lacie followed after her, not knowing what would happen when she opened the door herself-- for all Lacie knew, the air itself could begin talking to her and describe the appearance of people and things in abnormal detail, as though it was a narrator who was hiding things; but for Lacie now, there was only time for action-- action that was not simply motivated out of curiosity, or guilt, or fear.. but courage.

~ * ~

Lacie woke up in her bed, groggy from the feeling of oversleeping. Her dorm room was only lighted by one or more college streetlights and faint crescent moonlight sneaking through the dusty window blinds.

She sat up with memories that seemed too long and vivid to be from normal dreams and peaked through the window blinds at an ordinary outside.

Instinctively, the college student held back a surge of emotions. She feared that if she cried a gargoyle would blindly charge through one or more walls and into her room-- and maybe this time run her over.

When Lacie realized the absurdity of her thought she sat there and quietly laughed there in the dark. Something smelled iffy but she couldn't figure out what it was. She reached for her familiar glossy spectacles, got out of bed, and got dressed-- finding her clothes clean and back to normal in the process, including her green shirt with its normal cursive name, but not noticing that underneath it now read in very small print: “Restaurant and Laundromat”.

After this, Lacie pulled out a calendar from between the mattresses in her bed; it said June, the student picked up a permanent marker and put a final 'X' on Tuesday. Then she picked up the prescription bottle from the floor, ripped the sticker off with her fingernails, and threw it all away.

Lacie turned the lights on, and went to the bathroom, where she noticed an open bottle of strawberry shampoo.. the hair ooze smelled rotten and that's when she realized that the smell of spoiled strawberries was coming from her hair. She threw the bottle into the trash, not knowing what to think of it. Then using some other shampoo, she turned the sink handle to wash her hair; she stood there, and stared at the running water, and found herself half-disappointed that hot chocolate didn't pour from the faucet.

Lacie pulled out some week-old leftovers she had in her mini-fridge and threw the plastic container at the light, but no invisible limbs grabbed it, and it simply fell on the floor. The room felt cluttered, gloomy, and inanimate. And it seemed like it might be a good idea to get outside, get some fresh air, and see if everything outside was as normal as it looked.

Lacie got her boots out of the dark closet, struggled to tie them in the bad lighting, and opened the front door.

On the other side of the door was Elizabeth. She was still dressed like "She", but with no tape on her eyes or turtle biting the back of her hair, and no images on her strange dress. The English girl had a plain, white bag of donuts in her hand and a bunch of luggage behind her in a white laundry bin on wheels with donuts painted on it.

Both of the young women were stunned

at first, didn't move, and had comical expressions of shock on their faces.

But then the girls smiled at each other, both of them too nervous to say hi. Their smiles said that they were friends and not strangers. But their eyes said something different, that they were friends who were meeting for the first time in this universe.

They hugged. And through the dusty window blinds, intense light emanated from the road outside.

A moment later they let go of each other.

"Look!" Elizabeth noticed the light shining from outside and ran to the window, still not noticing the key to the donut shop in her pocket. Lacie followed her and raised the windows blinds, and they stared at the road glowing brightly with white light and the hint of faint, small rainbows in the darkness of night, while a few strangers gathered outside to see the strange occurrence.

"It's The Ultra-Violet Road." Lacie said with a faint smile, touching her glasses before looking over at Elizabeth who tried to smile back, but whose face was stuffed with a donut.

Elizabeth held the bag out and let Lacie grab a donut, and they ate and watched as the road of light began to flicker until it disappeared.

"Any trace of N'Qevna disappearing is

for the best." Elizabeth said before turning her face to Lacie again. "You might've been the reason we were both saved, but do you think any of the others were?"

Lacie felt despondent and looked down, and that's when she noticed some sparkly-blue salad dressing on her boot.